MY SILVER FOX PROTECTOR

AN AGE-GAP ROMANTIC SUSPENSE & ACTION
ADVENTURE ROMANCE

LAUREN COLE

CONTENT WARNING

This book has violence and heavy themes.

Sensitive readers please read mindfully.

For a complete list of content warnings and scenes you can visit: LaurenColeBooks.com/ContentWarnings

BLURB

I got knocked up by the Navy SEAL next door. He's my dad's bestie, and my new bodyguard.

I'm a professional hacker for the CIA, with a Diet Coke addiction, and the saddest social life you've ever seen.

Recently, I got myself into BIG trouble. Now, a six foot wall of tall, dark, and handsome is the only thing standing between me and prison.

Meet my savior: Mason Reynolds. A trained killer.

Sharing a bed with him was easy. Trusting him... impossible.

We each have our own secrets. And now that I've discovered his... I think I'm his next target.

I'm far from a trained assassin, but if he thinks he can end me, I might just kill him first.

My Silver Fox Protector is an angsty Action, Adventure Romance. You're going to love the exciting twist at the end!

Standalone/HEA/Heavy Themes - Sensitive readers please check the content warnings.

CONTENTS

WELCOME: DISCOUNT CODE

Thank you for reading a Lauren Cole Romance!

Visit LaurenColeBooks.com to grab your next book or bookish merch!

Discount Code: RomanceReadsy10

When you shop direct from the author, you're supporting a small business! YAY! Please enjoy this discount code as a thank you!

You can shop exclusive audiobooks, ebook bundles, or browse cute and hilarious, bookish merch!

Dedication:

To the good girls who've been through hell and back, and still hold space for their softness. To hell with the people who underestimated you, you're anything but weak.

1

EMMA

"WHAT?" I yelled over the thundering beat of the base. The lights at the club strobed around us in colorful bursts.

Olivia, one of my old high school friends I was trying to reconnect with, grabbed my arm, and leaned into my ear. "That guy is totally checking you out. You should go talk to him."

I looked to where she was pointing. "Who, him?" I rolled my eyes. No way. He wasn't really my type, anyway.

"Yes way." She raised her eyebrows up and down at me with a grin. "It's high time you had a little fun, don't you think?"

Just then, my apple watch buzzed with a notification. "Oh, shit." I turned towards Olivia. "I'm so sorry, I gotta jet." This is what I got for actually leaving the house for once.

She looked at me for a moment, before registering that I was leaving. "Seriously?"

I hated that look she was giving me. It was a look I had seen from everyone I had slowly grown away from over the last few years. "Yeah, sorry. Thanks for the invite, I really appreciate it. Truly."

"You know, you make it next to impossible to spend any time with you." She said it with true annoyance, not playfully. It was laced with subtext, almost like 'this is your last chance' or 'maybe I'm going to stop trying to be your friend because you're making it so difficult to get close to you.'

The thing was, she wasn't wrong. It *was* impossible to spend time with anyone when I was always on call twenty-four seven; tethered to my job, just waiting to sprint to my computer to resolve another security breach.

I grimaced, "I'm sorry Olivia, I really have to go. Thanks again."

"Sure. Whatever." She shrugged and made her way back over to the group of friends she'd invited me out with.

Fuck.

I was burning one of the last friendship bridges I had left.

I called an Uber, and while I waited for my driver to pick me up, I opened my phone. It was another security threat, but pretty run of the mill for me at this point. I shook my head. It would probably take me a mere ten minutes to divert it, but I couldn't do it from my phone. Once again, I was missing out on having a life because of my job.

The Uber driver dropped me off in front of my house and I quickly made my way inside, annoyed that I hadn't even had enough to drink to warrant taking the Uber in the first place.

I didn't bother turning the lights on, I made a beeline straight for the fridge and grabbed an ice cold can of Diet Coke, and cracked it open. I took a sip, savoring the way the carbonation burned down my throat, and sat at the kitchen table with my laptop.

Let's see who ruined my night.

I quickly checked through the system and found the breach in under ninety seconds. I shook my head.

So sloppy. What a waste of breath.

I went to work sealing off the breach and flagged the hackers' information up to my team leader for review. I checked the time on the microwave's clock.

Nine minutes flat. Thank you, asshole, for making me come all the way back home for this.

I went upstairs, taking the steps two at a time, and peeled off my tight black bandage dress, and chucked my sky high heels into the closet.

I hope you had a good time. I doubt you'll see the light of day again.

I hung the dress up in my closet and threw on a pair of soft sleeping shorts and a cami, and headed back downstairs to veg out. I went into the living room with my laptop and flicked on the TV.

I scrolled the streaming service for a moment before giving up and settling on a trashy reality show. I wasn't really watching it anyway; it was just for background noise, the comfort of human voices. I was alone so often these days, and any attempt at social interaction was often interrupted by an event like this evening. Aside from my dad, who was overseas for work for a few months, I had a hard time keeping in touch with anyone anymore.

Being employed against your own will for the government had many downsides. One of which was that I didn't have much of a social life. I often found myself lonely and bored.

I opened up a new browser on my computer and started online shopping.

The work I did for the agency was critical, but it was easy for me. I had to be on high alert at all times, but it was always a false start because the breaches were usually routine and easy enough to fix.

Nothing I couldn't handle.

I searched through the Versace website and landed on a deep red evening gown. It was quite expensive, but I could easily afford it. I made more than enough money than I knew what to do with. Being paid well and hardly ever leaving the house meant I was just stockpiling paycheck after paycheck. I hardly ever went out, and after investing in my retirement portfolio, I had ample funds to do whatever the hell I wanted. The problem was, I just didn't have the time freedom to do whatever I wanted.

I looked at the dress, and my finger hovered over the trackpad, deciding. With a plunging neckline and a plunging back, it was a showstopper, and it hugged the model in all the right places. I knew I'd never have anywhere to wear it. I added it to the cart anyway and checked out.

Why the hell not?

Hell, I could wear it around the house if I wanted. I opened a new tab and went to another online shop, and started looking at skincare. I wasn't really a makeup girly, but I did take good care of my skin.

Suddenly, a notification flashed up on my laptop.

Another security breach.

I sat up, surprised, and opened the notification.

Interesting.

I quickly assessed it, and sealed off the breach, but before flagging it to my team leader, I started digging around a bit. It was definitely the same person as earlier, and they were hacking right back in.

I smiled to myself, feeling mischievous. I wasn't supposed to dig further into the security threats. My primary job was to catch the breaches as they happened, isolate them, and send them up the chain of command so that another division could assess the individual security threat. My job was to protect the data. Simple and boring.

So *very* boring.

But every once in a while, I snooped anyway. I was slowly gathering information and data that I might be able to use to buy my way out of the predicament I was in. I was always on the lookout for a way out.

Besides, the agency wasn't even using half my skill for this damn job. I suspected that they kept everyone's roles extremely isolated. No one person touched too much information, they spread it out to make us less dangerous.

I didn't even know who my team leader was, aside from their username on the secure chat line we used. We communicated *exclusively* over our secure chat. We never spoke over the phone, and we'd never met in person. I had no idea if my team leader was a man or a woman, old or young.

The only person I'd actually met from the agency was Viktor, who I occasionally reported to when I'd screwed up. He was the one who had hired me in the beginning and he was there for the occasional wrist slap, and that was about it. I didn't even know Viktor's last name, for that matter. He was just Viktor, like the all powerful seeing Oz. Only a first name, a floating head bossing me around, despite how much I hated it.

I knew I should be grateful. Working a job that paid me super well was a generous alternative to the terrorism charges I was being faced with when they forced me into the agency. It was this or prison.

Even living in the free world, I hated how trapped I felt just the same.

My fingers hovered over the keyboard for half a second before I went for it.

Fuck it.

I sealed off the breach and went down the rabbit hole to see who was after the information. I quickly hacked through their security wall, but before I could start digging around, I was booted out.

Hmmm. Not half bad.

I smiled to myself and cracked my knuckles.

Let's see what you can do.

I quickly set up a trap door for the other hacker. Once they came through it, I'd be inside their computer before they knew what was happening. I'd be able to access everything on their hard drive. If they had a camera on their computer, I could even turn it on and watch them. I wasn't sanctioned to do this kind of hacking, but if I could identify who this was, give the agency a nice big fat fish to fry, maybe it'd earn me some privileges. Perhaps a break, or some time off. Or maybe some blackmail I could store away for a rainy day. Whatever it took to secure my freedom. I was facing terrorism charges if I didn't play their way, at this point, blackmailing someone would be cupcakes and rainbows. I didn't like it, but over the last few years, I'd learned that no one was going to take care of me, but me.

I took a sip of my Diet Coke and waited anxiously to see if they would take the bait.

I bit my lip and smiled.

Too easy.

They went straight for it.

I quickly hacked into their system and traced the IP address. It looked like they were in Iran.

Suddenly, my entire computer corrupted and went black.

My skin broke out in goosebumps, and my stomach dropped.

Oh fuck.

Fuck. Fuck. Fuck.

How?

I closed my laptop and stood up in horror, staring at it. Those little shits had set me up with their own trap door, and like an idiot, I'd walked right through it.

I grabbed my phone and opened the secure chat line with my team leader.

> Analyst04: We have a problem. Respond ASAP.

I quickly sent the message off and waited for a response.

I paced around the living room. My phone dinged, and I snatched it up.

My stomach dropped once more.

The hacker was all the way in, and they messaged me via my secure chat line.

> Not bad, but you got sloppy. You've been so successful at pushing me out the last few months, I'm quite impressed. But I am over your little games. Maybe you should sleep with the lights on tonight. It gets awfully dark on Allen Lane, don't you think? Night night, Emma.

THE HAIR on the back of my neck raised, and I quickly terminated the chat.

Holy fucking shit, I was in big trouble.

With my secure chat line terminated, and without my laptop working; I had no way of communicating with anyone from the agency. I had no phone number for my team leader. I had no way of getting in touch with Viktor.

Holy fucking shit. What did I get myself into? I grabbed a pocket knife and quickly pushed furniture in front of the downstairs doors, and ran upstairs and locked myself in my room. My pulse pounded in my ears as I peeked through the blinds in my room. The street was quiet, and the only noise was the soft hum of the glowing street lamp. It was after midnight and most of the lights in the other houses on the street were already off.

I knew because I had no one's information at the agency that I was highly disposable to them. As an off-book branch of the CIA, it was part of the gig. Protocol was to contact my team leader if something went south, and I prayed they would get the message and contact me.

I wasn't supposed to contact emergency services, but at this rate, screw the rules. If someone broke in, I was calling for help. I wasn't just going to sit here like a waiting duck to get picked off. Maybe that made me a shitty patriot, but I didn't care. I hadn't gotten into this work honestly, anyway.

I settled into the corner farthest from my bedroom door with my phone in one hand, ready to dial emergency services, and my knife in the other hand.

Eventually my breathing evened out and as I strained, I didn't hear any noise. I felt my eyes getting droopy as I sat there in the dark, and I tried to fight it as I felt myself getting more and more sleepy.

2

MASON

DING! I groaned and threw my hand over to my nightstand and searched blindly in the dark for my phone. The sound of a security breach alert.

I checked the time. Two in the morning. I rubbed the sleep from my eyes and checked the secure chat line.

> Analyst04: We have a problem. Respond
> ASAP.

THE CHAT LINE was terminated after the message.

Oh shit.

I frantically got up and went to the window, and peered through the blinds at Emma's house. All the lights were off and it was dark on the street.

What the hell did you get up to, Emma?

Suddenly, my phone rang. It was Viktor, my boss from the agency.

Aww fuck.

"Viktor."

"Did you see 04's message?"

"I did."

"I had 06 check out what she was doing before the chat went corrupt."

"And?" I held my breath, knowing this would not be good. If Viktor had another analyst check up on her, it was *not* any indication of anything good.

"She was digging again, Reynolds."

I groaned and paced in front of the window, rubbing my temples. Of course she was. She just couldn't keep her head down and do the work. She was always getting bored and seeing how far she could push the limits. "What do you want me to do?"

"Nothing. I'm sending a team in."

Shit.

"Just wait a minute." I snapped.

"It's already done. I've dispatched the team." Viktor said calmly, though I could sense a hint of pleasure in his voice.

"Viktor, just wait a fucking minute." I frantically searched, looking for a way to stall him. "Come on. There's got to be another way."

"The other way is that I cut her loose all together."

"If you cut her loose..." I searched for a way to reason with him. As the sentiment settled, I realized I wasn't entirely sure what he meant by cutting her loose. This was not good. Not good at all. "She's done everything we've asked, at least consider dropping the terrorism charges then." I paused, and Viktor said nothing. "She's good. You know that. We need her."

"She's messy, and she continues to step outside her scope, Reynolds. She's a liability. And if she can't keep the terms of her contract, then I can't keep the government from pressing charges."

"Just give her one more chance *for me*." I pleaded. I never pleaded. But for Emma, I pleaded. "You know she's the best on the team."

"Fine, but this is the last time I'm granting her special treatment after this. She'll be your responsibility. You'll be accountable for her actions."

"Done. So you'll call off the team?"

"No."

"For Christ's sake. Viktor, she's hardly a buck sopping wet. She doesn't need an entire team."

"She needs to learn a lesson. You know as well as I do, there are consequences for stepping outside of scope."

I clenched my hand at the thought. He was right. I did know the consequences. If the agency had any doubt in you... you were either intimidated into submission, tortured into submission, or just eliminated all together. *I* was equipped to handle that. *I* was strong enough to take the literal beatings and to withstand the psychological torture. *Emma,* on the other hand, was not. She didn't choose this life. But being in this life did give her choices. It was this, or prison. And Emma, spunky as she was, was not built for prison. "Who did you send?"

"The usual."

"Who?" I demanded, as I anxiously watched her house through the blinds.

"James, Brandon, and Andrew."

"What the fuck, Viktor. She doesn't need three guys." I leaned against the wall, feeling my stomach sink. If they were going the intimidation route, it could get ugly, really quick. My stomach clenched at the thought of her at the mercy of all three of their hands. With someone as small as her, things could get out of hand quickly. Too quickly. Those guys were used to bringing men like me to tears. Men like me, who didn't cry for anything, ever. If they applied even a fraction of the force I knew they were capable of, she might not recover.

No, I couldn't let him send them. I paced in agitation. There was only one way to protect her now. "I'll do it."

Viktor sounded pleased. "*You'll* go?"

"Yes." I gritted my teeth.

"Good. I'll redirect the team."

"Thank you."

"Don't thank me, Reynolds. If you go easy on her, I'll send the team out for both of you. Understood?"

"Understood." I clenched my fist. *Fucking asshole.*

"Good. Send me photos of the job when it's done."

The line went dead.

Fuck!

I gritted my teeth and threw my phone across the room. I sat on the edge of the bed and ran a hand over my face, steeling myself for what I was about to do. I hated this. I hated that it had to be me. But at least if it was me, I knew she wouldn't end up with any broken bones, and she'd keep all her teeth. So that was something, I tried to convince myself. I'd scare her, and try to make it look worse than it actually was, for Viktor's sake. But I *would* have to scare her. Hot anger boiled through me. This was the best I could offer her, and it was unacceptable. But at this point, hurting her was the only way to keep her from getting hurt.

I pulled on a dark shirt and dark pants and made my way down to the basement. I put together a bag, throwing in the essentials. Among my smash and bash kit was duct tape, zip ties, and I threw in a couple flash bangs, and some foggers. I hesitated before grabbing a small pouch that contained a syringe and a few vials of sedative and I threw them in the bag, too. I holstered my gun and pulled a mask over my head that had a voice modulator as I went out my backdoor. I went through the gate in the fence that divided our backyards, and I rolled my eyes at the theatrics of it. Normally I'd sneak in, but here I was going to make as much noise as possible. Alerting Emma of what was to come, another layer to the intimidation.

I stood outside her sliding glass door, and from my phone; I disabled hers. She had a company phone and laptop, so that if the agency ever wanted, it could pull all communication at the simple tap of a button. One of their many ways of controlling you. I stood there for a moment, and tried to shut my brain off, shut off the dread that filled my body. I had to dissociate whenever I did targeted intimidations; I had to disappear into a place where emotion didn't exist. Though I didn't disappear this time with the intention to harm, no, this time, I disappeared to cut off the guilt that rolled around inside me.

I gritted my teeth, and I smashed the sliding glass door in. I grabbed a stick from the yard and clanged it around, making as much noise as possible. I shook my head and stomped inside and dropped a smoke bomb. As I slowly stomped up the stairs to her room, I rolled a flash bang down the hall in front of her door, if nothing else, then to scare her. Finally, I stood in front of her door.

I shut my mind off and kicked the door in.

I looked around, and the sheets on the bed were mussed up. I reached under the bed and fished around until my hand locked around a flailing arm, and my stomach curdled at the sound of Emma screaming in terror.

I was the one making her fearful, and it made me want to vomit.

I chanted in my head, you're protecting her, you know that. This is an act of kindness. Over and over.

3

MASON

I DRAGGED Emma out from under the bed with a bruising grip.

"Please, what do you want?" She begged, pleaded for an answer as I hauled her up.

I didn't say anything; even with the voice modulator I could hardly speak, I could feel my emotions welling up in my throat, threatening to make my voice falter.

The lump in my throat tightened as I threw a screaming Emma over my shoulder and carried her downstairs.

Fight Emma, fight me. Don't give in.

I pleaded with her silently in my mind, knowing this was just as likely to happen again. She never was any good at staying out of trouble. Part of me wanted to see how much of a fight she had in her.

And fight me, she did. She screamed, and clawed at me, and thrashed as I bobbed down each step with a death grip on her.

Suddenly, there was a searing pain in my side. And I groaned and stumbled into the wall at the bottom of the stairs. Then another searing pain.

Emma grunted as she drove a knife into my side for the second time. "Let me go!" She screamed.

I momentarily lost my grip as I winced from the stab wound.

Good girl.

Emma scrambled off me and sprinted for the front door. She struggled to shove a dresser she'd pushed in front of it to the side. I grabbed my gun and fired a shot just above her hand, and she froze.

"If you want to live, you won't touch that door again." I growled. But this was good. She was fighting.

Before she could respond, I was across the room. I gripped her throat, pressing her into the wall. Not enough to truly choke her, but enough to scare her. With my other hand, I twisted the knife out of her hand.

"If you do that again, I'll use this knife on you. And I'll do things you couldn't fathom. I'll inflict so much pain that you'd be willing to confess to crimes you didn't commit." I growled, as she stared at me wide eyed, holding my wrists as I gripped her throat, and I watched as one giant tear streaked out of the corner of her eye.

Fuck.

I gritted my teeth and continued. I released my death grip from her throat and she collapsed down to the ground, coughing. I grabbed a leg, trying to ignore how buttery soft her skin felt against my palm as I dragged her into the kitchen. My heart sank when she stopped fighting me. She froze, terrified, and let me drag her into a chair, trembling as I zip tied her hands behind her back, and zip tied her legs to the chair.

She looked at me trembling, but the terror in her eyes was palpable, and as I stood across the room, I slowly removed the metal instruments from my bag and set them on the counter one at a time. It was a simple method, really. I wasn't even touching her. But I watched as her eyes roamed over the metal instruments as I placed them on the counter, one by one.

I, of course, wasn't going to get anywhere near her with any of these. Not a chance in hell, but she didn't know that. No, these instruments I had used to pull information out of the most tight-lipped of men. No, I wouldn't touch her with these. When these instruments were being inflicted, even the strongest of men would break, eventually. As she trembled watching me, I knew that even in her wildest dreams, she couldn't fathom the pain that could be inflicted with these tools.

Finally, with all the mental instruments laid out, I leaned against the counter and stared at her. Really looked at her. Though we lived next door, I didn't see her terribly often, mostly in passing. She was the daughter of one of my dearest friends, and I gladly kept an eye on her for him, but we were rarely in the same room. We'd never had much reason to be social outside of me hanging out with her dad. And at this moment, I realized, I didn't know if I had *really* ever *looked* at her.

Her dark long hair hung wildly over her shoulders and dipped over the soft curve of her breasts. She was wearing a *tiny* little tank top and *short,* little jersey shorts. Her skin was flushed as her chest heaved over and over. I realized she had grown into a woman and was quite beautiful, quite filled out now. I felt surprised as my cock strained against my zipper.

I caught her eyes again and shook my head, remembering to keep up the ruse. They were wild with terror, darting all around, assessing, looking for a way out.

"What are you going to do to me?" She whispered.

I brought myself back to the present. I knew her life wasn't in any real danger, but she didn't. This was all *very* real for her. I gritted my teeth, remembering Viktor wanted photos. Just scaring her wasn't enough; I'd have to leave some physical evidence that I was here.

I felt myself softly uttering, "I'm sorry." Before I could even catch the words. I struck her hard across her cheek. The easiest way to get big obvious bruising with minimal true damage.

She sucked in a sharp breath and looked at me with fury in her eyes as tears welled up. "What the hell do you want?" Her voice bordered on hysteria.

"What do you want?" She screamed at me.

I grabbed a knife off the counter and twirled it around in my hand as I squatted in front of her, putting us at equal eyeline. "What did you dig up?"

Her chest heaved. "I don't know what you mean?"

I sighed and walked around behind her. I grasped her throat, tilting her chin up to me, as I rested the cold blade against her skin. I leaned into her ear and lowly repeated, "What did you find?" The smell of her skin was intoxicating. I could feel the heat radiating off her neck. I found myself wanting to taste the skin where my blade was resting. So soft, so tender. The blade I held was sharp. Extremely sharp, and as I held it at her skin, a small bead of blood dripped down her neck, where the blade easily broke the first layer of her skin.

She jerked with a sharp gasp.

"Easy now, sweetheart. You move like that while I have this blade here. Well, let's just say our fun would be over a little quicker than I had planned." She held very still, but I could feel her pulse in my other hand. Her heart was racing, and her breasts heaving. At this angle, I had quite the view. I flicked my eyes away, feeling conflicted at the war raging inside me.

Was this attraction I was feeling?

It couldn't be.

"I don't know anything." She gritted out.

"Well, sweetheart, we both know that's not true."

"I don't know anything." She dug in hysterically.

"Well, if you're not willing to talk, I guess I'll have to start taking things from you with this knife."

Her voice broke. "Please, I don't know what you're talking about. I'll do whatever you want. Please."

"It's too late for that." I trailed my hand over her jaw and wound it through her hair, wrapping my fist through the length of it once, and then twice. Then, in one swift motion, I sliced the length off at her shoulders and she gasped as I dropped the cut length of her hair in her lap.

"Next time you go digging where you shouldn't, it'll be your fingers I'm dropping into your lap." I came around in front of her, and she was boiling angry, and even more scared.

I was done. I was over this. I couldn't bear to look at her face when she looked at me like that. I quickly gathered the zippered pouch from my bag and pulled out the syringe, quickly filling it up.

"Wha— what is that for?" She stuttered. "Please, I'll tell you whatever you want. Just please. I don't want to die."

"Shut up." I growled. And I did need her to shut up. She was breaking my heart.

She broke out screaming as I turned back towards her. "Help. Somebody help me." She eyed the needle. "No, no, no. What is that? Please."

I injected her and very quickly her eyes started to get

heavy and finally they closed, and her head dropped forward.

I leaned against the counter and looked at her. She was so small, so tiny. I shuddered, wondering how much worse it would have been if the team were here. I walked over to her and lifted her chin, inspecting the damage. I quickly snapped a photo and sent it off to Viktor.

Me: It's done.

Viktor: She doesn't look very banged up, Reynolds.

Me: Come on. This is good enough.

Viktor: You've always had a soft spot for her. Finish this job right, or I'll send the team in for you both.

Fuck.

I gripped the counter angrily before I suddenly became aware of the pain in my own side, and I stumbled into the kitchen, lifting my shirt to inspect the damage. As I packed paper towels onto my bloody side, I smiled to myself. She had a fighter in her, that was for sure, and I had two knife wounds to prove it. As I pulled my shirt back down, I looked at my bloody hands and back at Emma and knew what I was going to do.

I quickly went to work wiping my blood strategically on her, making her look bloody but believable. I snapped another photo and quickly sent it off to Viktor.

> Viktor: Very good, Reynolds. Very good.

I SMIRKED, knowing my little trick had worked. I had Emma to thank for that.

> Viktor: Bring her into the facility

> Me: You can't be serious.

I STOOD STARING at my phone, waiting for a response that never came.

Fucking hell.

There was no end to this. I shoved my things back into my bag and quickly cut the zip ties off Emma, and then scooped her limp body up against my chest.

It didn't miss me, how her warmth seeped into me as I cradled her against me, willing some form of comfort to be transmuted to her.

"You're ok, you're safe." I whispered softly to her. "I got you, baby girl. You were never in any real danger." As I slipped out the back, I carried her into my house through the back door. I swiftly moved through the house and into the garage, where I loaded her into my jeep. "I'm so sorry." I stroked her hair as I gently laid her across my backseat.

～

I STOOD STOICALLY, with my arms crossed, watching Emma through the one-way glass. As soon as I'd gotten to the facility, they'd loaded her up and taken her from me. After they processed her, they'd strapped her to a table and locked her in a cell.

I gritted my teeth. This was all so unnecessary. The intimidation was more than enough. This was overboard.

Emma slowly stirred, and her eyes fluttered open. I watched through the one-way glass as terror flooded her face as she woke up, and then relief at recognizing the facility, and then terror again, at the realization that she was strapped down.

She shook against the restraints as two agents entered the room.

"Why am I strapped down?" She spat, shaking against the restraints. "Let me go."

One of the agents spoke. "We have some questions for you before we make any decisions about your status."

"My status." She roared, "What the hell is that supposed to mean?"

"You've put the agency in a difficult position."

"Bullshi–" The intercom suddenly cut off, and the door into the observation room clicked shut.

I spun around to face Viktor, who gave me a stoic nod. "She's bloody. But maybe it would have been better if it were hers." Viktor pursed his lips knowingly.

"Fuck off. What is all this? You already know what she got into. What's with the song and dance?"

"We're being thorough, evaluating our risk."

"She's not a risk." I spat.

Viktor jabbed my stab wound, that had been bandaged over by a nurse in the facility. "Is that so?"

I bit my cheek so hard I tasted blood, but I wasn't giving him any satisfaction in a response.

"This is it, for her. This is the last time I'm going out on a limb like this. After this, her deal is null. And if she causes any further damage, you'll be responsible for the repercussions, personally."

I watched as Viktor disappeared out of the observation room and reappeared inside Emma's cell.

4

EMMA

"Viktor, tell them to let me go. I haven't done anything." I didn't know if I was terrified or relieved to see the only familiar face I knew.

Viktor walked over to the tray of metal instruments on the counter, and I found myself recoiling, not sure what he would do. He was cold and calculating. He did look like the type of man who would do terrible things to you with tiny little metal instruments.

He fingered the metal. "You're a liability, Emma. I took a chance bringing you in here, and you've done nothing but repay me with headache after headache."

"I'm not a liability, Viktor. I'm an asset." I asserted, and it was true. "If you'd just let me spread my wings a little more. I could help the agency so much more. A monkey could do my job, let me help go after these people. It's the same group. I know it. I think there might even be someone on the inside helping them."

"You know it?" Viktor mused. "You're very confident. What proof do you have?" He spun around with a sharp instrument in his hand, his eyes narrowed.

"Well, nothing yet, but if you'd just let me–"

"Enough Emma!" Viktor snapped. "If a monkey could do your job, tell me why I'm holding off the government on your behalf. What value are you adding to the agency? Hmm?"

"What do you mean?" I swallowed hard, watching him turn the instrument over in his hands.

"Why would I go through all this effort to offer you a deal, if you're just going to throw it in my face?"

"Viktor, please. If you just let me– the hackers... I know they're in Iran." I was using my one small piece of valuable information, trying to get a bargaining chip.

"You think I don't know that, Emma? You have one job. And this is your last chance, and if you can't do it, I can't offer you protection. Not from the terrorism charges, and not from the people who now seem to be after you. I won't give you another chance. This is it." I swallowed hard as he reprimanded me. "Do you understand?" He placed the instrument back on the tray.

I nodded.

"Good. Don't forget I own you." He towered over me. "Don't forget where you'd be without me." He turned around and headed for the door. "Now that's enough with all this. You'll stay in here until I believe, that you believe, what you just agreed to."

My head spun. "Stay in here? For how long?"

"Oh, and if anyone asks about the bruises on your face, you know the drill. This is classified, not a peep to anyone."

"But Viktor–" He was already gone, and the door firmly shut behind him.

I struggled against my restraints and rattled them hard, screaming out in rage. But no one else came. Eventually, I got tired, and I laid back and stared at the ceiling tiles. It was my own fault that I was stuck working for the agency. I'd gotten myself into this mess. And over a stupid boy, no less.

In my defense, I was much younger, and didn't fully understand the weight of what I had been doing at the time. I'd always been good with computers, and my mind was basically built to be a hacker. I'd always been a bit more introverted, and tended to stay home, which lent itself to my growing skill set. Over the years, I got better and better hacking into whatever I wanted, and I got confident, cocky. And it had cost me.

It had started when I was younger, and I'd credit myself more tokens for whatever computer game I was currently playing. Then it had escalated in my early teenage years to updating grades. When word had caught on at school that I had a special skill set, that's when I'd been paid to start hacking into things for other people. Then, as I got older, the jobs got sketchier, and I got more and more numb to the reality of what I was doing. The lines between right and wrong became extremely fuzzy.

Next thing you know, I was hacking into air traffic control like it was no big deal and changing my ex-boyfriends flight. I was seventeen at the time, and I'd been heartbroken when I found out he'd cheated on me. Everyone knew about it before I did, and it was humiliating. And when I'd heard he was taking his new girl on the family vacation that I was supposed to be joining him on, I snapped. If I couldn't be with him, and go on that trip as his girlfriend, no one was going on that trip.

I'd rerouted his family's plane from Cancun to a small town outside of Mexico City. My goal was to just fuck up their vacation and mess with him. At seventeen I probably shouldn't have been able to do what I did, but because no one really knew what I was doing, not even my dad, there had been no one to guide me back onto the straight and narrow until it was far too late. I'd completely missed out on the wrist slap and gone straight to the prison sentence.

What I did *was* a big deal. I knew that. But it was made even *worse* by the fact that there was a prominent government official onboard the plane, and I'd unknowingly delivered that plane into cartel territory. And because I'd been much younger, I'd gotten into the air traffic control system just fine, but I hadn't mastered the art of covering my tracks quite as well, and I got caught.

My dad's best friend, Mason Reynolds, was an ex-Navy SEAL and now worked in cyber security for the CIA. My dad had pleaded with Mason to pull some strings and try to help me out. Mason insisted he couldn't do anything to help, but my dad and I both knew he was behind the call I got, offering me a deal.

That's when Viktor had contacted me. He'd promised me a full-time, well-paying job, and that the terrorism charges would be dropped, so long as I continued working for his division, a black op cyber security team that was under a branch of the CIA. The division executed and protected classified intel and missions that most people couldn't stomach knowing about. It was off book and integral to the agency. It was a lifeline, but if I grabbed on, it would require devoting my entire life to the job. Otherwise, I'd be right back where I started.

With this job you were either in, or you were out. Complete and total devotion or bust.

As I stared at the ceiling, I felt enraged. One poor decision and here I was trapped for life. Maybe going to prison was the better option. Whether I was working for Viktor, and the agency, or I was locked up on terrorism charges, I was trapped either way. I was in a prison of my situation, and there was nothing I could do about it. I hated how help-less it made me feel.

I laid there not knowing what time it was, or how many minutes or hours had passed. I felt utterly alone. My dad didn't know what I *really* did. Even though I knew Mason worked in Cyber Security, I doubted Mason knew what *I* really did. Even if he did know, I couldn't risk talking to him about it, not that we saw each other regularly these days.

My job was highly classified, and I was strictly forbidden from discussing it with anyone. I was utterly isolated and alone in it. Tonight was proof of that. Maybe I needed to do what Viktor said, just put my head down and do the work. Maybe it wasn't all that bad. Maybe it was my own fault for pushing the limits.

I tried to push the bubbling desire for more down and out of my mind. I looked at the bruises down my arms, and the blood smeared down my tank top and shuddered. The memory of what had happened earlier in the night slowly pushed past the pounding fog in my head.

What was worse, getting attacked in my own home, or getting attacked in prison, if I kept this behavior up. I wasn't really sure.

I mulled over the situation. Who had come to attack me? And how had I ended up here at the agency facility? Had they gotten my message and found me just in time? Why didn't I think to ask Viktor about my attacker? See if he knew anything. I huffed, that was probably my only chance to get any information out of him about the events of tonight. After this, it would be a death sentence if I brought it up with him.

The events were fuzzy, and it didn't add up. There was something I just couldn't put my finger on, something almost familiar, maybe even hesitation from my attacker. I couldn't be sure, but something about the whole situation didn't sit right with me.

I had stabbed my attacker, and when I'd tried to escape, he'd shot at me, but he didn't shoot me. He had held me at knifepoint, but hadn't– and then I remembered my hair.

With my hands strapped down, I couldn't reach up and feel the damage, but I cried. Of all the things, it was silly, really. Hair grew back, and thank God it wasn't a finger like he'd threatened. But it was violating all the same to have your hair cut off like that. My hair was a bit of a security blanket for me, and my cheeks felt acidic as the tears streamed over them. And maybe I was crying about my hair, and maybe I was using it as an excuse to release the emotion of what I'd just been through; thinking I was about to be murdered in my own kitchen.

I jolted as the door to my cell suddenly clicked open and in strode a tall, muscular man, with warm tanned skin, and muscles that strained deliciously against the edges of his T-shirt. I sucked in a sharp breath as his warm brown eyes caught mine, and I felt a flush of heat splash up my chest and cheeks, and I squeezed my thighs together as that flush trickled into my core with nervous longing.

"I heard you weren't doing so hot." His deep voice washed over me, making my insides swirl.

"Mason." I whispered, looking around. "What are you doing *here*?" I was completely caught off guard and baffled as to why he would be allowed in here.

"How you holding up?" His gaze swept over me as he approached the table I was strapped to. I flinched at being unable to move, while my dream man hovered so closely over me.

He unclasped the straps around my wrists, and then I tried to steady my breath as his hand momentarily touched the skin on my waist as he unclasped the restraint across the middle of me. I pushed myself up to my elbows and watched as he moved down to my feet, and his thumb grazed the soft inside of my ankle as he undid the strap. I felt my center tighten with slick heat in response.

"I'm fine." I managed to squeak out.

"You don't look fine."

"I'm fine." I ground out. I said it to convince myself just as much as Mason. I couldn't afford to crumble, not when the stakes were this high. I had to keep my head on straight and keep moving forward. My life depended on it.

He stood at the foot of the table, leaning on the edge, causing the corded muscle in his forearms to fan. I sat propped up on my elbows, finding myself momentarily distracted by the salt and pepper strands streaking their way through his perfect dark head of hair. He was so fucking handsome, and he took my breath away, I'd imagined what it would be like to be with him more times than I could count. Imagined those muscular arms pressing me up against the wall while he thrust into me. I shuddered at the thought and swallowed hard.

Mason was my dad's friend, and he'd known me since I was younger, more awkward, and immature, and I was sure that was all I measured up to now. Especially being strapped to this table like a toddler having a tantrum.

Mason was so out of my league, and I tried not to think about how much that hurt. I'd never wanted anyone more.

My hand, now free, shot up to my hair, and I felt the blunt short ends that fell around my shoulders.

"This line of work can be dangerous." He rumbled. I flicked my eyes up and could have sworn I felt his gaze flick across my chest, but it happened so fast I thought I might have imagined it. "You need to be more careful."

I eyed him, not sure exactly how much he knew. My understanding was that Mason worked for the CIA, but I didn't know where or what he did exactly. It was a lot of smoke and mirrors for both of us. What I did know was that he was a medal awarded soldier. He had honor in what he did. I, on the other hand, was not even technically acknowledged by the government. I was the black sheep that they hid, and if need be, would dispose of, without a trace, if they needed.

"Let's go." Mason walked around the table to help me up.

"Where?" I asked, confused.

"You'll be staying with me."

"What, why?"

"Your dad called me and asked me to keep an eye on you."

"My dad knows what happened?"

"Well, yes, that you were robbed." Mason looked at me pointedly. It was almost a question, another test.

I slowly nodded my head, trying to decipher if that's what Mason believed, or if that's just what he was saying. If he was here, part of me wondered how much truth he actually knew. The fact that he was standing with me in this facility was evidence that he knew more than he'd let on in the past.

Not just anybody waltzed into the agency. Not even me for that matter. I only came here when I was invited or in trouble. Both of which I tried to keep to a minimum if I could.

I got up from the table and my head started to swim, causing me to stumble forward.

"Easy." Mason grabbed me and stabilized me. His big,

warm hands gripped my waist and planted me firmly against the table.

The room started to spin.

"You good?" Mason ground out, but his eyes were flashing over me with heavy concern. I squinted at him, trying to bring his face into focus.

"Yeah, I'm fine." I gripped the side of the table and felt the cool linoleum under my feet. I realized I didn't have any shoes. "I don't know where my shoes are..." I mumbled out, clutching my head as it pounded.

Mason gripped me tighter as I swayed.

"I'm just– I need to sit for a second..." And then I passed out.

5

EMMA

I FELT MYSELF BEING LIFTED, and I inhaled the warm scent of Mason as he pulled me into his chest. In his arms, I knew I was finally safe. Not only was he a family friend, he was an ex-Navy SEAL, for Christ's sake, nothing was getting past him.

With that realization, and my head still pounding, I found my eyes fluttering shut in exhaustion. As he carried me, I relished in the way his body heat seeped into me, warming me. He deposited me in the passenger seat of his Jeep and buckled me in. The soft hum of the car lulled me to sleep, and I awoke briefly to the sensation of being carried again before I slipped back under.

When I finally awoke, it was glaringly bright outside; the daylight filtered through the cracks in the blinds in white hot beams contrasting against the dark room. I groaned and pushed myself up to my elbows. My head was no longer pounding, but I felt so incredibly groggy and sore. Likely the aftermath of whatever drugs I had been injected with, though I had taken a few hits to the face, so it could be related to that as well.

I looked around the room. I didn't recognize it. I guessed I was in Mason's guest room, and it certainly looked like the guest room of a middle-aged bachelor. There was a simple dresser and a nightstand with a small lamp. The bed had a thin comforter, and it was gray. I smiled to myself, thinking how funny that was.

On the nightstand sat an aspirin and a glass of water. I took the aspirin and quickly downed the entire glass of water, suddenly realizing how thirsty I was.

I sat there for a moment fully waking up and absent-mindedly raked my hair away from my face, gasping when my fingers met the blunt ends of my hair so much faster than I expected.

I stumbled out of bed and towards the ensuite bathroom. I flicked on the light and gaped at my reflection in horror. This was the first time I was seeing myself since the attack. I gingerly pressed a finger to my eye and winced. My lip was busted up, and there was dark bruising forming all over my arms and face. I stared down at my tank top, at the smeared blood on it, before grazing my hand up to the knick on my neck. And then there was my beautiful hair, that was hacked off, and it now hung unevenly around my shoulders, rather than well down my back, as it had just twenty-four hours prior.

I heard a soft knock on the door. "Yes?" I called out suddenly, flushing at the realization that Mason was at the door.

"Can I come in?" Mason cracked the door, calling through it.

"Sure." I felt my heart rate skyrocket as soon as Mason rounded the corner into the bathroom. His jaw flexed as his eyes roamed over me in concern. "You should see the other guy." I joked.

Mason came to stand in front of me, and I stilled when he took my chin in his hand. He was inspecting my face, but he was standing mere inches from me. The heat was radiating off him. "I have some arnica cream that may help with the bruising." He patted the counter, and I looked at him with uncertainty. "Up." He commanded.

I rolled my lips over my teeth and felt a surge pulse through me at his command. I complied with his demand and pushed myself up onto the counter. He reached into the bottom drawer I had been standing in front of and pulled out a tube of arnica cream, and began applying it with surprising gentleness to my bruises.

I involuntarily sucked a sharp breath in and winced as he went over a particularly tender spot.

"I'm sorry." He ground out, his eyes glaring.

My eyes roamed over his face while he loomed in front of me, delicately applying the cream. He was *so* focused on applying the arnica cream, and he was *so* close I could feel the heat of his breath. His lips looked incredibly pillowy and soft, and so terribly inviting. We were close enough to kiss. As he focused on applying the cream, I was free to let my eyes roam all over him. The veins on his forearms bulged as he maneuvered around to the other side of my face. I tried to steady my breathing and distract myself.

"I'll need my things." It came out as a whisper, and I immediately regretted speaking.

Mason continued, his voice husky, "I've already brought them over."

"How'd you get in?"

"The backdoor was busted up, so I let myself in."

"Oh, right." I let out a small laugh. "I guess I should have someone come fix the door, so raccoons don't take up residence while I'm gone."

"I've already booked someone."

"Oh, thanks." I fidgeted, not knowing what else to say. While I had known Mason most of my life, he was my dad's friend. We hadn't had much one-on-one interaction, just the two of us. Now his presence was dominating my space, and I couldn't think clearly.

He stepped back and his eyes were dark, his face scowling. I felt heat pool between my legs as his gaze dragged over me. There was no escaping it. "There are towels in there." He pointed to the cabinet. "Why don't you clean up, and I'll meet you downstairs." He quickly disappeared and I let out the breath I didn't realize I'd been holding.

While I showered, I found it odd that I had so much blood on me, because as I washed myself, I couldn't find a cut anywhere on me. I cataloged that fact away, to reconsider later.

When I got out of the shower, and I had scrubbed the blood and sweat off of me, I found a couple of bags on the bed, filled with my clothes, and odds and ends from my bathroom. I blushed as I pulled on a pair of panties, thinking about how Mason had gone through my things, and selected these very underwear for me. I pulled on another pair of jersey shorts, a cami, and threw a giant graphic T-shirt over the top before making my way downstairs.

"Are you hungry?" Mason called out from the kitchen as I hit the bottom step.

I came into the kitchen and leaned on the counter. "Actually, yes." I instinctively went to reach for my hair to twirl it, one of my nervous ticks, and I grabbed at nothing. I quickly looked down, embarrassed at my mistake, and also because I suddenly felt naked without my security blanket. I tucked my hair behind my ears and smoothed it down in the back, as my neck burned with humiliation.

"You know it's not a bad look on you." Mason smiled at me, and I could see he was trying, but his eyes didn't smile with his mouth. His eyes still looked dark and troubled.

I made a face and softly smiled. The truth was, I hated it, and I hated how I felt without my long hair.

I sat on the bar stool, not quite knowing what to do with myself in Mason's house. He called and placed a takeout order while I ate him up with my eyes like it was the only meal I was going to eat tonight.

We sat across from one another eating our Chinese take-out, and I couldn't help but watch Mason's lips as he tipped a beer bottle against them. Those damn soft pillowy lips again.

The trouble was that I knew *exactly* what those lips felt like. I had tasted them before, just once, when I was sixteen, and he was thirty-two. He had been my first kiss. And I had committed the feeling to memory. But it left me wanting more.

Well, maybe that's not exactly how it went. But that's how I had cataloged it in my mind, anyway.

I had been doing a flip off the diving board at one of his summer BBQ's, trying unsuccessfully to get his attention and I'd miscalculated and hit my head on the way into the pool.

When I came too, I was lying on the concrete and there was a crowd of people all around. Mason was hovering over me. His lips were on mine, and his hands were on my chest, giving me CPR. After I'd vomited up the bleachy pool water, he'd wrapped me in a beach towel and carried me home.

Of course, my dad had been none the wiser when Mason carried me through the front door. He thought his best friend had just saved his daughter, and that's exactly what had happened.

Except that for me, it had solidified my obsession with Mason. It was the first time he'd looked at me, like really really looked at me. And the way he had tenderly held my face, and checked my head, and what it felt like to be pressed against him. It was bittersweet. I was hot for Mason Reynolds, but I knew I couldn't have him.

I knew he wasn't into immature teenage girls like me. He could have any woman he wanted. After the diving board incident, I continued to see him at one neighborhood BBQ after another that summer, with one gorgeous woman after another, and after weeks of growing moodier and grumpier at my predicament, I had finally vowed to get myself a boyfriend ASAP. I was determined to get over my crush, and fast.

My one and only boyfriend had pissed me off so much that I now had terrorism charges on my record. So that went exactly nowhere fast.

After I'd started working for the agency, I'd been too busy with work to really date. I'd gone on a few dates sure, but nothing I was really serious about. And now here I was, seven years later, and still pining after the same man. And once again he'd cradled me against his chest, and loomed in front of me while he tenderly checked my injuries.

And now, sitting here, across from him, watching his lips on that damn beer bottle, I couldn't help but wonder what they might feel like pressed against my collarbone, or what his hands would feel like tangled through my hair. I felt my center throb at the thought.

"You alright?" He asked, and I realized his gaze was on me.

Damn it, why'd he have to be so observant? "Yup great." I

lied and quickly threw my takeout container away before practically sprinting up the stairs to hide.

That night, as I laid in bed, I considered asking Mason how much he really knew. If he'd shown up at the agency today, maybe he worked for the agency like me. After debating for a while, I decided otherwise. If I wanted out of the agency, I had to be much more careful moving forward. I couldn't afford to get caught snooping around again.

6

MASON

WITH MY GUN COCKED, I softly opened the door and inched down the dark hallway. It was well after midnight. Maybe Viktor had decided to send the team, anyway. Or maybe whoever Emma had been snooping around on had actually sent someone to finish the job I'd started.

I peered into Emma's room. The door was open; the lights were off, and no sign of Emma. My pulse quickened. If anything happened to her on my watch, after what I'd done to her myself, I could never forgive myself. I quickly made my way to the end of the hallway and pivoted around the corner.

My heart caught in my throat.

Not because of an intruder.

But because of Emma.

She was standing illuminated by the soft glow of the hall night light in her lacy little underwear, with her giant T-shirt hardly covering a thing as she strained on her tiptoes. She struggled as she reached for a blanket on the top shelf of the linen closet.

I knew I should either help her, or go back to bed, but I

couldn't help but stand frozen, as I admired the soft curve of her ass. I shook my head, willing my thoughts to change.

Emma whirled around. "Holy shit!" She breathed. "You startled me."

"What are you doing?" I could hear the huskiness in my own voice as I spoke.

"You keep your house mother f-ing freezing. I was trying to get an extra blanket down." Her eyes flicked down to the gun in my hand, but she said nothing more.

I turned the safety back on and set the gun on the hallway table. "Here, let me." I closed the space between us, and she stood wedged between the closet and me. I could smell her sweet coconut scent as I reached around her. "Which one?" I huffed.

She turned around and pointed to the one she was reaching for. "That one there, the fuzzy one."

I leaned forward over the top of her and reached for the blanket above her. Our bodies momentarily pressed together, and my cock lit up at being pressed against her back for a moment. I stepped back and handed her the blanket.

"Thanks." she whispered, looking up at me with big doe eyes. She was so innocent, so inviting. The look in her eyes was uncertain. And there she was, standing in front of me, half naked. I ate her up with my eyes silently. Her breathing was fast and shallow. Even in the darkness I could see how dilated her eyes were, looking at me.

Fuck.

I found myself imagining things, all kinds of things I shouldn't be. I could push her up against the door frame right now, and sweep those thin little panties to the side so easily. And that's all that stood between us, just a thin little piece of fabric. Based on the way she was breathing, I had a pretty good idea of what I might find on that fabric, too. A warm damp spot.

Get it together, man. This is your best friend's daughter, for Christ's sake.

And then my eyes flicked back up to her face, where I could just barely make out the bruises across her face that were developing into a deeper blue hue. I felt hot shame pour through me. If being light years older than her wasn't enough, if her being my friend's daughter wasn't enough, then the fact that I had made those marks on her body was. I didn't deserve the thought of fantasizing about being with Emma, not after what I had done to her.

She deserved someone who would touch her tenderly, who would never leave a bruise on her body. But something in me felt the urge to be the one to make all those bruises and pain go away. Something in me felt the urge to leave different kinds of marks on her skin.

I felt myself trying to break the trance I was in. "You shouldn't be skulking around the house in the dark." I barked, and it came out more aggressive than I intended, but I was trying to do anything except get seduced by sweetness itself. And that's what Emma was. She was sweet and pure, and yes, sometimes spunky. But she was quintessentially good itself, even if she did have a habit of getting into trouble.

Her expression shifted to one of irritation, and she pushed past me roughly. "Maybe *you* shouldn't be lurking around in the dark with *that*." She waved to the gun as she walked past and went back into her room and closed the door firmly.

I went back to my room and closed the door even harder.

Fuck.

This was going to be more difficult than I anticipated. She had always been my best friend's daughter to me, but suddenly I realized she was a woman now. She had the body of a woman, and she wasn't the little girl I used to know anymore. Even with sheer terror in her eyes the other night, she was so fucking beautiful. Even pissed at me and covered in bruises. She was so fucking tempting.

The next morning, I got up around six, and when I came out of my room, Emma was nowhere to be found.

Fucking hell. She knows she is not supposed to disappear. The whole point of staying with me was so that I could keep an eye on her. I felt myself getting more and more agitated, wondering if this was her being rebellious, or if she was actually missing.

After numerous calls and texts, she finally appeared. She came gliding through the front door with her headphones in. She had her hair crammed under a hat and she wore tight leggings that perfectly wrapped around her curves; she was zipped into a tight fitted athletic jacket that accentuated her breasts. She looked like a sleek panther, her hips swaying as she walked into the kitchen.

"Where were you? You can't just up and leave like that." I grumbled. I was mad she had disappeared, but I was having a real hard time holding onto my irritation as she sweetly responded.

"I was just blowing off some steam. I'm fine really." Emma opened the fridge and pointed to the OJ. "May I?"

"You don't have to ask. What's mine is yours." I shook my head. "While you're here, I mean." She was getting more under my skin this morning than she had last night.

"Right." She tried to conceal a smile as she poured herself a glass. She sat at the kitchen table and opened her laptop.

I came over and leaned on the table. "Are you being good?" I prodded. "Staying out of trouble?"

She shifted uncomfortably, "Uh, yeah." And she gave me a look.

"What are you working on?" I prodded again. I wanted to see how tight-lipped she was going to be.

"You know I can't tell you that." Her shoulders were tense as her eyes scanned me, evaluating. "I'm just doing boring ol' data management. Nothing exciting, Mason." The sound of my name in her mouth made my core tighten hungerly. But she was doing well. She was keeping her head down and not saying too much. Though I could sense she wanted to.

The team I ran was a black op cyber security team, and she was one of a handful of analysts who supported the team. I knew she was good, but I was also worried about her. I didn't want her to accidentally stumble into something she wasn't supposed to see. That's why our division was under the radar, because sometimes the government needed us to do things, that were exactly that, under the radar. If she started digging too much, just like the general public, she might not like what she found. She'd find information, documents, contracts all containing more of what I'd been forced to put her through the other night; intimidation, torture, and secrets.

Emma was far too sweet to be diving that deep. No, she needed to stay on the surface where she could breathe, and let me troll the underwater for those predators. She had to have blind faith in the system, trusting that her team leader, me, wouldn't let anything come up from the depths to hurt her.

I caught her eyes, and she was studying me. "Do you work with Viktor?" She asked cautiously.

Fuck.

She's not being quiet at all, she's being cautious about how she asks. "Sometimes." I responded somewhat truthfully.

Except the truth was that I worked with him extremely closely. He was the main person I reported to. Viktor currently had me working to get more information from a terrorist group that was acquiring military weapons at an alarming rate. Emma shouldn't be getting tangled up in that anymore than she already was, certainly not with her track record. I could see her getting unknowingly tangled up in bigger charges, and wrongfully taking the blame for things she wasn't even a part of. She had to be smarter than this if she was going to last in this position. And she had to last in this position, or I couldn't protect her anymore.

"I'm going to work from home today." I let her know as she made her way up the stairs, presumably to shower.

"Oh?" She spun around with her eyes with a question in them.

I felt the corners of my mouth twitching. "So I can keep an eye on you."

She chewed on her lip for a moment and then went upstairs without another word.

After she had showered, she came back downstairs. She sat quietly, working for a long time, before she finally spoke.

As I sat across from her, I opened a new secure chat line as her team leader and initiated with her. She perked up right away and began to type furiously.

Analyst04: Where the hell have you been? You didn't respond and I got freaking assaulted and kidnapped. I think I have a lead on something too. The guys that hacked me were in Iran.

FUCK.

She wasn't lying low at all. I gritted my teeth and typed out a response, watching for her reaction.

CSTeamLeader: You shouldn't be going down rabbit holes. You need to lie low. Just keep your head down and do the work.

SHE HUFFED and furiously typed out a response.

Analyst04: This is big. I know it. I think someone from the agency is allowing these breaches. It's too coordinated and repeated. Something is not right.

CSTeamLeader: Leave it. Do your job. There's a reason you have the security clearance you do.

Analyst04: If you would just let me look at
some of the contracts, maybe I could get a
better idea of what they're after.

CSTeamLeader: You're not cleared to view
them, and do not let me catch you hacking
into our own system. There will be
consequences. I will not say this again. Do
your damn job, and let everyone else do
theirs.

I WATCHED her as she huffed and slumped back in her chair.
Her eyes were fiery. I meant what I said in the chat, but I
couldn't help chuckling a little at how worked up she was.
"Everything alright?" I asked her across the table.

"No." She ground out, rolling her eyes. I didn't speak,
letting her respond again. "It's just– ugh! My boss is driving
me insane. They're so ignorant. I have something, something is not right. And they don't even care." She placed her
elbow on the table and propped her cheek up using the heel
of her hand. She blinked at me in irritation.

"Want to tell me more?" I pushed. I needed to see how
much of a loose cannon she was, how much she was willing
to step over the line.

She thought for a moment and sucked her teeth. "I
can't."

"That's alright." I nodded.

Good girl.

"It's just that they're not even using me to my full
capacity."

"Maybe you shouldn't work so hard." I responded.

"Maybe you should mind your own business, Mason."
She said it with a coy smile that was playful. I felt my dick
light up, and I swear she could feel my turn on, because her
eyes flicked down to my lips for a moment before she met
my eyes again.

7

MASON

I WATCHED Emma as she milled around my kitchen barefoot, in those damn shorts again. As she turned her back to me to stir a steaming pot on the stove, I unsuccessfully fought the urge to look at her smooth, firm thighs. I wanted to walk around this damn counter and pull those thighs apart, and pull her warmth onto my tongue. I blew out a breath and tried not to think about what her pussy tasted like. What was wrong with me?

"Almost ready." She whirled back around with a smile that could rival the warmth of the sun. Her smooth pale skin, her curves that dipped in all the right places. With her short hair, she looked even younger now, as it swayed and moved with her while she spun around the kitchen, getting dinner ready.

It had been a few days of her being here, and we'd fallen into a rhythm of passing glances and light, polite conversation. After the first night of takeout, I'd cooked for the two of us, and I had made my staple of chicken, broccoli, and rice. After three nights of that meal, she'd offered to cook.

Clearly, she was over chicken and broccoli three nights in a row, and I didn't blame her.

It's not that I didn't know how to cook, but I was a busy guy, and I ate for nutrition more than taste. I had to keep my body sharp and fueled, and I wasn't keen on spending more time making food than was necessary. Typically, my fridge was stacked with my standard meal in five or six meal prep containers, ready to go.

She slid a wine bottle and a corkscrew in front of me. "Can you open this?" She whirled around and reached up on her tiptoes to grab two wineglasses from the cabinet. I stifled a groan as the bottom curve of her ass peaked out, just begging to be bitten. My eyes lingered on her firm thighs, and the warmth I knew I'd find at the apex of them. This was so wrong. I shouldn't be imagining what the warmth between her legs feels like. But it didn't matter what I knew was right, because I felt my cock strain against my zipper all the same.

She returned with the two wineglasses, sliding them towards me. "Here."

I poured a modest pour of wine in the first glass before she protested. "Come on, what are you? A lightweight? We're celebrating." As I poured the second glass, she grinned and lightly tipped the bottom of the bottle I was pouring up, so that I filled the second glass much fuller. "I'll take that." She said as she swiped the full glass from me.

I raised my brows at her. "What are we celebrating?"

"That I'm alive, that I didn't get murdered in my house the other day. That I got a haircut." She rolled her eyes and lifted her hand to show off her hair. She had used kitchen scissors last night to even out the hack job I'd given her. And I did feel bad about cutting her hair, but better her hair than something that wouldn't grow back. She continued, "That

we don't have to eat another one of your *meal prep* meals."
She teased.

"Hey, those meals are perfectly nutritionally balanced." I
chuckled.

"I'm not saying they're not. I'm just saying they're bland."
She put her hands up and shrugged mischievously. "I just
think you're going to like this a whole lot better."

"Can't wait." I smiled before taking a sip of my moderate
glass of wine. I was genuinely excited to eat whatever she
was cooking. But I was more pleased to see her in my
kitchen barefoot. Something about it felt primal to me. I
could get used to this. Having a beautiful woman cook me a
meal, and sharing it with me over a glass of wine. Though
not meant to be romantic, it was.

And after a steak dinner with braised asparagus and
buttery mashed potatoes, I leaned back in my chair, thoroughly satiated. I watched as Emma worked on her second
full glass of wine. She wandered over to the stereo and
turned the music up, and began twirling around the living
room, dancing.

I could feel my eyes gleaming as I watched her dance.
She was beautiful; she was a woman now, and her body had
all the curves to show for it. I tried not to lick my lips and
she let her head fall back, exposing her long, soft neck.

I got a notification on my phone, and I quickly pulled it
up. I blew a breath out. I had to leave for a mission tomorrow. I watched Emma innocently swaying to the music and
wondered what to do with her. I could leave her here. I did
have my place locked down with security cameras so I could
watch her that way. Though, I didn't feel great about that
option. If she was in any real danger, yes, I'd be able to see,
but I wouldn't be able to do anything useful.

Obviously, her attack had been coordinated by the organization, and carried out by me, but she had been genuinely threatened by the hacker she was goading. I didn't know how real that threat really was.

I was fast and clean when I went on my missions. I could keep her at the hotel, so at least she was with me.

Suddenly, Emma stumbled over to me and grabbed my hand. "Dance with me, Mason. Don't make me dance alone." She sang giddily as she placed her wineglass on the kitchen table and stumbled forward towards me, grabbing my hand.

"Easy." I reached out and stopped her from falling over.

As I sat with my hands on her hips, keeping her upright, she now stood between my legs, balancing herself with one hand on my chest. She chewed her lip, and her eyes went hooded as her chest heaved. Each breath accentuated the soft curve of her breasts as they strained against her tight camisole. I felt my pulse shoot through the roof. I could pull her into my lap right now and taste her. She stood swaying in front of me, as if she was waiting for me to do just that.

I cleared my throat. "I have to leave for a work trip tomorrow. I'd like you to come with me, so I can keep an eye on you."

She nodded, and her gaze was back on my lips. "Ok." She whispered out.

Fuck.

She *was* checking me out. I wasn't sure earlier, but now I was confident that she was waiting for me to kiss her. I gritted my teeth. Too bad I wouldn't. It was my job to protect her, and kissing her while she was drunk was not high up on the list of ways to do that. Or kissing her ever, for that matter.

Her eyes scanned my face, and she stepped forward. I could bury my face in her tits from where she stood. She was that close. I tried to steady my breathing, but she was such a fucking temptation. I realized my thumbs had been kneading her hips as I thought about her, because her eyes suddenly fluttered shut and she let out the softest whimper.

FUCK!

Oh, how I could make that moan even louder. I could have her screaming and moaning and chanting my name. The sound of that soft little moan made me feral.

"I think it's time for bed." I grunted out.

Her eyes flicked open, and she breathed rapidly at me. Suddenly I registered that it almost sounded like an invitation.

"For us to go to bed... in our own rooms." I clarified gently.

"Right." She whispered, but she still stood there in front of me, and I still sat there, gripping her hips. She blushed and dropped her eyes suddenly. "Want to know something embarrassing?" She questioned softly.

My pulse was through the roof. "Yes." I wanted to know every thought that popped into that pretty little head of hers.

Her eyes flicked back up, and she hesitated before she spoke. "Um..." She laughed again, "I used to say that you were my first kiss."

I racked my brain for a moment in confusion.

She searched my face. "You know, because of the whole pool thing."

Pool thing? What was the pool thing?

"When you saved me from drowning, and you gave me CPR." She smiled so big her eyes closed. "Isn't that funny?"

Something in me liked that she considered me her first kiss. Now I definitely knew she was thinking about me like that, and clearly had been for quite some time, seeing as I pulled her out of the pool when she was maybe sixteen or seventeen, I couldn't recall exactly. I needed to put an end to this right now before I did something stupid. I pulled a chair up with my foot, and gently pushed her down towards it, but she was locking her knees.

"Sit." I instructed gently but firmly.

She stood defiantly pushing against my grip; She was breathing heavily. I could have easily made her sit, but part of me didn't want to push her away. She continued, "I've always wondered what a real kiss with you would feel like." She slid her arms up around my neck and into my hair, and she shifted forward.

Oh, for Christ's sake, I did not have this kind of strength. The feeling of her hands raking and pulling through my hair with desire nearly broke me. "Emma." I said it softly, as I tried to let her down, easily, gently.

"I think you feel it too, Mason." Her lips hovered over mine. I could practically taste her sweetness in the air. She was so close.

"I don't feel that way about you, Emma." It was a lie, but it had to be said, it was for the best.

Her body language shifted, and she looked hurt. She let me gently guide her into the chair across from me. When I released her hips down onto the chair, I felt an immediate longing to touch her again. To feel her warmth against me.

I changed the subject, "I'll need you to stay in the hotel when we go on this trip, ok?"

"Yeah sure whatever." She was leaning on the table, tracing the wood grain with her finger now. She wouldn't look at me.

"It's really important. We'll be in Iran, and–"

"Iran?" She perked up way too much at that.

"Yes..." I drew it out, wanting her to clarify. She darted

her eyes away, and I pressed, wanting to know why she was so interested, "Why? Why is Iran significant to you?"

"Oh, it's not." She lied. It was my training to know when someone lied to me, and she definitely knew something. She was drunk, so it was even less hard to tell that she was lying.

"I just need to know you can stay put in the hotel, otherwise you could put yourself in more danger than you'd probably be in here." I studied her. "You think you can do that?"

"You just want to keep me locked up all the time. I'm tired of being trapped, Mason." Her eyes were getting heavier and heavier.

I shook my head. She was one hundred percent a flight risk. Over the last few days, she'd disappeared without telling me where she was going or when she would be back. Whether she stayed or came with me, I needed to know where she was at all times. I shook my head. I didn't like it, but I was going to have to track her, and not just on her phone.

Emma got up and started dancing to the music again. She was getting her second wind. I got up and quickly went to the basement. I leaned against the drawer for a moment and groaned. It had to be done, though. I opened the drawer and grabbed a sedative and a tracking chip, and headed back upstairs.

While she was twirling in the living room, I grabbed her glass and dissolved the powdered sedative into her wine.

"I topped you off." I called out to her, and she came back and slammed down the rest of the wine in one gulp. She grinned at me, and I shook my head. But this was good. She'd be out in no time, and she wouldn't feel a thing.

After a few minutes, her eyes got heavier and heavier. I

got up and came over to her in the living room. "You look tired. Why don't you lie down on the couch?"

She started to stumble. The sedative was pulling her under and she was fighting it. "Dance with me, Mason." She grabbed my arm and pulled me to her.

I pulled her tightly into my chest and wrapped my arms around her as we swayed in the living room, and then she finally went limp against me. I gently laid her on the couch, on her side, and injected the tracking chip into her shoulder. She murmured as it went in. "I'm so sorry, baby girl. I keep hurting you. I'm so sorry." I looked at her somberly before I slid my arms under her and pulled her against my chest.

I slowly made my way up the stairs, and deposited her in the guest bed, and pulled the covers over her. I tucked her hair behind her ear and found myself leaning forward, pressing a kiss to her forehead. It was the only stolen kiss I was going to take from her, ever. I took a deep breath in and sat there for a moment, watching her. Her mouth was slightly parted and a soft snore whispered out. I chuckled and gently rolled her over to her side, and the snoring subsided.

This was for the best. I needed her to stay close to me, and I needed to know under any circumstance that I could locate her.

Viktor said she was getting a second chance, but I didn't fully trust him. Viktor was going to do whatever he thought was best for the agency, even if that meant cutting Emma loose or worse. I owed it to Emma's dad to keep her safe. It had been me that got her recruited into this mess, even if it was her best option. I owed it to Emma to keep her safe, and that's exactly what I intended to do.

If I could get in and out, extract the information I

needed from the parties in Iran, and possibly eliminate any threats, it would slow down if not cripple the terrorist group that continued to steal the weapons we were tracking. It would remove the incidents Emma had been tracking, and maybe if it turned up to be a dead end, she would just leave it alone.

8

EMMA

I STOOD NERVOUSLY in the line to go through the TSA check. I held a fake passport, and I wore the clothes that Mason had given me. They were functional, but neutral, so that I'd blend in when I got there. I tried to steady my breathing as I approached the agent. I looked at the photo again and wondered if they would know this was a fake ID.

I smiled as the agent gruffly waved me up and looked back and forth between me and my photo. I held my breath, and then he finally snapped it shut and handed it back.

"Have a good flight."

"Thanks." I said softly as I put my things on the conveyor belt to send them through the x-ray.

When Mason had told me to travel with a fake passport, it had seemed exciting. Now I felt like my insides were going to be on my outsides. Mason was bringing me on the down-low, and I suddenly started to feel nervous.

As we ascended into the air, I closed my eyes. I was grateful that Mason was keeping an eye on me. I appreciated being able to stay at his house after what had happened, and I would be lying if I said I didn't enjoy staying there for other reasons. As the days had passed, I'd grown more and more attracted to him. I felt a small sting resurface as I recalled trying to kiss him last night, and the way he had pushed me away. At least I could blame it on the alcohol. I could certainly blame my boldness on it.

I felt my cheeks flush in embarrassment, and I tried to focus on other things, like how it was possible that the hacker I had tracked was in Iran, and that now Mason was going there on a mission. I didn't know exactly what that entailed, but it couldn't be a coincidence. There was just no way.

By the time I was finally standing outside the airport with my bags in Iran, I was exhausted and stressed. A very salesy man who I couldn't understand flagged down a cab for me, and I showed him the address Mason had written down for me. Mason assured me he would be there already when I arrived, and I hoped that was true, because I had no idea where the hell I was or where we were going.

As the taxi edged out of the city and closer towards my destination, the buildings got sparser and sparser until we were driving down a dirt road. I glanced at the driver. For all I knew, he could be taking me in exactly the opposite direction I needed to go.

I cleared my throat. "Are we close?"

He nodded his head.

I had no idea if he spoke English or not, if he understood me, or if he had good or bad intentions. I sat back in my seat and fiddled with a hangnail on my thumb.

Finally, we approached a small town, and as we drove further in, I felt a bit of relief at seeing people walking around again. I texted Mason.

Me: I think I'm close, but I'm not sure.

Mason: I'll be here.

I FELT immense relief as the taxi slowed to a stop and I spotted a tall, broad man approaching, and then he leaned over to peer at me through the window. Mason. He opened the door for me. "How was the trip?"

"Long." I squinted at him, shielding my eyes from the sun.

He took both my bags from me. "Let's get you inside." I followed him down a long alleyway, and at the edge of the alley, he pointed to a building across the street. "See that building there?" I nodded as he explained. "I want you to go up those stairs on the far side, and we're in room 214. It's on the second floor." He handed me a key.

I looked at him confused, "You're not coming up with me?" I felt anxiety creeping in. I'd never been to another country, and traveling alone was already a big deal for me, and now he wanted to send me to the hotel alone.

"I'm going to watch you from here, and then I'll meet you up there."

I chewed my lip and looked up at him.

"What's the matter?" His eyes flashed with concern.

"Uh, nothing." I tried to steady my breath. Why was I being such a big baby about this? He was just asking me to walk across the street by myself. But I didn't know exactly where I was going. What if I went in the wrong building and what if we couldn't find each other?

He encouraged me, "I'll see you up there."

"Ok." I took one of the bags Mason handed to me, and he kept the other.

I quickly made my way across the street where Mason could still see me and walked down the road to the building he had pointed at. I glanced back, and I didn't see him anymore. I felt my stomach tighten. I took a deep breath and made my way up the steps to the open air hallway on the second floor. I quickly found the room halfway down the hallway, and I steadied my hand as I pushed the key into the lock and the door swung open. I stumbled in with my bag and quickly shut the door behind me.

Before I even had a chance to look around the room, there was a sharp knock at the door. I peered through the peephole and quickly opened the door.

"You didn't lock the door?" Mason quirked a brow as he came in and shut the door behind him.

I threw my arms around him and hugged him. I didn't care. He had dragged me to the other side of the world, and he could be as grouchy as he wanted. I just needed a hug. I needed to regulate my nervous system. "I mean, I just got in here." I said quietly, realizing I definitely should have locked the door.

"Always lock the door, Emma. Always." I was surprised when Mason smiled and wrapped his arms around me, squeezing me tightly. "You did good."

His praise and his touch made me slick between my legs, and I licked my lips. "I'm really thirsty." I realized I hadn't had much water since yesterday. I didn't want to have to pee on the plane, or on the way over, and now in the heat of this room I was suddenly feeling overheated and thirsty.

Mason let go of me and pulled a bottle of water off the shelf. "You're going to want to stay hydrated." He grabbed a packet and emptied the powder into the bottle before shaking it up and handing it to me. "Electrolytes." He responded to my questioning eyes.

"What was that all about?" I waved my hand around.

"Coming up separately?" He asked, and I nodded. "Let's just say we shouldn't be seen together, and I don't want anyone figuring out we're staying together. It wouldn't be good."

That made me anxious. What exactly did he mean by that?

I took the bottle from him and quickly downed half of it, suddenly feeling a little lightheaded.

"You don't look so hot." Mason felt my forehead. I was suddenly feeling clammy. He guided me over to the bed. "Here, lie down for a little bit. Your circadian rhythm is all messed up from the time change. Sleep for a little bit and you'll feel better." The edge of the bed dipped as he sat on it, and I closed my eyes.

I awoke groggily, and could see through the window that the sun was starting to set. I'd slept the entire afternoon. So much for adjusting to a new time zone. I doubted I'd be able to sleep tonight now.

It was extremely hot in the room, even with the ceiling fan running. I sat up, and my clothes stuck to my body. I realized my throat was so dry, and I quickly found the second water bottle Mason had placed on the nightstand for me and I smiled and downed it. There was a note from Mason.

Stay inside. I'll be back tonight. If you get hungry, I set out an MRE for you. Use the bottled water and the teakettle to rehydrate it. I left my dessert for you. :)

I QUIRKED MY BROW. I could smell the food wafting up from the street, and Mason wanted me to hide inside and eat freeze-dried cardboard. Maybe it wasn't so bad, I decided. I'd never tried one, but I didn't have high hopes.

I grabbed a bottle of water and boiled it using the electric tea kettle Mason had left out for me. I poured the hot water into the spaghetti and meatballs MRE and sealed it shut like the instructions stated, and waited. After five minutes, I squished the bag up to mix it and opened it up. Woof, it was spaghetti, but not what I was used to.

I took a small bite. It wasn't bad, but it certainly wasn't good. No wonder Mason was used to eating the chicken, broccoli, and rice he'd meal prepped in quantities large enough to feed an army. What he had made was far better than this crap.

Despite the flavor, I found myself taking the last bite before I'd realized I hit the bottom. My system was all messed up, and I hadn't realized how hungry I'd been. I smiled to myself, looking at the two packets of cookies he'd set out. He'd left his for me, in addition to mine. It was small, but it was sweet, and it made the butterflies swell in my stomach.

After taking a quick shower, I opened my laptop at the small table across from the bed. Suddenly, I looked around the room, and that's when it hit me.

There was only one bed in this room.

One freaking bed.

My eyes darted around. Was Mason going to sleep in the room next door, perhaps? Or were we stuck together in one bed? My heart raced at the thought. The thought of brushing against him. Of lying down next to each other. My panties were instantly soaked at the thought. I nervously chewed my lips, wondering how tonight was going to go.

I checked the time. Where was Mason, anyway? It was getting late. It was well after dark, and I found myself nervous, hoping that he was alright.

I focused my attention on my laptop. If I was alone, I might as well use the time wisely, before Mason got back and I risked him seeing what I was working on.

Just then, I got a security breach notification. I sat there staring at it for a moment. I couldn't be sure without digging deeper, but this looked like the same footprint. It had to be the same person or group.

If I couldn't hack into our own system without being caught, maybe I could just watch and see what the hacker was looking for. Maybe they'd lead me straight to the answer. It was risky, but maybe I would get a little closer to figuring out what was going on.

I watched as they wormed deeper and deeper in until I got uneasy and sealed off the breach. They'd gone after the military contracts. But what was in those contracts I didn't know exactly.

My fingers hovered over the keyboard, and my heart raced as I went back and forth. If it was the same person, they could be here right now. Maybe what Mason was working on was connected to this. Maybe this information could help him.

Maybe if I couldn't hack into the system internally, maybe I needed to get in from the outside. I knew I could do it. I just had to get to a library or anywhere that had a different computer I could use. I doubted I'd be able to find one close enough to me, at least not in this small town. I closed my laptop and went to stand near the balcony. I didn't walk out in case someone was watching, but I peered out the glass door and up and down the street, just taking in my surroundings.

Suddenly, Mason burst through the door, and I whirled around and gasped, seeing he was covered in blood.

9

EMMA

MASON SLAMMED the door behind him and locked it. He didn't look at me as he went into the bathroom, and slammed that door too.

"Mason?" I got up frantically. He didn't respond, but I heard him banging around in the bathroom. "Mason, are you alright? What happened?" I cautiously pushed the door open.

I caught my breath for a million reasons when I saw him. He was washing so much blood off his hands, and the sink was tinted pink. His bloody shirt was on the floor, and he stood there with his rippling abs, bulging arms, and his neck flexed as he gritted his teeth and rinsed his wound.

I stood there wide eyed, taking it all in. "Mason?" I whispered as I reached out and touched his arm, and his gaze snapped up to me cold and terrifying and I sucked a sharp breath in and recoiled.

He peered at me like that for a moment before he finally relaxed and his eyes changed and softened as he looked at me. He said nothing, but he went back to rinsing out his wound. He had a few small wounds bleeding over his shoulders, but he had one deep, long gash on his forearm.

"What can I do?" I hated seeing him injured like this. He was tense and distant. "Are you ok?" I said with a little more force.

"I'm fine. Most of this isn't even my blood." Mason gritted out.

His response made me sick, and I gripped the counter.

"In my duffle there is a small green zippered pouch. Grab it for me." He instructed.

Without asking questions, I quickly went back into the room and dug through his bag. I quickly returned with the zippered pouch.

"Open it for me."

I unzipped the pouch to reveal gauze, a needle, suture thread, small medical scissors, and a bottle of clear liquid, among other medical items. He grabbed the clear liquid with his good hand and twisted the cap off with his teeth. I watched as he poured the thick clear liquid onto his wound and he spat a string of curse words as he smeared it over the gash.

I leaned with my back against the bathroom counter, watching him as he leaned forward on the counter for support, while the liquid slowly dried.

"Glue?" I asked softly, and he nodded.

"Fucking piece of shit." He hissed, examining the wound. It didn't look like the glue was working. One side of the gash appeared much deeper. He irritatedly grabbed the suture needle out of the kit, and I snatched the thread before he could.

"I'll do it." I said firmly, and I gently took the needle from his hand and he nodded.

I'd never sutured someone before, but I figured I'd do a

better job than Mason doing it to himself. Maybe. I wasn't sure, but I wanted to help. I pushed myself up onto the counter and pulled his arm across my lap. I tried to ignore the zing that sliced through my core at his heavy arm resting on my bare thighs. He was hurt, and I needed to help him. That's what I needed to focus on. I hesitated with the needle above his arm for a moment.

"Go ahead." Mason said firmly.

I took a breath and looked up at him standing in front of me, shirtless and sexy as hell. "I've actually never done this before, I admitted."

"I'll guide you." He nodded.

I went to work and quickly pulled the thread through his skin. The glue was keeping his wound together on the more shallow end of the cut, but not on the deeper side, and now as I pulled his skin back together the dried glue dug into his tender flesh and he didn't say a word, but I could tell it didn't feel good based on his rapid breathing.

"We should have started with this." I mumbled as I concentrated. Mason talked me through the basic stitch, and I worked my way along the wound. Twelve uneven, oddly spaced stitches. "I'm sorry. This probably isn't going to heal very well. I think you'll have a scar." I apologized.

"Then I'll always have a memory of this trip with you, won't I?" Mason stood with one arm across my lap, and one arm braced against the counter, and I suddenly became aware of his hungry gaze on my lips.

"All done." I whispered, barely able to get a word out. I was thrumming with energy for Mason. We were so close, we were touching even, but not in the way that I wanted.

Mason stayed leaning in, even as I set the kit to the side. He slowly slid his arm across my thigh, until it was his hand that was resting there, and I felt like my heart was going to leap out of my chest. My eyes flicked back and forth, reading his, and he flicked back-and-forth, reading mine. His breath was fast, his eyes lusty, his desire clear.

His hand slowly caressed my thigh, and I couldn't suppress the soft sound that bubbled up out of me. He was touching me with intention, with need, and it was everything I thought it might feel like.

I watched as his hand slowly trailed down my leg to my knee, and he gently pushed my legs apart and came to stand in between them. His hands worked their way back up to my hips, and I felt my arms instinctively go around his neck in an attempt to draw him closer to me. His hands worked up over my stomach and he kneaded my breasts through my cami.

I felt like I was suffocating in the best way possible, like there wasn't enough oxygen in the world to give me the breath I was trying to pull in. Mason's touch stole my breath away, and I loved every second of it.

I closed my eyes and let my head tip back, and that's when I felt his delicious lips descend down to my neck. I felt a gush between my legs and I clenched around nothing as his mouth worked its way over my jaw, and then hovered over my lips.

I thought I might explode from the tension, and I let out a small whimper, longing to taste his mouth on mine, and that seemed to push him over the edge and his mouth crashed down onto mine.

His lips were exactly as I had remembered them, but better. They were pillowy and soft, and suddenly his tongue swirled around mine, and I felt my own desperation and desire increase as he claimed me. I'd had my one boyfriend in high school, but this wasn't anything like that. The way he was touching me, where he was touching me. It was like he knew exactly how to prime me up, to set me up exactly how I needed.

His hands were everywhere, his mouth was everywhere, and I relished being wrapped in Mason Reynolds arms, the man I had pined after for ten years.

His mouth stayed on mine, and I heard his zipper. My heart pounded. Would he be rough? Would he be gentle? Would it be big? Would it be *too* big? Would I know what to do? All these questions swirled around in my head as his hands slid my shorts down. My center longed to be filled by him and it was about to be.

"Mason, I have to tell you something–" I started, as his thumbs looped through the sides of my panties, but I was cut off by the ding of a security breach on my laptop.

"Fuck." Mason pulled away, his breathing ragged as he leaned over me on the counter. "You should get that."

I panted, feeling the energy between us dissipate.

"Mason." I said, feeling disappointment wash over me.

He took a step back and put his hands behind his head, and nodded toward the room. "Go."

I looked at him for a moment before regretfully sliding off the counter and over to my laptop.

As I worked, I felt the irritation rise up. I didn't bother digging into this one. I wrapped it up as quickly as possible in an effort to get back to Mason. I heard the shower turn on, and I slipped back into the bathroom. "Mason?"

The water sloshed against the shower wall, but he said nothing. Finally, the water turned off, and his hand reached out and pulled the towel into the shower. The curtain opened, and he stepped out wrapped in a towel, covered in glistening water droplets. And once again, I felt my center clench around nothing.

His face was cold again, and hard. I fidgeted, not sure

what to say. Finally, I reached out and put my hands on his chest, and tilted my head up in an attempt to kiss him again. Mason grabbed both of my wrists against his chest and held me like that for a moment. "I shouldn't have kissed you, Emma. This is wrong."

"But you did," I breathed, "and I wanted you to. I still want you to." I tried not to sound too desperate, but I pleaded with him, anyway. "Mason, kiss me. Please." I said it softly, as I could feel my heart breaking at the realization that what had just happened, what was *about* to happen, was probably over for good.

Mason removed my hands from his chest and slipped around me into the room. I turned towards the mirror and leaned on the counter.

I fought it, but I felt a hot tear slip down my cheek. I suddenly felt so embarrassed, so humiliated, so rejected. I was in my underwear, exposed, and vulnerable, and Mason didn't want me. I gripped the counter, trying to will myself to not cry, but it came anyway. I felt like the least desirable piece of shit.

Mason materialized against the door frame. "Don't cry, baby girl." He said softly.

"I know I'm not like the bombshell woman you normally date, but am I really that bad?" I spat.

His brows went up and his eyes softened, and he pulled me up against his bare chest. My cheek burned as it pressed against his taught muscles.

"It's not like that and you know it." He said gently as he stroked my hair. "It isn't right, you and me." He kept me pulled tight against him. "I shouldn't have done that. I shouldn't have kissed you. I'm sorry."

"Why'd you do it if you didn't want me?" I sobbed

against his chest. I was humiliated and yet I was still finding comfort in the way he held me.

He pulled me back and looked at me with surprise. "Emma, I do want you. But shouldn't."

"You do want me?" I repeated back to him, and he nodded.

"I'm *very* attracted to you, Emma."

My heart swelled at the sentiment, and I felt the hope blossom in my chest again. I reached out and palmed him over his boxers and he growled, and like a vice he had my wrists in his grip. "We can't, Emma. I shouldn't have led you on like that. This is for the best." He said it sharply and firmly.

I bit my lip, and he let my hands go. I went into the bathroom and got ready for bed, and when I came out, Mason was sitting on his laptop at the small table.

"So we're sharing a bed?" I scoffed as I climbed into it and glared at him.

He sighed, "Yes, and I am sorry about that, especially after... I am sorry."

I huffed and pulled the covers up, but it was too hot and I immediately pushed them down. I was still in my cami and undies, but I didn't care. He'd already seen that much, and worst case scenario would be that he caved and gave me what I wanted, anyway. A girl could hope.

After a long while of me tossing and turning, I finally sat up in irritation. "Are you coming to bed? Your glowing screen is keeping me up."

"Right, sorry." He closed the laptop and came over to stand on the other side of the bed.

I knew nothing more was going to happen, at least not tonight, but my pulse shot through the roof all the same when he slid into the bed next to me.

The bed was just large enough for two people, and with Mason's massive body, it creaked and protested under his weight as he adjusted. I could tell he was uncomfortable. He was trying to give me as much space as possible in this tiny bed. I had over half the mattress real estate, but with Mason's size, he should have been the one spilling over into the middle. But at this rate, I didn't care. I was tired and emotional, and if he was going to let me take half the bed, then I'd take it.

10

MASON

AS THE HOURS TICKED ON, I couldn't sleep. My mind was running a thousand miles a minute. I'd killed a man, and then I'd come back and nearly fucked Emma. I was such a moron. But the adrenaline had been pumping, and she'd been sitting there so lusciously tempting. The heat of her thighs sending chills down my spine. The heat from her likely soaked center radiated off her. I could practically smell her want and not only had I been stupid enough to kiss her, I'd been stupid enough to make her feel bad about it when I hadn't followed through.

I'd meant what I said. I did want Emma. But there was no world in which it was appropriate for us. I was a good man. I had values, integrity. And fucking the little girl I'd watched grow up did not align with any of those values. No matter how much my cock demanded a taste of her, now that she was a woman, I had to be stronger than that.

I tried to steady my breathing as I recalled how she'd been putty in my hands, her big wide eyes gleaming and timid as I'd let my hands roam all over her. Touching places I shouldn't have. Awakening things in her I shouldn't have.

Emma grumbled, tossing and turning next to me. I could already feel my resolve slipping. Sharing the same bed for the next few days was not an ideal follow up to what just happened.

Finally, I rolled over, and found Emma sound asleep, sprawled out next to me. I chuckled. She was not having any issues taking up the extra space I'd given her. Her brows were crunched together though, and she mumbled incoherently and whimpered in her sleep.

I felt a pull on my heartstrings as I watched her, likely having a nightmare.

"Please, no," she begged in her sleep, and then she mumbled something incoherent again.

I let out a breath and reached out and stroked her hair softly, trying to soothe her. She was probably reliving the attack in her dreams. Just another way I'd hurt her.

As I stroked her hair, she slowly quieted and stilled, slipping back into peaceful sleep.

I AWOKE the next morning and suddenly froze. Not only did I have the stiffest morning wood, but it was pressed against Emma's stomach, and I groaned at the contact as I twitched in realization. She was intertwined with me, her head on my chest, softly snoring. She was still sound asleep and her legs were threaded around my top leg. My leg was angled up, leaving my knee snugly wedged against the apex of her thighs. Or more accurately, against the heat that radiated out from between her legs. I clenched my teeth together, and I tried not to imagine what that heat tasted like, felt like under those tiny little panties that were now bunched up around her waist, leaving her ass exposed, the skin just begging to be stroked. I tried to ignore the thought that said she'd be so tight and wet for you. I tried to ignore what I knew too, that after last night she'd be thrilled if I woke her up with a million soft little kisses on all those exposed areas of skin.

I gritted my teeth, trying to ignore *all* those thoughts.

Here we go, another day of temptation.

Despite my best mental effort, she stirred, and I tried to ignore the buzz that pushed through me when she brushed against my dick, leaving me twitching again. I could feel her stirring and I sucked a breath through my teeth as I tried to ever so gently shift her off of me, so I could quickly get up before she realized.

I headed into the bathroom to check the bandages on my growing list of wounds. I quickly peeled off the bandage from the wound that Emma had given me via two stabs in the back that night. It was stitched up and healing nicely, but still tender. Then I checked on the newest gash on my arm, the one Emma had stitched up as best she could, and I smiled, knowing that it would indeed leave a scar, and that I didn't mind in the slightest. It was a record of her concern and care. Even if I couldn't ever have that for myself, I'd stolen a moment of it, and now I'd carry it with me forever. I quickly swapped out the bandages, throwing the dirty ones in the trash bin, and I stuffed the bloody ones to the bottom so they were not easily visible.

When I came out of the bathroom, Emma was propped up on her elbows, rubbing the sleep from her eyes and looking incredibly sexy. Too sexy.

I had to get out of this room before I lost my will. "I'm headed out. I'll see you tonight." I quickly grabbed my

things and then snuck a look up at her. She was watching
me quietly. "Don't forget to stay here. Seriously, don't leave."
I said it firmly, a command.

"What am I supposed to eat?" She questioned, suddenly
realizing what she already knew.

"There's more food in that bag."

"Really?" She made a face. "I'm supposed to live off
MREs, you did not include that detail before we left." She
huffed, "I can smell all the good food down there, though."
She lifted her chin towards the balcony, and the smell of
food that was sneaking through the closed door. "Can't
you?"

And I could smell it, but right now I didn't have the time
to play host. That's not why we were here. "I know, but the
less we can leave the room, the better." I'd feel a whole lot
better once I could get Emma back home and on more
familiar ground. I didn't love leaving her here alone all day,
but it was the best option I had at the moment.

She squinted with sleepy eyes. "*You* left yesterday." She
emphasized with a wave of her hand, "Why can't we grab
something, just quickly?"

I came to sit on the edge of the bed and felt her eyes
sweeping over me with longing. "And look how I came
back." She nodded, her eyes flicking down to my arm.
"Promise me you won't leave, ok?" I said it more softly than I
had before.

"Fine," she grumbled and plopped back down on the
bed in frustration. "I'll just rot in here, I guess, eating
cardboard."

I smiled at her, despite her concentrating on the ceiling
and avoiding my gaze, and then locked myself out.

I quickly made my way up the street and over a few
blocks. I headed into a small cafe I'd been to a dozen times

before and gave the cashier a code word. They nodded discreetly, and I headed out and around the side of the building. After waiting for a moment, the gate buzzed open. I latched the gate behind me and made my way down the long, narrow alley. The blue sky was a long thin slice between two buildings, the sun not yet high enough in the sky to fully illuminate the dark pathway. At the end of the alley, in the building on the right, I knocked on the metal door; the sound echoing hollow and sharp.

After a moment, a man whipped the door open and greeted me with a big white toothy smile, a stark contrast from his dark cropped beard. He wasn't particularly tall, but he was sturdy and broad, and I knew from personal experience how strong he was. What he lacked in height, he certainly made up for in strength. I grinned at my friend, whom I'd worked with many times while I was a Navy SEAL, Arash.

"I was wondering when the big man himself was going to come knocking on my door again." Arash slapped me on the arm, and I winced as he made contact with one of my smaller injuries.

I clapped him on the back. "Good to see you, too." And it was, with the work we both did, it was too often that we'd part ways, not sure if that was the last time we'd see each other. It was something we both knew, but never discussed.

He raised his eyebrows. "I thought you were retired." He gestured for me to follow him into the building.

"That makes two of us." I grinned. "I'm working in a different capacity now."

He nodded. "They make it hard to leave, don't they?"

I tilted my head. "Yeah, you could say that." My eyes widened and dilated trying to adjust to the darkness inside, even being as early in the day as it was, it was hard to see, my eyes struggled to adjust to the difference between the bright daylight, and the dark cool of the building.

He led me into a room in the back and gestured to the table. I pulled up a chair.

"Tea?" He asked with a raise of his brows.

I nodded, and he gestured to someone who disappeared into the hallway, presumably to bring the tea.

"You well?"

I grinned, "About as well as I can be..."

"Because you look like shit." He threw his head back and laughed, deep and throaty, clearly amused with his own joke.

I rolled my eyes and chuckled.

Someone returned with the tea, and then Arash excused everyone and closed the door, leaving us in privacy.

His gaze sharpened. "What do you need, friend?" He got straight to the point.

"It's a big ask." I warned him. "I'm looking for the leader of a terrorist group. I believe it is known as The Crescent?"

Arash clicked his tongue and nodded in recognition.

"So you know them?" I prodded.

"Are you after information, or is this a kill order?" He questioned.

"Does it matter?"

"No, I suppose not." He shook his head. "Though I'd advise against leaving loose ends at all possible costs. If you know what I mean."

And I did. It was a serious warning from a wary soldier. Maybe not the soldier of any government now, but a soldier nonetheless. "Do you know where I can find a man in the organization by the name of Armeen?" I asked.

He nodded. "*I* don't, but I think I know someone who can get you that information. But I believe the man you're *really* after is someone they call The Viper. I believe Armeen pulls the trigger, but only as The Viper commands."

I scoffed and shook my head.

Arash scolded me. "I know, I know. On the nose... *maybe*. But this group, Reynolds... everything they touch is poisoned, *so* much death, *so* much violence." He smiled warily at me. "Do be careful, friend. I'd hate to see you get bit." He stood up.

"No promises."

He swung the door open. "Give me a moment. Let me see what I can find out about Armeen."

Arash returned a short while later with a scrap of paper and an address. "A meeting. The Viper will not be there, but Armeen should be."

I nodded and thanked him for the information.

He walked me back to the front door. "They've been acquiring military weapons at an alarming rate, you know."

"I know. That's what I'm trying to slow down."

Arash threw a couple of play punches at me. "I'd like to see you breathing the next time I see you."

"So would I." I stepped out into the bright daylight, and I turned towards him sheepishly. "You wouldn't happen to be willing to loan me a car, would you?"

Arash grinned and tossed me a set of keys before I'd finished the question. "I was waiting for you to ask, old friend. I was just waiting for you to ask." He chuckled, "Don't get her too dirty now," and disappeared behind the closed door.

I made my way down the alley and found the gate at the other end already unlocked. I pushed it open and into a small parking lot, where I quickly found the matching car to the keys he'd given me. I shook my head and laughed; the car was absolutely caked in mud and dust.

I had a couple of hours before the meeting time Arash had given me. I'd be able to scope out the location and hopefully find a good spot to listen in during the meeting.

I got a text from Emma

> **Emma:** What do you recommend for breakfast? Eggs and hash browns or Eggs and peppers.

I CHUCKLED TO MYSELF. Breakfast was not one of the better foods to enjoy with MRE's, something about rehydrated eggs wasn't a big winner in my book. I usually ate a dinner meal for breakfast for that very reason, but I deviously decided to let her figure that out on her own.

> **Me:** The hash browns are more filling. Depends on how hungry you are.

> **Emma:** Alright, I'll give it a try. Thanks :P

I CHUCKLED. I was definitely going to hear about this later. I'd try to make it up to her later and grab something for dinner, give her a taste of authentic street food before we left. I debated telling her about the dinner plans, but decided to keep it a surprise instead. If I could wrap this up cleanly this afternoon and make it back early enough, we could enjoy a nice meal together, and I'd only have to endure one more night with her in that damn dollhouse bed. Otherwise we'd be pushing our luck, if we shacked up together much longer. I tried to push the thoughts I'd had this morning out of my head, as I remembered the feeling of her pressed against me.

After driving for a bit, I found myself approaching the address Arash had given me, and I stopped a ways away, opting to approach on foot. The address was a large abandoned warehouse, with a few scattered buildings around it, all quite dilapidated, but overall the location seemed to be a low traffic one. After making my way around the building, I slipped inside, and once again my eyes worked to adjust to the change in light.

I quickly placed a few discrete microphones in various places in an attempt to record the conversation that was about to take place. Then I made my way up into the rafters and positioned myself behind one, in an effort to stay concealed. I pulled out my sniper rifle and set it up, and then I waited. If all went well, I'd record the conversation, and if Armeen did show up, I'd evaluate my ability to take him out right here and now. It would require taking out whatever security was inside, as well as the guest he'd be meeting with, necessary casualties. I was here to gather up as much information as I could, and then, as Arash had suggested, tie up the loose end when I was done. I'd have to feel it out. But hopefully I could take down Armeen.

I shifted up in the rafters. It was a hot day, and it was even hotter all the way up here now that it was well into the afternoon, and even hotter with all the gear I wore. I felt a bead of sweat work down my neck and disappear into my shirt collar.

My mind once again wandered to Emma, and last night, and back to how good she'd felt against my chest when I'd woken up this morning. I blew a breath out. I was glad I could keep an eye on her, but in hindsight, it probably wasn't the best idea to bring her to a place where we had to share a room, share a bed. It would be too easy to slip up, when we both wanted each other so deeply.

Plus, if she ever found out what the stab wound on my back was from, that it was the one *she'd* given me. I didn't know how she'd respond. She'd probably never speak to me again, and I'd deserve it.

The one silver lining to coming back injured last night is that I now had a variety of injuries across my body, so hopefully she'd be none the wiser. Not that I planned to go shirtless around her more often than I needed to, but personal space was certainly difficult in that tiny room.

I pulled out my phone and checked the microchip I'd injected into her shoulder.

Another secret I was keeping from her.

I shook my head.

The GPS dot showed her hovering over the apartment.

Good girl, staying put.

I nodded to myself, feeling relieved that she'd listened to me. I warily slipped the phone back into my pocket, knowing the day was young.

I checked the time. We were nearing the appointment.

Suddenly, the doors to the warehouse creaked open, and a man entered with one security guard in front and behind him. I stilled as I watched them through the scope. I didn't recognize this man. A short while later, a second man entered with security escorting him as well.

This man I did recognize through the scope.

My target.

Armeen.

I watched as he waved the security off and they excused themselves outside.

Fuck.

I was hoping they'd stay inside. It'd be far easier to pick them off that way. I counted six and wasn't sure how many were outside.

11

11

EMMA

I FINALLY PULLED myself out of bed and dug around in Mason's bag for breakfast. After texting him about which egg meal I should eat, I settled on the eggs and peppers. It was supposedly a little lighter than the other. I boiled more water for my breakfast and hoped I had picked well.

I stood hugging my arms across my chest, watching the tea kettle hum away, working so hard to boil water. I felt a sadness settle in the pit of my stomach about Mason stopping things last night, and the longer I stood there, the more pissy I felt about it. He'd freaked me out, storming in here covered in blood, and then he'd gotten me all hot and bothered, and then just left me with a burning, throbbing, aching need. I needed a release so badly, and I wanted him to be the one to give it to me.

He had admitted that he wanted me, so that was something. It made me feel a little less humiliated. Then the image of his bloody clothes flashed through my mind, and my stomach clenched. Even if we weren't together, he was still someone I cared about. I'd known him most of my life. But getting closer with him over the last week, especially after kissing him, knowing he was restraining himself, everything felt heightened, and the thought of him out again today, doing God knows what; it made me anxious.

I poured the water into the pouch and sealed it shut while it rehydrated. I squished it around and opened it. It smelled okay, but it looked worse. I took one bite and gagged, quickly chucking it into the trash.

No way.

I sat in front of my computer and munched on the left-over cookies Mason had shared with me yesterday. If I couldn't dig through the contracts without getting flagged, maybe I could dig through Mason and Viktors' records and figure something out that way.

I spent the entire morning scouring, and I found nothing. The amount of nothing I found was *so* much nothing that it could only mean someone had taken all that information and made it into nothing. The lack of information I found was just as telling as finding the information itself.

I stood up and paced. What could this mean? Was it possible that Mason also worked off book, that he was part of a black ops team, was it possible that he was part of *my* black ops team?

I raked my hands through my hair. That would certainly make the most sense. He was the one my dad had begged to help me, and had been the last resort we'd gone to before I'd been in contact with Viktor. If he was working for or with Viktor, then that was exactly how he'd gotten me hooked up with the position in the first place.

I dove into an expired contract, knowing it was a far safer place to start, and checked the records for all the breaches. There were some variations, but there were similar ones that kept showing up on the records again and again. I chewed my lip. If the same person was doing this over and over... Why wasn't it being dealt with? Unless someone didn't want it to be dealt with.

There was no way the agency didn't know. I may not have been allowed to track the source of the breaches down, but I flagged them up the chain of command every time. My understanding was that there was someone responsible for dealing with the source of the breaches. But maybe there wasn't. Maybe everything was so separated out at the agency that they'd unwittingly created a hole. It was highly unlikely, but it was certainly a possibility with the data I was looking at.

And if it was in fact someone internal, then this was getting extremely dangerous, extremely quickly. I wondered how much Mason knew. I needed someone to talk to. The isolation of everything was wearing me down. Something wasn't right, and if I could just bounce some ideas, some thoughts off of someone, anyone, maybe I could get to the bottom of it. It was a huge risk to bring it up to him though, because if someone at the agency was involved, they were covering their tracks extremely well. If Mason even had context for any of this, I could possibly be putting him at risk, and that was the last thing I wanted. To drag him into my mess. But even still, something in me felt like he'd probably be the perfect person to talk to about this.

I'd have to feel it out with him, I decided.

But the one thing I knew for sure was that something was *definitely* up.

There were just too many pieces that didn't add up. The more and more I thought about the night of my attack. I played back Viktor's words in my head, trying to remember exactly what he'd said. It was all so fuzzy, though.

How had I ended up in the facility?

How had my attacker gotten to me so quickly?

The attacker had to be well connected. There had to be an organization or a network if the breach was made here in Iran, but I was attacked within hours back home. This was organized, there was no doubt about it.

I sat there with my feet up on the chair, leaning on my knee as I pondered, and suddenly realized I had been at this for hours, and I became aware of the pressing need to use the bathroom. I wandered into the bathroom absentmindedly, still thinking about everything. When I reached for the toilet paper, I let out a low grumbling noise from the back of my throat. There were all of four squares of toilet paper left.

I stretched, still sitting, and leaned around and peered into the bathroom cabinet, willing there to be stocked rolls of toilet paper.

Fuck.

I took the last four squares off the roll and used them before hunting around the room for extra toilet paper anywhere.

Nothing.

As I looked around, I peered into the bathroom trash, and noted the bloody bandages, at how many there were in there. More than I had put on Mason last night. My stomach clenched at the thought. I caught my reflection in the mirror and gazed at my own fading bruises. I diverted my eyes away to avoid the fear that twisted in my stomach whenever I remembered the events of my attack.

Finally, I gave up searching, realizing there was clearly no toilet paper, and stood with my hands on my hips. I had zero idea what time Mason was going to be back, and how long I'd be stranded here. I quickly texted Mason.

> Me: There's no toilet paper here!!!!!!

I WAITED A FEW MINUTES, and there was no response. So I texted him again.

> Me: I don't want to drip dry for the rest of the day, you know. When will you be back??

STILL NO RESPONSE.

I grumbled again and got up and peered through the glass door leading to the balcony. I hesitated for a moment and then slid the door open and stepped out into the hot sun onto the small balcony. I peered up and down the street. People and cars lazily made their way to wherever they were going, and no one so much as glanced up at me. I chewed on my lip for a moment, wondering what I should do, if I should go out. I thought I spotted a drug store at the end of the street, though I couldn't read the sign. If I hurried, it probably wouldn't be a big deal, and I certainly would need toilet paper again at some point today, especially if all I was eating was those nasty MREs.

Seeing as I still had no response from Mason, I'd have to take matters into my own hands. If I was going to have to survive on two more MREs today, I certainly wouldn't be able to make do with four sheets of toilet paper. Not that there was even that left now.

I went back into the room and pulled on the clothes Mason had instructed me to wear; neutral pants and a lightweight button up I pulled on over my tank top, and finally I fumbled as I wrapped the headscarf loosely over my hair once again. Mason had made sure that I wouldn't stick out as much as possible, but as I stared at myself in the mirror, I wasn't entirely sure how convincing it was, especially with the remaining bruises on my face.

I dug through one of Mason's bags and found some money, and shoved it into my pocket, not knowing remotely how much it was. It could be enough for a pack of gum, or it could be enough for the down payment on a car for all I knew. I was about to push myself up off my knees when a glint caught my eye. One of Mason's pocket knives. I only looked at it for a moment before shoving it into my pocket. Just in case. Next to it were a couple of passports. I opened it up to see my photo and an entirely new name, different from the fake one I'd used yesterday. Curious, I unzipped another one of Mason's bags and found it filled with weapons and guns, and I quickly zipped it shut and stood up.

More confirmation that Mason *was* special ops. No record of anything anywhere, and a bag full of military grade weapons.

Who are you, Mason Reynolds? What do you do?

With the knife and the money in my pocket, I took a deep breath, and I opened the door. I peeked my head out into the open air hall and was blasted with that same warm air again. As I peered back and forth, I didn't see or hear anyone, and I stepped out into the hall. It suddenly dawned on me that I didn't have a key.

Fuck.

I quickly went back into the room and softly shut the door, my eyes darting around, searching for the key. Mason had locked himself out this morning, and I wondered if that was the one and only key we had for the room. I pulled out my phone, still no response from Mason. I texted Mason again.

> Me: I'm going to run up the street for TP. Is there a key????????

I PRESSED my head against the door, and then whipped the door open again, and still no one was in the hall. I shook my head and stepped into the hall and closed the door behind me and prayed a silent prayer that no one would realize the door was unlocked. I'd be gone for a mere 15 minutes, maybe less.

I didn't like it, but what other choice did I have? Mason should have set me up better before he locked me in here. Keeping my head down, I quickly made my way to the corner where I thought I had spotted the drug store. I opened the door, and quickly realized it was a small eatery, and my mouth watered, and my stomach growled as I realized I hadn't eaten more than a nibble of a shortbread cookie for breakfast. I sighed and stepped back to the street, knowing I didn't have much time, and I needed the toilet paper most. I looked around and walked another block up, and felt a surge of relief when I spotted a small convenience store.

I stepped into the cool air of the store and nodded to the cashier, who looked me up and down before going back to whatever he was doing before I'd disturbed his peace. I stood on my tiptoes and surveyed across the shelves in the middle of the store, hunting with my eyes for what I needed.

My gaze swept over snacks and drinks, and I eyed them hungrily. I walked around one of the shelves and on the bottom; I spotted what I needed. I quickly grabbed a pack, and decided if I was here, I might as well get a few snacks. Because why not?

Some of the packaging was in English, some not, and even still I could recognize what the chips and snacks were. I reached for a bag of what looked to be similar to a sour cream and onion chip, and I felt my pulse quicken as I became aware of a second man in the store. He stood nearby, looking at an item, but I suddenly realized he'd been watching me, and for how long, I didn't know.

A shiver went up my spine and I felt a pulse of anxiety shoot through me. I left the chips and as I approached the cashier, I'd already dug out a wad of bills to pay for the toilet paper. As I stood there, I felt the man's shifty gaze on me and my anxiety bloomed a bit more; I waited just long enough to see that the money covered the amount for the toilet paper, and I quickly moved for the door, leaving the cashier with whatever amount of change he was counting to give back to me.

I whipped the door open and stumbled onto the street, not daring to look back. I walked quickly with purpose, and crossed to the other side of the street as I got back onto the block we were staying on. Only then did I sneak a look over my shoulder, and what I saw made my chest seize up, and my limbs go numb. The man was definitely following me, and I panicked as I neared the apartments.

I needed to get away from him as fast as possible, but I also didn't want to lead him straight to where we were staying. I veered around the far side of the building I'd originally come up yesterday and sprinted up the steps, my thighs burning with the frantic exertion as I pounded down the hall and finally stumbled into the room.

I froze.

Someone was bent over Mason's bag, rifling through it.

Rifling through our passports, and money, and whatever other secret things Mason had in there. They stood up and spun around hearing me, and I felt the tiniest tinge of relief at seeing it was a young boy, maybe thirteen or fourteen. His eyes went wide, and he threw his hands up.

Suddenly, I became aware of pounding footsteps, and before I could whirl around, my headscarf was yanked off, and then someone was yanking me back by the hair, and shoving me to my knees.

12

MASON

ARMEEN and his associate moved to an area of the warehouse that the microphones I planted couldn't quite pick up. I groaned to myself as I peered at them through the scope. Where they were standing, I couldn't hear a damn thing, from up here, or through the ear piece I had in my ear.

My phone buzzed in my pocket in a specific pattern I'd set up as my alert to see if Emma was on the move. I gritted my teeth.

Damn it. Why couldn't she just stay put?

I softly set my rifle down and eased my phone out of my pocket. I tapped on the notification and quickly saw that she was two blocks up from the apartment. I zoomed in and looked at the location. I shook my head. She was at a convenience store. She'd no doubt given up on the eggs and decided to take matters into her own hands. While I understood that the eggs didn't make the most appetizing of meals, I'd eaten them for years and learned to put up with it.

I swiped out and saw a slew of messages from Emma.

Emma: There's no toilet paper here!!!!!!

OH SHIT, I chuckled, realizing I hadn't remembered to tell her there was extra toilet paper in one of my bags.

Emma: I don't want to drip dry for the rest of the day, you know. When will you be back??

Emma: I'm going to run up the street for TP. Is there a key????????

OH FUCK.

I'd locked her into the room this morning. There was an extra key, but I didn't specifically think to mention it to her because she was instructed to not leave. But she'd left anyway, and she'd left the God damned door unlocked, it seemed. With all our valuables, all *my* valuables inside.

I flexed my jaw and swiped over to the GPS. She was headed back to the apartment. I sent her a quick text.

Me: Sorry about the TP. I had some in my bag. Text me when you're locked back in the room, please. I'll be back soon, hopefully.

I FLIPPED BACK over to the GPS and watched as the dot quickly moved back over the apartment. I waited for a moment as the dot stopped feeling my chest loosen, but still no text response from her. I felt my chest tighten as I watched the dot move back up the street and then quickly, *too quickly,* up the next road. I quickly texted her, not sure what I expected.

> Me: Emma?

> Me: Emma, please respond and let me know where you're going.

I SWALLOWED hard as I watched the dot move too fast for her to be on foot, and I tried to steady my breathing at the realization that she was in a car.

In my hiding spot up in the rafters, I laid my head on my forearm and focused on my breathing for a moment. Terror swept through my body as my mind filtered through every horrible explanation. I shook my head. No, there had to be a reasonable explanation for this. Maybe she took a taxi. I texted her again.

ME: Emma? You there?

STILL NO RESPONSE. I quickly cross checked her phone's location, and was further horrified to find that it was at the apartment. She was in a car, and she didn't have her phone.

I dragged a hand over my mouth and picked up the rifle once more and eyed Armeen through the scope. I couldn't hear a damn thing they were saying, and they were moving towards the door like they were finishing up, anyway.

Suddenly, I heard several gunshots outside, and I tensed, finger on the trigger of my own gun. I peered through the scope, watching the door. The warehouse door slammed open, and a man stepped halfway through it and fired two shots in rapid succession. Armeen went down, and so did the man he was meeting with. I stayed still, just watching, observing. The man dragged one body out, leaving a trail of smeared blood, and then returned and dragged the second out, firing an additional shot into Armeen as he struggled before going still.

I heard a car engine start, and I swiftly came down from the rafters, as a car with no plates sped away.

Fuck.

I sprinted to my own car, and when I saw where Emma was on the GPS, I thought I might vomit. She was miles away from the apartment and headed into the middle of nowhere. Where she'd be isolated in the desert.

I sped past the city and into the desert as I followed her. I was thirty to forty minutes away. It was too far. It was too long to leave her without help. I gripped the steering wheel and tried to focus on what I would do when I got to wher-ever she was. I tried to ignore thinking about what might happen to her if I couldn't get to her quickly enough.

She was traveling with *me*, and if anyone knew that, it was a risk on its own. But she was a young single woman, and that was reason enough for not going unescorted here. I pounded the steering wheel until my palms ached, angry with myself for even bringing her here. Angry at myself for not protecting her better. For not making the risk crystal clear. I hadn't wanted to scare her, and if she would have just stayed in the room, she would have been fine. But as my palms ached from slamming them into the wheel over and over, I realized that I should have scared her. I should have made the risk clear as daylight. What might happen to her if she was spotted alone? Here.

I roared at no one as I floored it to where the dot had now stopped on the GPS, and I counted the minutes and the miles until I reached her. If anyone had laid a finger on her, I would do terrible, terrible things to them.

MY HEART THUNDERED in my ears as I pressed my back against the wall of the long single story concrete building. I stood in the shadow and gathered myself, settled my mind for what I might find inside.

I had instructed Arash to come after us if he didn't hear back from me. I had to ensure I could get Emma out, even if I couldn't get myself out.

I peered around the corner and watched the man guarding the door. He mindlessly paced back and forth, not alert, not ready for what was about to hit him.

I closed my eyes for a moment and breathed out. As I breathed out, I emptied all the emotion out of myself; I shoved the panic about what I might find inside into a tight box that I sealed the lid on.

I flicked my eyes open and moved quickly and softly, coming up behind the guard. Before he could make a sound, I slit his throat and softly lowered him to the ground. Dragging him around the corner to bleed out, I carefully kept an eye on my surroundings and then used my boot to kick dirt onto the trail of blood I'd left, effectively covering it.

I wiped my knife on my pants and pulled out my gun as I slipped inside, willing my eyes to adjust to the darkness more quickly, willing my senses not to betray me. Not here, not now.

I breathed in a slightly foul smell, not quite placing exactly what it was, but knowing it was not a good sign. I blinked as I worked my way down a long, wide hallway, pausing at the first doorway to listen. I knew from the tracker I had placed in Emma's shoulder that she was about halfway down this end of the building.

I quickly scanned and worked my way past several doorways. In some, I spotted various metal tools and instruments laid out on tables, much like the ones I'd used to extract information many times before. The sight of it made my stomach roll, and I steeled myself, clenching my jaw as I kept moving. I couldn't think about it, couldn't think about the possibility of Emma being in this place, where they used those types of things.

I moved past a few more doors with cell bars imprisoning limp people, cowering on cots, facing the wall, away from their doorways. Avoiding eye contact and attention, no doubt. I swiftly scanned each cot as I slipped by, looking for Emma, and that's when I heard it... and my blood ran cold.

A guttural, desperate scream.

Emma's scream.

My pulse thundered in my ears.

The screaming was followed by gasps and weak coughs, and then, what I didn't think could be worse than the screaming... it went silent.

The silence was a dagger through my heart.

Fear like I'd never felt before consumed me, overtook me.

Terror shredded through me as I quickly approached

where the source of the sound had been, and as I rounded the corner, gun drawn, eyes like a scope, that's when I saw it.

Saw what they were doing to her.

In the moment that I realized she was still alive, relief flashed through me, but the moment was almost too brief to count, because it was immediately suffocated by blind rage. Rage so hot and purpose driven that it snuffed out everything else.

Something in me broke and as my body took over, I watched Emma's tiny hands clawing, flailing, fighting for her life with all her might as a much larger man jerked against her, holding her head under a bucket of water.

He lifted her, pulling her back by the scruff of her neck, a bag over her head, and she gurgled, choked and struggled to pull in breath against the sopping wet fabric against her face. Her clothes were ripped in various places, exposing her, and small splatters of blood speckled her clothing. Before she could unleash another scream, or pull in another desperate breath, her head was back under the water.

The shots simultaneously rang out in the air.

I fired one, two, three shots.

I heard gunfire spraying around me.

Four, five shots.

Silence.

And then, finally, the sound of splashing water and Emma gasping for breath again as she pushed herself up out of the water. Coughing, sputtering, gagging as she fought to pull in breath.

Tunnel vision.

Emma and only Emma.

My body took over again, and I moved towards her.

She was in my arms, pulled into my lap in a flash.

She clawed against my arms, leaving my skin open and bleeding as I held her tightly against me.

"You're safe, it's Mason, I've got you." I pressed her to me and chanted these words at her until she finally stopped fighting against me and her hands went frantically to the bag on her head.

I felt a growl bubbling up in my throat as I quickly pulled my knife out.

Not only had they put a bag on her head, but they'd zip tied it around her throat. It served two purposes. It made the bag impossible to take off, and even more impossible for her to pull in a full breath in the brief moments between her head being forced back under the water.

I quickly cut the zip tie and pulled the bag off her head.

The look in her eye as the bag came off shattered me.

Her dark eyes filled with wide terror, no relief that it was *me* holding her.

Just fear.

Just unadulterated fear.

She gripped my shirt and finally collapsed against my chest, alternating sputtering coughs with heart wrenching sobs. My heart ached at the sight of her small vulnerable frame trembling in my lap.

We had to hurry. "That's right, just breathe." I kept my tone calm, soothing. I flicked my eyes around. I had to get her out of here. Someone would have heard the gunfire. "There you go, that's it, I've got you." I breathed the words into her hair as it touched cool and wet against my lips.

Just before I could pick her up, she turned away and vomited mostly water onto the ground beside us. "You're alright. I've got you now." I chanted it to her, over and over. An attempt to soothe her.

As I stood up, she was weak against me, hardly able to

stay upright, and so I swiftly threw her over my shoulder, but before I could reach for my gun, I pivoted towards the door and my heart sank.

We had company.

I watched in frustration as men with guns drawn on us filed into the room, and one man without a gun finally filed in last.

The unarmed man wore an amused look, smug perhaps. Though the only unarmed person aside from Emma in the room, he seemed well at ease.

I quickly pulled Emma down against my chest and she turned, pressing her face into me, refusing to engage with what was happening in the room. She continued to cough up the water in her lungs, but her breathing, while still rapid and frantic, was slowly starting to come in more controlled gulps.

The unarmed man who stood blocking the door spoke first. "Such a shame." He motioned to the men I'd murdered in cold blood who laid on the ground bleeding out around us. "They were good men. They were my men."

"Then they shouldn't have laid a finger on her." I spat. My eyes swept around the room, evaluating.

One door.

One window.

Eleven men.

Ten guns.

Eight bullets left in the chamber.

One clip just out of reach, on my right hip.

I slowly shifted Emma around me, and she clutched me, hardly letting me tuck her behind me, hardly allowing me to shield her body with mine.

"She's quite stubborn." He said, raising his eyebrows at Emma.

I glared at him, willing him to disintegrate with my gaze as I also watched the armed men as they stood watching us. They were calm, not entirely disrupted by the dead bodies that laid around us, bleeding onto the concrete.

"You know, it's in your best interest to let us walk out of here." I growled.

The man paced to the other side of the room and looked out the window. "Perhaps." He waited for a moment before turning back and continuing, "Perhaps not... I know you're U.S. intelligence."

"Then you know there will be heavy consequences if we don't walk out of here." But I was getting the sense he already knew that, and he didn't care. My chest tightened as my mind raced, considering the options, the possibilities.

How many could I put down before I'd have to reload? They'd put more bullet holes in me than I could count, but if I could reload just one more time, perhaps I could finish them. I might not walk out of here, but Emma might.

He turned towards us, his hands behind his back, "You know, I just love the USA. They're so forward, so modern. But we are well on our way here..." A sinister smile crept onto his lips. "Though I must admit, we do have some barbaric laws." I could feel his eyes drilling into me, analyzing, watching for a reaction. "For instance, did you know it's illegal for a woman to stay with a man if she's not married to him?" His eyes narrowed, watching me. "Unless, of course, they're family... which *you* are not." He paced to where he could see Emma standing behind me as she clutched me, silently trembling. "Such a shame she couldn't stay put, isn't it?"

I pivoted, once again pushing her out of his eyeline, and he smiled at me. The look dripped through my body like poison. "Well, it's a good thing we're married then." I lied through my teeth, but I had gotten us passports with matching last names for this very reason.

The man paced around to the other side of the room, not looking at me again, as he casually found interest in the light bulb on the ceiling, and then a crack in the cinderblock wall, "Wouldn't that be nice, if it were true?" He had a smug look on his face as he watched me.

I rehearsed the muscle movement in my mind's eye. Eight shots, reload, three shots, run. It was those last three that I was worried about. There were just a handful too many men in this room for me to take out, while still being able to keep Emma out of the line of fire. There were just too many, and if it were just me, I'd risk it. But it wasn't. "You're welcome to check on that." I pivoted around the room, keeping an equal distance between us as he slowly paced around us. "I think you'll find we share the same name."

The man chuckled, "You did come prepared, I'll give you that. But you and I both know those are false documents. No, I know that Miss Mitchell is not your wife, and as such, I'm afraid I have to do my duty to my country and take the girl with me. To carry out the consequences of this unholy abomination that she's committed."

"Like hell you do." They weren't taking her anywhere. I pulled my gun and fired, until the clip ran empty, then I slammed the next clip in and fired until the clip ran empty. Bullets came spraying back towards us. I gripped Emma behind me with my free hand, clutching her to the back of my body as she screamed.

An automatic gun fired all around us. I whirled around and dove to the ground, covering Emma's body with mine. I willed myself to become wider, denser, ensuring more coverage over her.

The gunshots stopped, and I panted as I assessed how badly we were shot.

"There will be order!" The man shouted in irritation. And I lifted my head to the wall behind us to see a circle of bullet holes in the wall, a halo around us, not directly at us. I peered over my shoulder and my heart sank as more armed men filed in, and now held a wide, impenetrable circle around us.

Underneath me, I could feel Emma trembling uncontrollably. I felt a gun press to my neck, and I lifted my hands up in surrender. Someone kicked my gun away while another grabbed the second gun I had and removed it from me. Another man grabbed Emma out from under me and dragged her up as she screamed. In one swift motion, I grabbed my knife and slashed his calves, splattering both Emma and me with blood.

I felt the hard butt of a gun as it contacted my skull, and I stumbled back, blindly, as my vision went spotty. I shook my head, willing the room to come into focus.

Two men held Emma up by the arms while the man in charge stood in front of her. He softly grazed his knuckles over her cheek and her lower lip trembled as a tear spilt over the rim of her eyes. "Such soft skin."

She jerked against the men and finally screamed, "Let me go." Her voice was hoarse and hollow.

"Don't you fucking touch her, you bastard." I tried to stand up, but was shoved to the ground again. I felt a warm trickle work its way down my temple and softly plop onto the floor in red taunting drops.

The man cocked his head, "So strong willed. Even after all that unpleasantness." He motioned to the bucket of water. "She still wouldn't speak." He continued, "I think my men will quite enjoy themselves with such a hellcat. It's always more fun when they fight. Don't you think?" His lips curved up in a soft smile at me as I registered the threat.

I roared and shoved the man standing over me into the wall and grabbed his gun, but before I could make another move, the man in charge cut me off. Each man holding Emma now had a handgun aimed at her head.

"Tsk, tsk, tsk." The man scolded, "I wouldn't do that if I were you."

"What do you want?" I said through gritted teeth.

His eyes lit up. "What do I want? Well, perhaps if you'd prefer my men didn't desecrate your little flower, maybe you'd prefer to do it?"

"What do you want?" I spat.

"If you want to prove to me she is indeed your wife, *show me*." His eyes were glimmering, as if he'd just come up with the idea.

My chest rose with tight, uneven breaths.

"You bastard." I spat. And the next few moments whizzed by us.

"If you're not inclined to cooperate..." He motioned to the men and one pulled out a knife and slid it into the space between the buttons on her shirt, and one by one, he sliced the buttons off, further shredding her clothing. Leaving her shirt open and exposed, as he ran the blade down her chest, she cried out as he let the blade break the skin. Finally, in one quick motion, slid the knife under the fabric of her bra, and ripped it open, leaving her completely exposed to all the hungry eyes in the room. "I'm sure she'll be compliant by the time we give her back to you." The man said. "If she lasts that long."

"Mason." Emma screamed with such force I thought I might dissolve from the sound. "Mason, don't let them take me." She fought against the men holding her, but didn't gain an inch of ground. That terror filled her eyes again.

"Fine." I roared.

The man's eyes glimmered again, and he motioned towards the gun in my hands, which I reluctantly laid down on the ground, and then he nodded towards Emma. The men released her, shoving her roughly to the ground, and I closed the distance between us and pulled her into my arms.

"Don't let them take me, Mason." She trembled as she said it over and over again. I pulled her tightly against me, covering her chest from all the watching eyes.

I turned her around, with my back to the men in the room, and pulled her face into my hands and forced her to look at me. She just nodded with understanding. I whispered to her, "We can find another way." She nodded into the room, and I looked over my shoulder as the walls became covered with soldiers as they filed into the room with smug grins. A shiver went up my spine at the realization of what was about to happen.

"You won't mind if we watch." The man stated, as he leaned against a table.

I turned back to Emma. "I won't touch you unless you ask me to." My heart was breaking.

Her lower lip trembled. "If you don't, they will." Her eyes went wide as an armed man approached.

"Don't you fucking take another step." While I no longer had weapons on me, I must have sounded menacing because the man didn't.

The man in charge checked his watch. "I've got a busy day, get on with it, or I'll let them have her before I execute her."

"You're going to fucking pay for this." I growled.

Emma reached up and grabbed my face in her hands,

suddenly looking at me, as if she wanted to soothe *me*. "Just pretend it's last night. I'll be ok, I promise. We just have to get through this."

Fuck.

But what I didn't have the heart to tell her was, even if we did play their little game, they might still try to take her anyway. I gritted my teeth. If they did try to take her, it would be over my dead body.

I warily eyed the cot in the corner and backed her up to it and gently laid her back onto it. Disbelief sweeping over me, at what I was about to do, what I *had* to do.

13

EMMA

"I'M NOT GOING to let anything happen to you, Emma. No one's going to take you." Mason gently scooted me up on the cot, gripping me under the shoulders. "Eyes on me," Mason instructed. "Only on me."

My lungs burned, my throat burned, the tears in my eyes burned. My chest burned from where the knife had broken the skin. But most of all, my pride burned, for not listening to Mason, for not taking his warnings seriously enough. I had been stupid, so, so stupid.

Lost in my own mind for a moment, a myriad of emotions raced through me. Fear, defiance, determination, uncertainty, shame.

Such shame that I had left when he told me not to. And another shame too, shame that as I laid on this dirty cot with Mason looming over me, that I couldn't help but feel the heat between my legs blooming. Despite the watching eyes, despite the danger, and maybe because of the danger, my adrenaline and desire bubbled to the surface.

I trusted Mason wholeheartedly.

I trusted him with my life.

I trusted him with my body.

I trusted him with my virginity.

I tried to steady my breath as I wondered if I should somehow whisper it to him, my secret. To warn him. I didn't know if he needed warning.

I wondered if I'd be able to push through the pain of my first time, wondered if I didn't tell him, if he'd be able to tell anyway. Wondered if I dared whisper it to him, if the others would hear, if they'd snarl and chuckle and if it would fuel their sick desires.

Mason lowered himself over me, angling his body to block as much of me from viewing eyes as he was physically capable of. And it wasn't hard, as I looked at his broad chest spread out in front of me. Seeing him on top of me like this, I realized just how big Mason really was. As I felt the weight of him sinking onto me, I realized just how dense and thick those muscles really were. He lifted a hand up to stroke my cheek with his thumb, and that's when my eyes darted down and through a sliver of visibility.

I gasped at what I saw.

Mason didn't look. He kept his eyes on mine, as I kept my eyes on what I saw.

He took my chin in his hand softly, and he whispered just as softly. "Don't look at them, look at me."

I finally flicked my eyes back to his. Those brown eyes were warm and sorrowful, regretful. "They're recording us, Mason." I breathed. As if being watched wasn't bad enough, as if giving my virginity to Mason, like this, in front of these men wasn't bad enough. They were recording it.

My mind raced a million miles a minute, trying to figure out, if I ever got out of this, how I'd track all these men and their phones, recording me, and wipe any record of this moment into oblivion.

"Focus on me." Mason said even more softly, and I had to stifle a soft gasp that threatened to escape when his thumb made contact with my hip bone, bare and exposed now that my shirt was ripped open. My eyes flicked to him. "That's it. Focus on me, focus on how this feels." He rumbled down into my ear and the heat of his breath swept me into all that was Mason.

As his hands worked over my stomach, up the side of my leg, I could tell Mason was going to do his best to prime me up before he buried himself in me. His mouth met mine, softly. So, so softly. He gently swept his tongue over my lips before he worked over my jaw, and then the delicious soft place between my collarbone and my neck. It was a chaste kiss compared to how he'd kissed me last night. An apology, of sorts. I shuddered as the warmth of his touch caused a slick pool to form between my legs; a dull aching, a hungry pulsing. I shuddered at the thought of what it would be like to take him. To take a man for the first time. To take a man as these armed soldiers watched us, recorded us.

"Lose the clothes." Someone grunted, and the others agreed.

Mason ignored them until I felt cool metal meet my cheek.

"Lose the clothes." The soldier with the gun snarled.

As Mason pulled back, he gave the soldier a look so dark that it should have leveled him to the ground, and the soldier stood back.

In one swift movement, Mason pulled his blood splattered T-shirt up over his head, and in a second swift movement, he stepped out of his pants. My heart pounded as I took in his chiseled chest, and then my eyes wandered south. I swallowed hard at the angry erect member that loomed before me. Mason stood fearless, naked, defiant.

As I laid there, I reached down and unbuttoned my own pants, and willed myself to just look at Mason, to not flick my eyes to the wall and watch the men's eyes as I undressed.

With one knee resting on the cot and one hand reaching for my waistband, Mason instructed me to lift my hips. In another swift movement, my pants were gone, and in the next Mason's body was looming over me, once again shielding me from the prying eyes mere feet away. Merely a second of exposed skin, and now I was safely cocooned underneath him again.

I became suddenly aware of his hard length pressing against me through my underwear, and I let my hands roam over his chest as I softly bucked my hips up to meet his friction. An invitation, permission, longing, forgiveness all wrapped in one discrete movement. I saw in Mason's eyes he understood.

"I don't have all day. Get on with it, or my original threat stands." The man in charge sighed like he was already bored with us.

Mason's hands lingered at the waistband of my underwear, his eyes asking, questioning. I nodded in response.

His thumb slipped under the fabric and I couldn't catch the whimper that slipped out of me when it connected with my throbbing center. I heard the men in the room shift and chuckle at the sound. I felt heat bloom in my cheeks.

Mason grumbled at their response, but I could tell there was a fleck of relief that I wasn't repulsed by his touch. He lowered his torso closer to me as he slid my underwear down around my knees. "Bite my shoulder if you have to. Don't let them win." He gazed at me a moment longer. "Ready?"

"Yes." I barely whispered as my back arched and his thumb circled my most sensitive spot so briefly.

One of his knees slid between my legs and nudged them just far enough apart to lower himself between them. I felt his head thick at my entrance, and I bit my lip as he so, *so* gently began to ease in.

I'd imagined this moment with Mason more times than I cared to admit, and now, as it was happening, I didn't know what I wanted. I was conflicted at my true desire for Mason, and at the horrific situation that my dream was unfolding in.

Mason kept his eyes on me, watching, monitoring, alert, as his hands roamed and continued kneading over me. My breasts pebbled at every stroke and every sensation. I struggled not to writhe under him at both the pleasure, and now also the burning stretching. I squeezed my eyes shut, and rasped in unsteady breaths as he sank lower and lower, the stretching, the burning consuming me. Here it was. I had wondered what it would feel like, and I started to sweat as I focused on my breathing to push through the pain.

Suddenly, Mason froze as if he could read my mind, and when I opened my eyes, I realized I'd broken the skin on his biceps, digging my nails into him.

"It's alright, keep going." I panted.

His eyes swept over mine, frantically; reading, interpreting, wondering. As if, as if he suddenly knew.

"Do it or they'll know." I hissed.

He hesitated for a moment, and I bit his shoulder as he gently eased the rest of the way in. He waited for a long moment, and then in a voice so soft, in my ear closest to the wall, he breathed. "I didn't know. I didn't know."

"I know." I hummed, and I wrapped my arms around his neck and gripped him to me. My shield, my protector, my savior, and he couldn't bear it, that he'd been forced to do this to me, to save me. I could feel it in the shakiness of his voice as soon as he'd understood what was happening. What he was taking.

More insults, more demands were hurled at us, and I braced as Mason pulled back just enough to look at me with such sadness, and then he consumed my mouth with his, as passionately as he had last night, and he snapped his hips into me.

As I gasped at the sudden fullness again, his mouth consumed any sounds of pleasure or pain as they slipped out of me. And then, before I knew it, it was over. He pulled himself into me one more time, hard and fast, and shuddered, jerking against me, his breath ragged in my ear.

That was it.

He'd come inside me.

It was done.

Mason stayed frozen in place, his body still blocking mine from view. I heard shuffling, and some clapping and crude talk; some of it in English, some of it in a language I didn't understand.

"Thank you for the material," a voice said." And then finally, it went quiet. The light in the room went out, and then a cold clanging of metal, locking keys, and then more quiet.

Mason turned over his shoulder, and swept the room with his eyes, empty, and then he slowly pulled out of me. I shuddered at the sensation.

He stood up, and handed me my pants, and quickly pulled his own on, and then his eyes flicked to my bare chest, and he didn't look away, he just once again kneeled on the cot. "Arms up." He instructed gently. And he pulled his T-shirt over me, covering me.

He looked at me quietly for a long moment before finally speaking. "Emma–"

I swallowed hard and quickly leaned forward and
pressed my fingers to his lips. "Don't." I whispered hoarsely.
I could see the pain swirling in his eyes. "We did what we
had to, and that's all there is." He took my hand from his lips
and he took it in his, kissing the back of my hand tenderly.
His gaze traveled over my face, and something, possibly
pride, flickered in his eyes briefly before he licked his thumb
and wiped my face. I looked at him with a question in my
eyes.

"Blood." He said and his eyes hardened again.

And then, he was all business. He stood up and surveyed
the room, the window, the door, the ceiling. He paced the
room over and over, taking in our surroundings, taking in
our cell.

I watched him quietly, letting him calculate, consider,
and hope. After some time, I finally laid back on the cot and
stared at the ceiling. I didn't know what they were going to
do to us, or what was going to come, but I found a brief
moment of peace. It was a brief moment of being able to
pull big full breaths of oxygen into my lungs, and for that I
had never felt more grateful.

I stroked my throat, presumably where the zip tie had
dug into my skin, and my heart raced at the memory of
fighting for air. Of thinking I was going to die, of thinking I
was so close to pulling in breath, but being unable to while
my lungs filled with water instead. As I laid there, I
suddenly felt so, so tired.

And then finally, I felt those big, warm hands snake over
and under my body, and I felt Mason wrap himself tightly
around me. The warmth of his breath sent another shiver
up my spine. "I'll be awake." He said. "You can close your
eyes if you need to." He spoke softly in a soothing voice.

"Did you find a way out?" I grumbled, not having the

energy to hardly get the words out, my throat raw and hoarse.

He sighed. "No, not yet."

I pushed myself back into Mason's body; I wiggled my hips back into his. I felt him tense as I rubbed against him. If I didn't have this, if I couldn't be even a *little* mischievous, what did I have?

Nothing.

And that wouldn't do at all.

Not at all.

14

MASON

HOURS LATER, my mind wandered to Arash, and I wondered if he'd come. If he did, I hoped it was soon. What had just transpired was horrific, but if we couldn't get out, I knew it would pale in comparison to what would follow. The things they'd do to us, the things they'd do to Emma.

There was no way out of this room, of this cell. Of that, I was certain. I'd have to wait until someone came to check on us, and hope that I could out muscle them. At this point, that was our best chance.

I gripped Emma to me as we lay on that tiny cot. I listened to her breathing, trying to decipher if she was awake or sleeping. If she was sleeping, I'd let her get her rest, but once she woke, I had questions I needed to ask her.

I reflected on the words the man in charge had said, that Emma hadn't given up any information. I wondered what they knew, what information they were trying to get from her. How they had known she was with me.

Emma shifted, mumbling incoherently, and began to whimper in her sleep. I gently shook her, but she didn't wake. Her breathing was fast and uneven. I roused her a little more roughly until her eyes finally snapped open and she shot up frantically, pushing herself away from me.

"It's me, it's me." I grabbed her by the shoulders, forcing her eyes to meet mine. Finally, recognition swept over them, and her shoulders slumped.

Suddenly, I heard an explosion. Emma looked afraid, but I listened a moment longer, and then I let myself smile.

Emma looked at me, confused. "We're getting out of here." I breathed.

WE RODE SILENTLY in a jeep with a man I didn't know, but who had cleared the pathway out of the prison in blood. I recognized the insignia on his uniform and knew he was with my friend, Arash. He deposited us in the parking lot I'd borrowed Arash's car from earlier. I walked with Emma's hand in mine as we waited at the gate to be buzzed into the alley, and then finally we stood in front of the door where I'd last seen Arash.

The door opened, and my friend looked from Emma to me with a grim look in his eyes as he waved us inside the dark building.

Arash agreed to drive us to the apartment, where I could scope out the building to see if I could retrieve any of our things, our passports, our ticket out of here. I had asked Emma to stay with him while I went to retrieve our things, but she'd refused. She refused to let go of me, let alone let me out of her sight. And I didn't blame her for it. After pleading with her, she'd agreed to stay in the car with Arash near the apartment while I gathered our things, but that was as far as she was willing to let me out of her sight.

I slipped back into the building and quickly threw our

things together. I couldn't tell what was missing yet. I'd just have to grab everything in sight and take inventory later.

I kindly thanked my friend Arash, as he dropped us off at an apartment in the next city over. "No one will bother you here, at least not for a few days." He assured me.

I pushed the door to the room open, and waited for Emma to go inside, before closing the door and firmly locking it behind us. She stood quietly with my giant shirt draped over her and waited for me to speak first.

I motioned to the bed. "I'm sorry, it's one bed again." I dragged a hand through my hair and realized how dirty it was. Caked in blood, dust, and sweat, most likely.

Her eyes flicked up to mine. "I'm not." She said it plainly. No desire, no spite, just content with the sleeping arrangement.

"We'll take an inventory of what was taken, and then we'll figure out how quickly we can get home." I assured her.

She nodded and sat on the edge of the bed.

I rubbed my neck. "You want to shower first?"

"Sure." She nodded and disappeared into the bathroom.

When the door closed, I blew out a breath and sat on the edge of the bed. I needed to talk to her, to check on her, but I didn't know how. I didn't know what to say. I didn't know the right words to use.

After what I'd been forced to do to her, I didn't know how to exist around her. She felt so breakable, like rare porcelain that was ready to shatter.

While she showered, I quickly went through the bags and did a once over inventory. All my guns were missing, the passports seemed to be gone, and various other odds and ends had been looted. I groaned as I squatted in front of the bags on the ground.

"What is it?" Emma asked.

Without turning around, I responded, "Our passports, and my guns are missing. Not good."

"Oh."

I finally stood up and turned around. Emma stood barefoot, her hair wet, the blood washed from her face, wrapped in a small towel. My gaze dropped to her chest, where her breasts heaved against that tiny towel, where the top of that cut started and then disappeared between her breasts. I felt anger flash through me for a moment. She just stood there, letting me look. I shifted as I looked at her, and she looked at me. Suddenly, it dawned on me that I was blocking her path to her clothes, and I awkwardly motioned to the bags while sidestepping out of the way.

I moved towards the bathroom, and as I closed the door, I saw Emma looking at me over her shoulder with a look I couldn't decipher.

I stood under the hot stream of water, watching the rust brown water pool around my feet and wash down the drain. I was grateful for this shower, grateful Arash had a place we could stay for a few days while we got back on our feet. There had been many days when I'd had to eat and sleep caked in dirt and mud and other people's blood. It was not something I looked forward to. It was a simple luxury to be able to shower like this.

I turned off the water and wrapped myself in a towel, eyeing the gash on my forearm, eyeing the stab on my side. I considered Emma's gash and realized we'd both need to do a little first aid tonight.

I stepped out into the room and Emma sat on the edge of the bed in one of my giant T-shirts and a pair of those soft little sleeping shorts she loved to wear. "I borrowed your shirt." She chewed on her lip.

I crossed the room and pulled out my own clothes. "I see that." I dared another glance at her, and she watched me, again with a look I couldn't read in her eye. She held my gaze for a long while and then finally turned her head the other way to let me change. "Nothing you haven't seen before." I mumbled.

"No, I guess not." She responded, and I felt her eyes flick over me before they shifted away again.

Clothed, I sat next to her on the bed. "Emma–" I started, and once again before I could finish she was closing my mouth, but this time it was with her lips, not her fingers.

She threw her arms around me and pulled herself into my lap as she hungrily pressed her mouth to mine. I gently pulled her back, looking at her. "We need to talk about what happened. I need to make sure you're okay."

She pulled herself back to me desperately.

"Emma, please, talk to me."

When she couldn't reach or get her mouth to mine, because of the distance I kept between us, she finally collapsed against my chest, her arms slipping down from around my neck. She sobbed against me, gut wrenching, soul crushing sobs.

"I'm not even remotely ok." She shouted into my chest and the vibration echoed through my body. "I nearly died. I thought I was going to die... I was so scared, Mason, so scared you wouldn't find me, that you wouldn't come for me." She pulled back to look at me, her eyes wet. "I can't imagine what would have happened, what they would have done to me, Mason. I'm so sorry I left the apartment. I shouldn't have. I should have listened to you."

"You didn't know." I breathed, "I should have made that more clear, but I didn't want to scare you, and that's my fault. I shouldn't have brought you–"

She cut me off "Mason..."

"Yes?"

"I need you. I need you *now*." She tried to pull me closer to her.

I stroked her cheek with my knuckles. "Emma."

"Mason. I've loved you since I was sixteen, ever since the first time you saved me and pulled me out of that pool."

My pulse quickened as she laid herself bare to me.

"I've imagined what it would be like to *be* with you, more times than I can count. When I touch myself at night, it's *you* I think of, *you* I want." She spoke slowly, emphasizing each word. "You're all I've ever wanted, Mason, and I got you, but not the way I dreamt of, not the way I wanted– the way I want."

The breath left my body. "Emma, it's not right. I'm so much older than you. I've known you since you were little..."

"I'm not a little girl anymore, Mason. I'm not." She breathed, her emotions tittering between hurt, and rejection, and desire. "I've never been with anyone–"

"And I'm *so* sorry for that. I'm sorry for all of it, but I'm especially sorry for that." I couldn't help but consider if I had just succumbed to temptation last night, maybe then her first time would have been the way it should have been, filled with pleasure and in the safety of an intimate quiet moment between two people.

I could hear the hysteria, the desperation in her voice, "We can– you can't let that be my first time Mason, I can't let that be the only memory that replays in my head over and over when I think about losing my virginity. Please." She begged, her hands roaming over me, tears spilling over her eyes. "Please, I know you don't want me. I know that." The sound of those words, of her thinking I didn't want her, broke my heart. She continued, "But please don't let that be my only sexual experience. Give me something good, give me something filled with love, to smother out all the horrible things that happened in that room, Mason."

My heart responded to her plea, and my body did too. When we had kissed the other night, I'd wanted to lay her out on the bed, and make her come in nine different ways, whether I should or shouldn't have. After today's events, I wasn't sure. But she was right. She didn't deserve for that to be the one and only sexual experience she'd had. What a terrible thing that would be.

As I let myself consider her in that way once more, as I released the seal on that box of my feelings for her, of my desire for her... I *was* attracted to her, more than I wanted to admit. I knew it wouldn't be hard to give her one night. What *would* be hard was letting it be *one* night. Could I have her coming on my fingers, on my tongue, have her riding my cock, and then just walk away after tonight? Did I have that kind of strength? I didn't know.

She must have sensed the shift in my resolve, my hesitation in my eyes, because she watched me carefully as she slowly, slowly leaned back in, and this time, I didn't push her away; I let her lips meet mine; I let her hands thread through my hair.

Fire, electricity, desire.

My dick lit up in approval.

I shut my brain off and let my body take over. Let my hands roam over her body, up her sides, and down her arms as she relaxed against me. I scooped her into my lap and grabbed the nape of her neck, and deepened the kiss, tasting her sweet mouth as her lips parted and she let my tongue explore her mouth before it danced with mine.

She pulled herself tighter against me, and I held her face

as I moved soft kisses over each eye, and then warm, tickling breaths over each ear. There was the sound of that erotic little whimper again, the one she'd given to me in that room, the one that had told me while the situation was traumatic, it wasn't my touch that would do the most of the damage.

I swiftly picked her up without breaking our kiss and deposited her into the middle of the bed, laying her back, so *so* gently. This time, when I touched her, it would be slow, it would be for pleasure. This time when I entered her, she'd be breathless and begging me to.

I took my time, tasting every inch of her face, her neck, letting my hands explore all the little bare places of her skin before we even started removing clothing.

"I want you, Mason." She breathed up at me through hooded eyes, her hips tipped up to meet mine. A request for more friction.

And I wanted her too, but I would take my sweet, sweet time, for her, and for me. "I want you too, Emma." I growled into her neck, and she shuddered at the sound. "I'm going to teach you." I let my hands trail against the waistband of her shorts. "Teach you how this should always be." I continued. "I'm going to start by teaching you how to come on my fingers." I worked my way down, pushing up the giant T-shirt she was wearing and kissed across her stomach down to her hipbones, giving her a hot open-mouthed kiss on each. She arched her back up and whimpered in response. "Then," I rasped. "I'm going to teach you how to come on my tongue."

She panted, barely uttering out the words, "Please, Mason. I need you."

I slid those little shorts down, dragging my hands down the sides of her legs before I slipped them down over her bare feet. Rubbing the soft sensitive spot on the inside of her ankles, I could see a damp spot forming on her underwear, and I continued, "And then I'm going to teach you how to ride my cock, until you come, over and over again. Until you're dizzy, and can't think, or breathe, you're filled with so much pleasure." I began a slow, torturous path up her inner leg with my mouth. A different kind of torture, the kind I was happy to inflict on her, over and over again, despite my better judgment. "Would you like that?" I growled as I got closer to her inner thighs.

She clutched the sheets in balled up hands and panted, "Teach me Mason, show me."

My hands snaked up under her shirt, and I palmed her butter soft skin under my fingers, finding a nipple and rolling it between my fingers until it was hard. Her back arched at the contact. I worked my mouth back up her stomach until I was at her face again. "Arms up." I instructed. She greedily complied, letting me slide my shirt off her, leaving her in nothing but her panties and her blushed skin.

My eyes went to the long shallow cut down her chest that trailed between her breasts. I kissed it from top to bottom, so, *so* gently, with feather light pressure.

My hands grazed everywhere except the sweet spot she really wanted me to touch, a buildup that she would appreciate later. As I worked closer and closer to her center, I was already met with that slick wet heat that had worked its way down her inner thighs. I slipped a finger into her underwear, and she violently arced up off the bed in response.

"Oh, Mason." She cried out, "Yes."

I gripped her underwear in my teeth and dragged them down her legs, only this time when I kissed a trail back up, I kissed until my mouth found that warm slick heat, and let my tongue taste her.

15

EMMA

I GASPED, feeling like I could ascend into the sky. "Oh, God." I breathed between moans. New uncontrollable sounds tumbled out of my lips one after another. Mason's mouth continued working steadily over my center. I couldn't think. I couldn't breathe, my muscles, my core, my body was tightening, urging me towards the edge. I clenched around nothing, the longing to be filled, burning brightly.

"That's right, you're almost there." Mason growled into my core, and I thought I might shatter at that feeling alone.

"Come for me, Emma. Be a good girl and come for me." He sucked my clit into his mouth and as his hands kneaded my nipples, I unraveled.

The room disappeared, and there was nothing but intense pleasure. A black hole of bliss was swallowing me up as all my muscles contracted and then uncoiled at once.

The room slowly came back into focus, and I panted as Mason nuzzled into my throat, sucking and tasting the skin there. "Again." He whispered into my ear, and his fingers dipped into me, one and then two. And then, to my surprise, a new sensation, deeper, different.

"Oh God. Mason…" I wrapped my arms around his neck as his hands pulsed inside me. His mouth met mine, hungry and wanting, and I tasted myself on him.

I had hardly caught my breath. I was already ragged from being unraveled once, and I felt my center tighten around his fingers, felt my legs tighten as he urged me closer and closer. Warmth spread through my core as I reached the edge again, blissful desire as I pushed myself down harder on his fingers.

He chuckled at the movement and breathed into my ear. "You're doing so good, gorgeous. That's it, come on my fingers, like I know you can." The words sent a thrill down my spine as they mixed with the heat from his breath.

Again, I couldn't think, I could hardly breathe, the only sound of my ragged breath and moan after moan, a crescendo of sound coming out of my mouth, and then his other hand slipped over my stomach, pressing down so that the pressure of his fingers inside me was met with the pressure of his palm against the outside of me. I screamed and exploded, crying out his name again and again.

I blinked, feeling lightheaded with my arms around his neck, as he shifted to my side and let me catch my breath.

"Mason, I want you inside of me. I need to feel you." I panted. I needed to fill more than just those long deft fingers. I needed all of him. Needed to meld with him, to not be able to tell where my body ended and his started. I needed him closer.

He nodded and slipped out of his pants and quickly returned, continuing to kiss me softly as I came down from my high. Once again, I felt his head at my entrance.

"It won't hurt this time." He nuzzled into my neck. "I promise."

He parted my legs, and he was right. This time, I was so

slick, so wet, so ready for him. He watched me carefully as he slid into me. I felt full, stretching, adjusting to accommodate him, and he slowly continued to ease into me, until I finally felt his hips tether against mine.

"So wet for me. So ready to take me in." I blushed at his comment, and I let my hands wander over his muscular, hard chest, his abs. I followed my intuition and wrapped my legs around his waist, and raked my nails over his ass. He shuddered at the touch.

"Easy, or this will be over before you've gotten a decent ride." He growled.

But I didn't care. I wanted him to come inside me again. I wanted him to fill me up. I wanted him to have a release as good as he'd given me.

I raked my nails over his ass and he slid out and thrust into me, his eyes filled with dark, glimmering desire. I raked my hands over his body, watching him now responding to my touch, as I squeezed myself tightly around his cock. I watched as his breathing turned ragged like it had before, and one of his hands reached up, gripping the headboard as he slammed into me over and over. And before long, I felt that tightening, and I gave way to his touch as everything within me coiled, ready to spring once more. My body, ready to dump me into the sea of ecstasy at any moment.

His mouth was on mine, my hands were tangled in his hair, his hands gripping my hips, my thighs with every thrust as we together shattered into bliss. I screamed out and felt his hand clamp down over my mouth with a chuckle as he groaned with his own release.

"Not too loud, or we might find ourselves in some trouble again."

In one swift motion, he rolled us over, still inside me, and he pulled me onto his chest as he laid on his back. I laid my head on his chest, draped over him, as his arms splayed out beside him. After a moment, those big warm arms wrapped around me, and he gently lifted me up off him and laid me back on his chest.

"That's my girl." He stroked my hair and kissed the top of my head.

"Thank you." I breathed, feeling enveloped in the scent of him. Earthy, and musky, and like you'd imagine, a big muscled man would smell.

"Thank *you*." He chuckled as he traced his fingers down my back and over my side. We laid there for a while in each other's arms, our breathing steadying.

I felt him under me, and bit my lip, looking up at him.

He smiled, a devilish grin that sent a blush through my entire being. He sat me on top of his hips, on my knees with my center draped over him, leaking out with his desire and mine, lubricated with my new desire to feel him again.

"Now I'm going to teach you how to ride my cock." He chuckled, guiding my hands up to his chest, and then the headboard. "Here, or here. You choose."

I squeezed my eyes shut, and my head tipped back as he lifted my hips and helped me lower myself onto him again. In this position, I felt him even deeper within me.

He gripped my hips as I shyly found my rhythm. He continued to praise me, his hands roaming over me, his eyes gleaming at me, admiring me, worshiping me as I took my pleasure on him. When I was almost there, I began to tremble, and he took my hips in his hands and drove me down onto him over and over until we could both once again find sweet release.

Mason cradled me in his arms, whispered sweet nothings into my ear, how beautiful I was, how he wouldn't have known what to do if he'd lost me, and over and over again he split me in half, guiding me to pleasure I hadn't known my body was capable of. I relished in every bit of it, of the fantasy come alive, of the tenderness of his embrace, how feral his eyes became right before I climaxed. I fell hard into the ocean of Mason's eyes, and I knew that I really truly did love him, and as he gazed at me, I thought, maybe he felt the same.

Hours later, I sat once again at the edge of the bed, and he ever so gently applied an antiseptic balm to the cut on my chest. His eyes, a mixture of guilt and hunger as he looked at me, and touched me.

He took my face in his hands. "I will never let something like this happen to you again, Emma. Never."

I gave him a soft smile. "I know." And I knew he meant it. I knew he would protect me from ever experiencing horrors like this again. My mind drifted to the men's phones in the room, the way they had snickered, the recordings they took. I had to get on a computer ASAP and figure out who this group was, maybe just maybe, I would have a chance of retrieving and destroying any and all evidence of the horror of what happened there.

He took my chin in his hand. "What are you thinking?"

"I'm thinking I need a computer... I need to try to scrub those videos off all those phones."

Mason raised a brow at me. "I wouldn't count on a high success rate for that."

I blew out a breath. "I know, but I have to try, at least." I hesitated for a moment. "Thank you, by the way." Mason waited for me to continue. "Thank you for covering me, for blocking me from their view."

"What else was I supposed to do?"

"Can I ask you something?" I eyed him. "You're part of

the black ops security team, aren't you, under Viktor... like me?"

Mason shifted, getting slightly tense.

"I looked you up. You don't exist. Which means... well, you know what it means."

"Em, you know I can't tell you that."

"No, but you could tell me if I'm wrong..."

Mason said nothing.

"What I'm working on, you, us coming here. It's not a coincidence."

Mason's energy shifted, and he got up. "You need to leave this alone. You keep digging and we're both going to end up worse than today."

"I think it's someone on the inside." I continued.

Mason snapped, "Don't you get it. If you're right, if it is someone on the inside, you're putting yourself in even more danger. Do you know who those men were? Do you?" I could feel myself shrinking at the tone he took.

"They..." Mason looked around and lowered his voice. "They are part of a terrorist group, Emma. Or at least they're closely associated with them. This isn't a game. We got lucky today." He shook his head, and his fingers grazed the cut on my chest. "Despite everything, we got really, really lucky. That won't happen again." He stood up. "We're disposable. Don't make it easier for them to do."

I chewed my lip, debating if I should reveal what I had discovered earlier, that I knew someone who went by The Viper was attached to the string of attacks. I didn't know how much I could get out of Mason, but it was a start, and knowing, even if he wouldn't outright admit it, that we worked for the same organization, the same agency, the same division, it made me feel a lot less alone.

16

MASON

"LEAVE IT ALONE, EMMA." I gripped the edge of my kitchen sink back home as she continued to dig.

"If you would just share some information with me, maybe I could figure this out." She huffed.

I spun around. "Don't you get it? I don't want you anywhere near any of this. It's bad enough that I got you a job here, but you just need to keep your head down and do the work. Stop digging, stop prying into everything. Please." I begged her.

"Why won't you tell me anything?" She pointed her finger at me. "I'm on to you Mason, I know you know far more than you're letting on." She shifted in her seat, her voice more soft. "Who was that terrorist organization, and what did they want to do with me and you? How did they know who we were?"

"I'm not at liberty to share."

"Why won't you help me?" She pleaded right back, "Why won't you help me get out of this?"

"What?"

"The agency. I want out."

"Emma."

"If I could just figure out who's behind this, maybe I can deliver Viktor a big win. Maybe he'll renegotiate my contract. Let me leave. I don't know, I'm desperate. I'd do anything to get out."

"Oh, Emma." My heart sank when I realized her main motives for why she was going after this like a hound. I closed the gap between us and hesitated before stopping in front of her. I nearly took her face in my hands, but after that night in Iran, I'd found my resolve and I hadn't slept with her again, but the tension between us remained taut and my desire to reach and touch her nearly broke my resolve. "There is no getting out. I'm so sorry about that. I wish... I wish I hadn't helped recruit you in the first place."

"Don't say that. If you hadn't, I'd be in prison. We both know that... but that doesn't mean I want to be trapped by Viktor and by this damn agency for the rest of my life. I want out."

"What would you even do?"

"I don't know. Anything. Everything. Just exist, have a life, have friends." She narrowed her eyes at me. "Find time for a lover, maybe." She turned away from me and went back to working at her computer on the table.

"I care about you, Emma, deeply. But we can't be together like that. We just... we can't." The amount of guilt I carried for not only what had happened to us in Iran in that cell, but then that I'd fucked her on every surface in that little room, whispering things I shouldn't have to her, trying to wipe away the pain we'd both endured in those moments.

I shuddered and tried to ignore the shiver that ran down my spine at the memory of those little whimpers and sounds she had made under my touch. The ones that made me hard just thinking about them. The only resolve I had was to try to make all of this right by never sleeping with her again.

She sat there silently typing, and then her shoulders slouched. She leaned on her hand. And then cautiously, "What do you know about The Viper?"

I ran a hand over my face. "For Christ's sake, how do you know about that?" This girl, this woman, she just couldn't help it. Over and over, she was flirting with danger.

"I know that he's linked to what happened to me at the house. I know that he's attached to nearly every security breach we've had in the past three years. And I'm almost positive that someone on the inside is working with him. *And* I know you have heard this name before by the look in your eyes."

This time, I did take her face in my hands. She stilled at my touch. Her eyes became softer, more hooded. "Emma, you're the smartest woman I know, but sometimes you can be a real dumbass." I couldn't help the corners of my mouth from twitching up, and hers did as well. And then I became more serious. "I mean it, I'm not going to tell you what you're saying is wrong, because you know better, but I am going to tell you that you're in way too deep. You shouldn't even know names like that. It's... it's not safe. Do you understand? Do you get what I'm trying to tell you?" She chewed her lip and her eyes drifted to my lips. "I've been trained, trained to deal with and handle what we went through in Iran, and worse. You haven't–"

"How do you know I haven't been trained?" She taunted, "I could be higher up in the organization than you." She raised her brows, and I chuckled. I had to be careful how I broached this subject with her. She still didn't know I was her team leader. "I just know." I responded. "You're not cut

out for those kinds of situations, nor would I expect you
to be."

She got quiet for a moment. "Mason, why *did* you bring
me with you?"

"I didn't want to leave you alone here." And I hadn't. I
didn't know if she was safe. I didn't know if Viktor would get
any bright ideas and take things further with scaring Emma,
or worse.

"Why not? You don't think I'm safe?" She spoke evenly,
but her eyes were combing over my face, searching, trying to
decode all the answers she could tell that I wouldn't
give her.

I sighed, "I don't know. I don't know if you're safe here
alone. That's why I brought you." She nodded and left it at
that.

I went back to doing dishes, and we were both quiet for
the rest of the night. Emma stayed furiously working away
on her laptop and I didn't bother to ask what she was
working on, and I had my own follow up to do after the
mission went sideways in Iran. I had to figure out who had
killed Armeen, and why, and who the man who had taken
Emma was. It could have been a random abduction, but I
seriously doubted it. He knew too much about Emma and I
for that to be the case. But I didn't bring any of that up with
Emma.

Emma said good night and then softly padded up the
stairs for the night. I watched from the dining table as she
walked down the hall and she looked down at me, before
softly closing her bedroom door behind her. I groaned and
rested my head in my hands on the table. What a mess. It
was taking everything in me not to burst through that door
and scoop her up and take her into my bed, where I wanted
to bury myself in her again. The look she'd given me when I

told her I wouldn't touch her again. She'd looked so hurt, and I just couldn't bear to keep hurting her. It seemed like that was all I did to her, hurt her, and I hated it. Staying away, I thought, would be the best way to take care of her. At least I tried to convince myself of that.

Finally, feeling frustrated after coming up with no further discoveries or information on the issues, I made my way upstairs. I couldn't help but hover outside her door for a moment. I could see the soft glow of the lamp from under the door, and I wondered what she was doing in there. I gritted my teeth and made my way into my own room, finally crawling into my sheets, alone.

I WASN'T sure what time it was when I awoke, but I immediately broke out in a cold sweat.

Screaming.

Emma was screaming again.

Faster than I could process what I was doing, I ripped the gun out of my nightstand and flung my door open. I could still see the soft glow of the lamp under her door, and she screamed again. I ripped the door open, searching, ready to pull the trigger, but no one was there, just Emma.

She thrashed in the sheets and I took her shoulders and gently shook her. She mumbled incoherently and cried out in her sleep.

"Emma." I shouted it to her, but she didn't wake.

I climbed into the bed and pulled her into my lap. "Emma, wake up. You're just dreaming."

Her eyes finally flicked open, and she thrashed for a moment, gasping for breath as her eyes met mine. She struggled to suck in full breaths as she hyperventilated.

"Just breathe, I've got you. You're right here, you're with me, you're safe."

When her breathing had finally steadied enough, I moved to get up. She slid her arms around my neck. "Don't leave me, please."

I blew out a breath, "Alright." I stood up and carried her down the hall to my bed. "Your sheets are soaked. Let's go to my room." She nodded.

"Here." I handed her one of my shirts, and she didn't turn as she peeled hers off and replaced it with mine.

I pulled back the sheets, and she climbed in and I pulled her to me as soon as I slid under the sheets. She settled into my chest.

"I keep having these awful dreams. I'm drowning over and over again. Those hands around my neck, shoving me into the water." She shuddered against me. "I'm so lonely, Mason." She tilted her head up, "I can't talk to anyone, and you... you won't hardly look at me since we got back."

I ran the pad of my thumb over her lips and then tilted her chin up to me. Her eyes fluttered closed as she waited for me. And I couldn't bear to have her feel alone any longer. I let my lips meet hers, and kissed away the tears. As my hand ran down her torso, she gave a little whimper, and my dick lit up at the sound.

"Make me feel better." She whispered.

"I will." I promised, "Be good, and let me take care of you." I rolled us over so she was on her back and my mouth quickly found its way to her sweet desire. The heat, the smell of her, the way she bucked her hips, and arched her back at my every touch. I pinned her hips to the mattress as I devoured her. And not until she was desperate and begging did I finally bury my hungry length into her tight, warm center. I tried to ignore the thought, but the fact that I was the only one who had touched Emma, who had tasted her. It made me feral. Her body was mine, and mine alone.

"What are we going to do about your dad?"

"He won't care."

"I seriously beg to differ."

"Let's not worry about him right now. We have too many other things to worry about." She sighed, "At least I have you now."

17

17

EMMA

My GAZE DRILLED into the gym mirror in front of me, my feet pounded the treadmill one after another. A meditation of sorts. Even from here, I could see the dark circles under my eyes. After so many nights in a row of waking up screaming, Mason had finally just moved me into his bedroom. And while I did sometimes wake up screaming, it had been farther and fewer, and when I did, he woke me up almost immediately, and in his arms I quickly settled back to sleep.

I could see the guilt, though, see how he thought of himself, about how he was so conflicted every time he touched me.

I had pushed Mason a bit, but I knew I wasn't going to get any further information from him, so I finally just shut up about it. Sweat trickled down my chest and burned where it met my healing injury, instantly reminding me and taking me back to that day in Iran. My lungs burned as I sprinted on the treadmill, another reminder at the privilege it was to suck in oxygen, to suck in breath.

I glanced down at the distance and as I crossed the two-mile mark, I finally pulled myself up and stepped on the railing while I shut the treadmill off.

I made my way into the locker room and stripped down, wrapping myself in a towel while I laid in the sauna. I needed to get out of this contract somehow. I needed to figure out who was behind all this. I needed out of this life. Desperately.

I knew Mason had recruited me, but I wondered who had recruited him, if he was just as trapped as I was, or if he chose this.

I laid staring up at the ceiling, considering all that I knew. The contracts, I'd mostly gleaned, were military weapons contracts, and someone on the inside was helping this terrorist group get their hands on these weapons. Someone was letting them bypass the system over and over again, and allowing them access to the locations and time of these shipments. As I laid there tracing the seams of the long thin wooden beams on the ceiling with my eyes, I let my mind drift to all possibilities. I let my mind wonder who it could be within the organization. The only two people I explicitly knew were Viktor and Mason, and I wondered where Mason really stood within the organization, if he was working for Viktor or if he was more of an equal.

There was so much guilt within Mason, and I suddenly wondered if Mason might be The Viper. I laughed as soon as the thought crossed my mind. Maybe Viktor, then? Maybe neither of them. I felt bad for considering either of them, but I didn't have much alternative when they were the only people I knew.

Mason was right, though. I didn't know who was behind all this, so I needed to be more careful.

∾

"HOW WAS YOUR RUN?" Mason asked as I came through the front door.

"Good."

"Feel better?"

"Sure."

Mason raised his brows at that. "I actually have something to tell you." I closed the distance between us and came to stand between his legs where he sat at the kitchen table. "What's that?" He put his hands on my waist, his thumbs tracing my hip bones. I tried to ignore the bolt of heat it immediately sent to my center. "I'd like you to be my date."

"Oh?"

"There is a gala, and I'd like for you to come with me."

"As your date?" I chewed my lip and tried to conceal the smile that tugged at the corners of my mouth. "You want to take me out in public, like as your... date?" I tried to suppress how pleased I was.

"Will you go with me, then?"

"Of course."

"Good." Mason went back to work at his computer. "It's black tie. Do you have something to wear? If not, I can take you to find something."

I thought for a moment, and then remembered. "Um, I think I do, actually." I grabbed Mason's car keys and headed out.

"You just got back. Where are you going?" He asked, and I loved how concerned he was about me.

"To my P.O. box. I had my mail forwarded while I'm staying here." I gave him a sly look. "I ordered a gown a while back that I think should be at the post office by now."

"Don't be long." Mason gave me an equally devilish look, but he sounded wary; he really hated letting me out of his sight.

"I'll be fine, I promise." I let my fingers graze along his shoulders. A promise of something for later.

18

MASON

The night of the gala...

"Oh God." Emma breathed into my ear as I thrust into her. Those little sounds and moans sent me over the edge. I held her against the wall, and she cried out, her head sagging against my neck as I emptied myself into her. I pulled out and carried her across the room, laying her out on the bed. I kissed her from head to toe, leaving a trail of licks and bites down her whole body, her back arching with every delightful touch. I sucked her nipple into my mouth and rolled my tongue over it until it pebbled. She raked her nails through my hair as I grazed my teeth over her other nipple and nipped it gently, earning me another little moan.

I loved how she disintegrated at my touch. I loved the smell of her desire, especially when I knew I was the only man to have ever smelled it. And most of all, I loved how she trembled under my touch as she begged me to let her finish.

My fingers found their way to my favorite place, and I

teased her round and round until she was begging me to give her exactly what she wanted. I quickly flipped her over and ran my palms over her perfect ass, her skin so soft. I used my thumbs to spread her open and her hips lifted off the mattress a plea for contact, which I greedily gave her. I quickly put on a new condom, and her chest relaxed into the mattress as I lifted her hips up to meet my own. I slid into her fast and hard, and she panted against the sheets.

"Oh God, Mason. I love it when you fuck me like you can't get enough." She panted.

"That's because I can't get enough." I growled as I leaned over and pulled her up to her elbows. I grabbed a handful of her hair and wrapped it around my fist, pulling her head back as I thrust into her again and again.

"Oh fuck, Mace, I'm–" She was right on the edge again, gasping as her core fluttered around me, telling me she was close.

The fact that I was the only one to have touched this body, to have fucked her like this, and every other way I'd fucked her, it made me feral. I was feral for her, to have her, to keep her. Emma buried her face in the sheets and cried out as she shattered around me. I pulled out of her and we collapsed on the bed, laying there in each other's arms for a long while, as our breathing came back to normal.

Emma sighed. "I'm going to have to fix my makeup."

I chuckled, "You'd better do it quick before I pull you on top of me, and make you ride me until you can't walk."

Emma slapped my arm playfully, but seeing the look in my eye, she quickly rolled out of bed and slipped into the bathroom. A wise decision if we were ever going to make it out of this bedroom.

We'd been getting ready for the gala and I had walked into the closet just as she was about to step into her evening gown. I'd taken one look at her in that red lace lingerie and the dress never made it over her hips. Her protests had quickly turned into betraying little whimpers right before I'd hauled her up against the wall.

Since I'd given up trying to keep my hands to myself, Emma and I had fallen into a fast and furious routine over the last few weeks. She'd quieted down about work, and we both seemed to be content to reserve our energy for the bedroom. Or the closest surface we made it to, at least.

We were in our own little bubble, and I was falling for her hard. Her determination, her sass, the gentle look in her eyes when she was concerned about me. I'd almost lost her, and everyday we grew closer, the realization of that fact haunted me deeper.

I'd been steadily at work trying to pinpoint what was happening with the terrorist group and everything had gone quiet after Iran; all the leads had just dried up and disappeared. But I'd gotten intel that one of the key leaders would be hosting this charity gala tonight; I shook my head at the thought of a man like that, who drove terror, chaos and death, and wondered if while he was rubbing shoulders with the wealthy and elite, if they knew who he really was. I assumed they did. The people who would be attending tonight, no doubt, had their hand in the black market sale of weapons, or were adjacent beneficiaries.

The shower turned off, and I heard the bathroom drawers opening and closing. I lazily made my way into the bathroom and stood behind a naked Emma, who stood in front of the mirror between the double sinks. She gave me a playful warning with her eyes, but I couldn't help myself. Just a taste, just a little taste, was all I needed. She watched me in the mirror as I wound my hand around the nape of her neck and tilted her head to the side, opening up that soft crook for another kiss. My hand snaked over her belly, wandering lower, lower, lower. Her eyes fluttered shut.

"I'm never going to finish getting ready if you keep doing that." She rasped. "Get in the shower. Now." She commanded me and as she struggled to steady her breath as she spun around to face me.

I placed my hands on either side of the counter behind her. "It's so cute when you think you can tell me what to do."

She bit her lip, and her eyes flicked down to my lips. "Mason." She begged me with soft exasperation alongside the thrill in her voice.

"Fine." I nipped her lower lip and went and turned on the shower.

I ran my hand under the water, waiting for it to warm, and I felt Emma's eyes on me. When I looked over my shoulder, I noticed her staring at the stab wound on my side. "You've taken all your other bandages off, that one must be pretty bad." She said, "Did that one happen in Iran?"

I tried not to flinch. If there was one thing that would fuck us over, it was Emma's determination to get an answer. "Uh yeah, it's doing much better now, though."

"Good." Her eyes flicked up to mine. "You're not going to swap out the bandages?"

Fuck.

"No, I did this morning." I said evenly, trying to end the conversation without sounding too curt to be suspicious.

"I could do it for you." She said.

I didn't dare look at her as I stepped into the shower. "That's alright." Whether it was concern for my wellbeing or if it was curiosity, or God forbid suspicion, I couldn't meet her eyes.

Finally, she wordlessly went back to curling her hair, and I quickly lathered up.

I knew better than to assume her silence meant she'd stopped thinking about things. In fact, it may have been worse. It meant she was silently mulling things over, sprouting theories and hatching plans, with no indication of what was to come.

I'd turned her questions down enough times that she'd stopped asking questions about everything going on, but part of me got the sense that she'd never been hotter on the trail. Her mouth stopped asking questions, but her eyes never did.

As I stood under the hot water and rinsed, I felt my chest tighten at the thought of her figuring out that I was her boss, figuring out that I was the one who had attacked her, even if it had been to protect her.

She may have forgiven me for what happened in Iran, and I knew a small part of us was even grateful that we'd been thrust into each other's arms. I wondered if we hadn't, if we'd still be in the little bliss bubble we were in. A small silver lining to a horrible circumstance. But the shame I felt ran so much deeper than that. I couldn't keep myself away from her. She was like an addiction, despite the many reasons we shouldn't be together. Amongst which was the fact that she wouldn't understand what I had done to protect her. The closer we got, the closer she was to piecing it all together. And the closer we got to it, all blowing up.

I wondered what she was thinking as she gazed at the bandage over my side, over the stab wound *she'd* given me. I wondered if she suspected. I couldn't tell. If she did, she wasn't giving anything away under that sweet little face. I'd have to be more careful to keep a shirt on until it was fully healed.

I wrapped a towel around my waist and over my bandage and walked out of the bathroom and into the walk-in closet. Emma was back in her red lingerie and I felt my cock brush against the towel as it lengthened hungrily, not even remotely satiated by the meal it'd had, not but twenty minutes ago. I leaned on the doorway with my arms crossed and drank her in, watching her as she tilted her head to the side and pushed her soft brown waves over her shoulder to put her earrings on, the motion exposing that intoxicating neck of hers. She was a tall, or perhaps a short, but very delicious, refreshing glass of water. She was like a Christmas present, sparkling and wrapped up in that damn lingerie again, like a big soft red bow, just for me. She straightened to look at herself in the mirror and startled when she caught my eyes behind her.

She whirled around with wide eyes. "Don't even think about it." She said sternly, trying to cover a smile. "I don't have time to start over *again*."

I put my hands up in surrender and gave her a devilish grin. "I wouldn't dare." She darted around me in the doorway, and quickly beelined back into the bathroom, and I heard the soft click of the lock shortly after the door shut. Insurance. Making sure that we'd actually get out of the house on time.

I slipped into my black suit and black bowtie and realized my hair was a post romp in the sheets, mess. After a knock on the bathroom door for my hair product, Emma cracked the door and shoved it through before immediately shutting the door again.

I drawled through the closed door. "I promise I won't ruin you again until you ask me to." I drummed the pads of my fingers across the door as I turned to go to the hall bathroom instead.

After a moment, the door cracked open, and I turned around to catch her giving me a glimmering look. "Who said it was you I was worried about? Don't tempt me, Mace."

"I would never, darling." My words were laced with subtext.

She grinned, and I gave her a wink before she quickly slammed the door with a giggle and the lock clicked into place again.

I went downstairs and a brief while later, Emma stood behind me, softly clearing her voice.

I turned around, "Shit." She gave me a shy little smile, and I drank every delicious inch of her in as she turned for me to admire her every curve. She was walking temptation itself.

"What do you think?"

"I think we'd better get going before I shred that thing off you." I closed the distance between us, and her eyes told me that her hands were struggling just as much as mine, to stay off each other. "You look beautiful." I chuckled. "You *always* look beautiful, but you look *particularly* beautiful tonight." She blushed at the compliment.

I placed my hand on her back and guided her over to the table in the hallway, and stood behind her as she faced the large mirror. "One more thing." I pulled a black lace mask out and lowered it over her eyes.

Her mouth parted slightly in surprise as I tied the smooth black ribbon securely around her face. "I see why you were willing to take me as your date now." She rolled her eyes playfully before biting her lip. "And yours?" She turned around and grabbed me by the lapels while I placed my own mask on. "You look so handsome." She breathed. Her eyes flickered over my chest and her hands slid over my biceps. "I've never seen you in a suit, it's..." She cleared her throat. "It's quite, the ah, turn on." I could hear the raspiness in her voice and see the change in her breathing.

I raised my eyebrows at her. "Just say the word. I don't mind being late."

She grinned, "Yes, you do."

"Not if it's for good reason."

"Don't tempt me, Mason Reynolds, be good."

I quickly closed the gap between us. "Again, it's so cute when you think you can tell me what to do." I pressed my hips into hers so she was pinned between me and the hallway table. She shifted so she could feel my length against her. My hands, propped up on either side of her, braced on the table behind us. I leaned down and brushed my mouth over the shell of her ear, causing her eyes to flutter shut. I whispered into her ear, "Tell me what to do again, and I'll have to teach you a lesson." I lazily stepped back as she struggled to catch her breath and I offered her my elbow with a wicked grin. "Shall we?"

WE ARRIVED AT A LAVISH HOUSE, and our driver dropped us off in front of the door. We made our way up the steps to the event. The plush carpet rolled out over the marble stairs dampening our every step. Finally, we reached the top step and, with Emma on my arm, we headed into the ballroom.

I shook my head, knowing blood had paid for this estate and all the lavish finishings in it. Further motivation to take down its owner.

As we stepped into the main ballroom, Emma tried not to gape, but she whispered to me as she gazed at the ornate paintings on the ceilings and the crystal chandeliers. "Holy shit."

We were surrounded by other lavishly dressed individuals in masks, no one the wiser to who we were, or that we weren't invited. And looking at Emma, in that dress, she was the most beautiful of them all. "You're more fucking beautiful than anything or anyone in this room, Emma." Her hand squeezed my arm in response.

And I was right because as we made our way further into the room, all the eyes slowly flickered to Emma. A shot of pride found its way to my dick. She was so damn beautiful, and as I watched everyone watching her and only her, I realized just how much of a bubble I'd been in. Every man in this room had lust in their eyes as they peered through their masks in Emma's direction.

Suddenly, I noticed a man in particular; he was dressed in a cream tuxedo, and had dark hair and warm skin that glowed from many hours in the sun. I kept my eye on him as he kept his eyes on Emma.

Suddenly I felt fiercely possessive, and placed my hand on the small of her back, and let it graze lower, lower, lower over her bare skin. A subtle but possessive hand placement that told everyone in the room to fuck off. She was mine, and mine alone. But with the steep dip of the front of her dress, and the extremely low cut in the back, I knew they would look. And I didn't blame them. Even the most disciplined man would have a hard time keeping his eyes to himself, but fortunately I didn't have to. Emma stood confidently, the smooth red of her dress, matching the red on her lips, and when she slowly turned to look at me, I had to stop myself from taking her into a dark closet and smearing that red lipstick over her entire body. I had to keep my eye on the prize. We were here to get information, and eat a few hors d'oeuvres and get out.

"Why are they all looking at us?" She asked a little

nervously. She touched the mask on her face, adjusting it. "I feel like I'm not supposed to be here, and they know it."

"They're not looking at *us*, they're looking at *you*." I chuckled, "Because you're the sexiest woman in this room. Get used to it. It's going to be a long night."

She chewed her lip and gave me a little smile. Even underneath that mask, I could recognize those sparkling eyes anywhere. Though I didn't plan to let her leave my side for a minute, I knew I wouldn't need to see her eyes to identify her. She was a beacon of beauty that stood out from all the rest. There was no mistaking her for anyone else tonight.

We milled around for a bit, drinking champagne, making small talk. A few men asked her to dance, and she politely declined. After a glass of champagne and realizing that I wasn't going to disappear without telling her, she'd finally warmed up and loosened her grip on my arm. With a little confidence from the mask, I assumed, I was delightfully surprised at the bits that Emma would come up with as we talked with each new person.

She'd kept an impressively straight face while weaving together the most detailed stories about our dating history. As the night went on, she got bolder and bolder. It had started with innocent stories of her saving my life as an EMT and how we'd fallen in love. Sweet, cliche, slightly believable.

But I'd nearly spit out my champagne as we spoke with a sweet white-haired older woman. Emma had decided to go real big, telling her how she'd been so excited when she got the call to come in for work. That she was a high end escort and how she was going to get an extra large bonus from her boss, if she gave me a happy ending tonight. I'd almost lost it and had to bite my cheek until I tasted metal as the older woman looked between us, mouth agape, and tried to so kindly offer Emma life advice.

Emma grinned and politely excused us and I guided us to a quieter spot in the ballroom, ready for a chit-chat break. "Wow." I chuckled as she laughed, so pleased with herself. "You are something else." Her smile up at me, the playfulness of her mood, the cleverness of her conversations, delighted me.

The man in the cream tuxedo continued to eat Emma up with his eyes. I noted him again as I placed my hand on the small of Emma's back. "Dance with me." I whispered against her ear. "Dance with me so that all the other bastards in this room know you're mine, so they know that it's my name you scream, late into the night. So that they know you only spread your legs for me."

She sucked in a sharp, soft gasp. "Mason." She blushed crimson red.

"Hmmm?" I hummed into her ear, already pulling her against me as I guided us to the dance floor.

I pulled her tight against me as we swayed, letting her feel my hard length, letting her know I burned for her and her alone. I ran long soft circles over her exposed back, and her eyes fluttered.

"The things I'm going to do to you when I get you home."

"What are you going to do? Tell me." She whispered in a hushed voice.

"Well, first I'm going to rip this silky little thing right off you." I gripped her hip and rubbed my thumb over her stomach."

"Mmmm." She hummed, her chest heaving rapidly. "What else?"

I leaned closer to her ear, letting my breath tickle her ear and her neck, "And then, I'm going to torture you until you're just begging for me to give you release... I'm going to taste every inch of your soft, smooth body, and then, oh, the things I'm going to do to you, with my fingers, Emma." I trailed them down the side of her hip as a reminder. "I'm going to wait until you're slick, until your thighs are so fucking drenched, and then you're going to count with me while I fill you up with as many fingers as I want and I'm going to turn you inside out, again and again." She trembled against me as I continued, "I'm going to fuck you with my fingers until you can't tell where one orgasm ends and the next begins. And then I'm going to let that sweet little pussy of yours get a taste of my–"

"May I cut in?" A man stood with his hand outstretched.

Emma's face was a shade of crimson and she was breathless as she gazed only at me.

"Does it look like she wants to dance with you?" I growled.

Emma glanced between us and quickly saved face. "Um, actually, I think I need a break." She broke away and headed for the table of hors d'oeuvres.

I followed her and grabbed each of us another glass of champagne from a server walking around with a tray of champagne flutes.

She gave me a grin and stuffed the entirety of a bite sized hor d'oeuvre in her mouth, before taking the champagne from me and washing it down. "This is fun. I like getting dressed up with you, and going out..." She eyed me somewhat warily. "What are we *actually* doing here?"

"We're having a date." I grazed my knuckles over her ribs.

She pretended not to respond to my touch, but I knew better. "What are you up to while we're on this date?" She said casually as she took a long time deciding which hors d'oeuvre she would devour next.

I sighed, knowing she was smart, so I didn't try to lie to her. "I'm scoping out a potential lead."

"Uh, huh." She said it evenly, as if she wasn't at all surprised. "Who?" She asked so innocently I knew she was being coy and not innocent at all.

I grumbled before lowering my mouth to her ear, and she shuddered as I hummed for a moment.

"You see that man over there– don't look right now." I explained, "The one in the cream tuxedo." I stepped back. "I have a lead on him."

She casually flicked her eyes across the room before scanning the rest of the room, as if she wasn't looking for anything in particular.

"I was planning on catching him in a dark corner, but I hadn't considered how much of a distraction you'd be."

"What do you mean?"

"His eyes have been glued on you since the moment we walked in here."

"No?" She said in modest disbelief.

"Uh, huh." I gave her a pointed look. "I need to go upstairs and see if I can pull some information off his hard drive, but I've been trying to decide how to best do that all night. I don't really care to disappear while everyone here is waiting for their turn with you."

She glanced around as if she suddenly noticed there were still eyes following her. "How long will it take?" I could tell she was trying to be helpful, but her voice was ever so slightly strained.

"Just a few minutes."

"Ok, go do your thing then. I'll be fine."

"Not a chance."

"Well, you've got to do it at some point, don't you?"

After much back and forth, I finally convinced Mason I'd be fine by myself for a few minutes. I hated the idea that he felt like he had to babysit me when he was really here to work.

I shifted as my feet started to ache from my heels. The thin straps were beginning to create blisters on my feet. That's what I got for being a T-shirt girl who decided to wear four-inch heels tonight. I never had the chance to dress up and go out like this, and I'd jumped at the opportunity, but now I was seriously regretting my shoe choice. I leaned on the side of the table and adjusted the strap to my shoe.

"Seriously, I'll be fine. Don't use me as an excuse. Go do your thing." I said it more sternly than I meant to. The pain of my feet was wearing off the glamour of the evening.

"Fine. But stay alert. I'll be gone for less than ten minutes." He grumbled and nodded towards the man in the cream tuxedo. "He's going to ask you to dance the moment I disappear."

"Should I say yes?" I popped another olive into my mouth and chewed it nervously. I didn't know who the man was, but something about him made me look a little longer trying to piece it together.

"I don't like it, but if you feel so inclined, it would buy me a little bit of a window."

"Ok." I looked up at him. "I really don't think he's going to ask me to dance, though."

Mason chuckled, "I guarantee he's going to." He leaned down and gave me a soft kiss, but he didn't take my invitation as I parted my lips slightly.

I made a face when he pulled back. "We'll see." I said. "If he does come over here, I'll try to keep him busy." I gave him a pointed look. "Don't leave me stranded for too long though."

"I'll be back before you know it." Mason kissed the top of my head. "Alright, be good." He turned and looked across the room and casually waved to someone, but I doubted he was waving to anyone at all.

I reached for another stuffed mushroom and popped the whole thing into my mouth. I'd just hover over the food, and hopefully, no one would bother me.

When I looked up, Mason was gone. My eyes flicked around the room, and that was it. I shook my head and hoped he'd be quick. I tried to ignore the eyes, but without Mason at my side, I suddenly felt like I was prey being sized up by the many male eyes in the room. I didn't want to make myself smaller. I hated that, but I also didn't have the energy to deal with anyone's attention right now. I kept my eyes on the food and continued grazing.

A deep voice sounded behind me. "Where did your date go?"

I whirled around, startled by the closeness of the voice. It was the man in the cream tuxedo, standing there, far too close for comfort.

I froze, suddenly recognizing his voice, the voice that haunted me in my dreams. I'd recognize it anywhere.

It was the man from Iran, the man who'd threatened Mason and me.

The man who'd questioned me about Mason, and then when I said I didn't know anything had proceeded to have me tortured, nearly drowning me.

The man who'd let all his men record us while he forced Mason and me to do *the deed* in front of them, like some sick sporting event.

I tried to steady my breath, not to give anything away. In this dress, in this mask, I looked different from how I'd looked in Iran.

I could be anyone.

I am supposed to be here; I told myself and struggled to steady my breath as I stuffed the scream that wanted to claw its way out, right back down.

His bodyguards hovered nearby, and he held his hand out. "A dance?"

A hard lump formed in my throat, and I couldn't speak. My eyes flicked around the room, looking for Mason.

The man stepped forward now completely in my space and chuckled, "I promise I don't bite." He winked at me through his mask as he gazed down at me, and it sent a sickening wave through my stomach. "Unless you want me to."

I was panicking. I didn't know what to do. I turned to go the other way, but his bodyguards stood in the way. I wondered if I ran what they would do.

He rounded in front of me and his eyes prowled over me, like a wolf sizing up its prey. "You wouldn't want to embarrass me in front of all my guests, would you?" He saw in my eyes that I didn't know he was the host. "Besides, if a lady as lovely as yourself is going to crash my party, I'd like to know who she is." Still, he held his hand out.

I looked at the guards nearby who looked like they were ready to pounce if I decided to kick him and run, and then around at the eyes watching us, watching me, watching him.

Mason will be back any second.

Against my better judgment, I took a breath in and steeled myself, reluctantly following him to the dance floor.

Knowing who this man was, I knew it was even more important that I bought Mason a window, because I didn't dare to think about what would happen if either one of us got caught red-handed. I nodded, forcing a small smile onto my face as he led me out to the dance floor.

He hadn't actually ever touched me, but all the same, I tried not to shudder when he slipped his hand around my waist, and took my other hand in his. And I tried to control the urge to kick him in the balls as he comfortably slid his hand down my bare back until it was far too low for *my* comfort. But aware of all the watching eyes, I didn't dare speak or shove his hand away. I felt like a deer frozen in the headlights. Or maybe I was a clever fox, keeping him busy while Mason gathered the information we needed to take him down. I wasn't sure if I was the predator or the prey. But I certainly felt like prey.

"So tense." He spoke into my ear, and his hand gripped my back tighter.

Suddenly, the room started to close in on me, and I tried to pull my hand from his, but his grip only tightened.

We began to move to the music, and I felt like I was going to puke. "I need to use the restroom." I whispered out. I was going to faint or scream or run. I wasn't sure. I had to get out of this room, get his hands off me, *now*.

"Well, why didn't you say so, beautiful?" The words came out like a threat.

He danced us to the edge of the room, and then guided me to the hallway and I breathed a sigh of relief when he finally released his grip on me, and I made a beeline straight into the bathroom without looking back.

I took my sweet time and dabbed my face with a single use hand cloth and some cool water. I gripped the edge of the sink and steeled myself.

Mason will be back at any moment.

Suddenly, a large, wide man appeared in the bathroom. "Mr. Shah wanted me to check on you."

I steadied myself on the counter and looked around. There was no one else here. I figured if there was going to be a scene, I'd rather be out in the hallway closer to people, not here in the bathroom where there was one way in, and one way out. "I'll be out in a moment." I glared at him.

"I'll wait." He said and crossed his arms and stood watching me, blocking the doorway.

I rolled my eyes and applied some lipstick from the tiny clutch that dangled on a thin, delicate chain from my arm. I had to pretend I was still doing something for the moment. I took my time, and finally, when I couldn't think of anything else to kill more time, I reluctantly motioned for the giant oaf to move and he escorted me back into the hallway.

Mr. Shah's body guard followed me out, but I breathed a sigh of relief when I didn't see Shah, and I turned to head back to the main ballroom. If Mason was done, he was probably in the ballroom looking for me, wondering where I was. I needed to get back to the main room with everyone.

As I started down the hallway toward the ballroom, my breath hitched as Mr. Shah appeared from a doorway in the hall and cut me off. "Feeling better?" There was almost a snarl in his voice.

"Much." I nodded and moved to walk past him. One of his other body guards appeared from the room and blocked my path.

"I'd like to show you something." He smiled, but his eyes were anything but smiling.

"I'd really like to get back now." I tried to say confidently as I went to sidestep him, but I felt my voice waver anyway.

"I won't keep you long, darling, I promise." His words were cunning and charming, but I didn't believe him for a damn second.

20

EMMA

I LOOKED AROUND, feeling more and more trapped and agitated as they herded me. Finally, Shah looped his arm around me and I tried not to shrink back as he did so. I tried not to give him the satisfaction, even though I was repulsed by him.

"It's just right down here, a little something special for a beautiful lady like yourself." He guided me further and further down the long hallway, and with the plush carpeted floor, the sounds of the ballroom got quieter and quieter. I debated screaming for help, but I didn't dare use Mason's name. The farther we got down the hall, the more I realized no one was going to hear me, even if I did scream, and the panic set in further.

It was all happening so fast, and I wasn't reacting even remotely quickly enough. Now I was cornered and no one was around to hear me.

We approached a tall ornate door and when he went to unlock the room; I caught his veiled surprise that the door was already unlocked. I prayed that this was where Mason went, and that he was inside already.

Shah ushered me into a study. The room had a large desk in the middle; the walls covered in books, ornate vases and statues were sprinkled around the room, and thick heavy curtains that went to the ceiling hung at the windows.

Shah all but dragged me into the room and my heart sank even more when the guards stayed in the hall. Then the guards reached in and pulled the doors closed, leaving just Shah and I inside, the plush carpet and curtains leaving us in muted silence.

My pulse thundered in my ears as I whirled around and pulled on the door, but it didn't budge. Shah was suddenly behind me, his hand wrapped around my stomach and he pulled me against him, breathing into my hair, smelling it.

"Don't fucking touch me." I hissed and tried to pull away.

He chuckled, but only gripped me tighter. "So feisty. I like that in a woman." He pulled us further into the room and he finally released his grip, causing me to stumble forward and brace myself against the desk. I swallowed hard, looking towards the windows.

He walked over to a bar cart and poured me a drink, watching me eye the windows. "They don't open." He grinned a reptilian smile, pleased with the look in my eyes.

He set a drink down on the desk, and he stepped back and leaned against the bookshelf, and motioned to the drink. I felt a small wave of relief at the distance between us.

"I'm not thirsty." I ground out.

His eyes narrowed. "Drink."

My chest heaved, and I sprinted towards the doors. I yanked the handles, and they didn't budge, so I banged on the door and started screaming for help.

Shah casually stayed where he was. "No one's coming to help you, sweetheart." His voice got low and aggressive. He looked at me like a predator sizing up prey once again. "I said drink," He snapped, saying it with such force that I knew there would be consequences if I did not.

But something in *me* snapped, and I became enraged. "I said I'm not fucking thirsty." I pointed at the door. "Let me out." I screamed it at him, but I could tell it only thrilled him more.

Fuming, I launched myself at one of the ornate vases sitting on a decorative column, and I pushed it onto the floor. It crashed to the ground, shattering into dozens of little shards.

"I said, let me the fuck out." I shouted at him as I moved to the next one.

"You're going to regret that." He growled. In a flash, he'd crossed the room and grabbed me, dragging me to the desk. He shoved me against the desk and pulled off my mask. I suddenly felt so vulnerable and exposed. "That's what I thought, my little plaything from the desert." He took off his own mask and chuckled. "That vase was very expensive. I'll expect you to pay for what you damaged." His fingers trailed over my bare shoulders.

I spit on him, and I suddenly became afraid as I sensed the animalistic shift in his temperament.

In a flash, he backhanded me across the face, and I stumbled back. Before I could right myself, he'd grabbed me by the hair and snarled in my face. "I didn't get to play with my toy in the desert. I do have a delightful video, but I think I'd like to try you out for myself."

I screamed and struggled against him, but I couldn't budge.

He shoved the glass towards me again. "Drink." He growled with venom in his voice.

Trembling, I picked up the glass, but I didn't drink it, but

I thought maybe playing along would buy me some time. Time for what I wasn't sure, hopefully for Mason to show up. I eyed the alcohol in the glass and debated pouring it out, but decided that might not be in my best interest. I could sense an even bigger explosion coming under his already boiling exterior, and I didn't want to egg him on.

He grabbed his own drink and threw back the rest of it, and then before I knew what was happening, his hand was forcing my glass up to my lips and his other hand was wound through my hair ripping my head back. I couldn't help the cry that escaped my lips at the surprise and the sting of pain as he gripped my skull by the hair.

"Drink, you fucking bitch." He growled at me, and pressed the glass to my lips, tipping the entirety of it into my mouth, and I choked as he poured the alcohol down my throat. It caught me by such surprise that to my horror I involuntarily swallowed the volume of it, and sputtered out the rest, coughing.

It was all flooding down on me at once, the feeling of liquid in my lungs, the burn of it, the sound of his voice, it triggered something in me. Suddenly, I was right back in that cell, about to drown again.

I lurched against him, but couldn't budge under his grip. His body pinned me against the desk, one hand still controlling me by the hair, and the other now gripped my wrist so tight the circulation was being cut off.

"I think I'll start now. I like a little fight before it kicks in." His breath was hot against my cheek as he laughed.

I was panicking; I was thrashing against him, and I couldn't fully process what he meant. Before what kicks in? Suddenly, I gasped at the realization that he'd drugged me. I tried to fight against him, and because I hadn't eaten much, I think the drugs had started to hit me, or maybe it was the panic and I was just losing a grip on reality. I wasn't sure which. My head got fuzzy and my legs felt wobbly beneath me.

He whirled me around and shoved my face onto the desk, holding me down by the neck and I felt the fullness of him press against me as his hands raked up my dress and he shoved the fabric up over my hips.

His breathing was thick and heavy as I screamed and struggled against him, feeling myself getting weaker and weaker by the moment.

"Such a little slut, I see." He was pleased by my red lingerie. Then I heard the sharp ring of his zipper. "There, there, you won't even remember this tomorrow."

I felt a hot tear slip down my cheek as I surrendered to what was about to happen.

Suddenly, two gunshots sounded. It was loud and yet it sounded so far away in my mind.

Then the doors exploded open.

"I'm going to fucking kill you." A deep voice thundered.

I felt myself slip to the floor as Shah's body was no longer pressed against mine.

A gun fired, and I covered my ears far too long after the fact.

I heard screaming, and I frantically and unsteadily pushed myself up off the ground and pulled myself to my feet, using the desk. My ankles refused to hold me upright in my shoes and I struggled to reach for the straps to kick them off, but couldn't muster the strength to remove them.

My vision started to swirl, and I tried to push the face in front of me away as wide, warm hands held my face. "Are you alright?" The face slowly came into focus, Mason.

He spoke so softly. *So* softly. "Did he touch you?" There was such strain in his voice, his eyes came into focus, such concern. I could feel those safe, comforting hands searching over my body, taking inventory, gently checking me.

"I thought he was going to–" I couldn't even finish the sentence, partly because I didn't want to speak the words and partly because my brain fought against my every thought, slowing them down, mixing them up.

More screaming and then Mason turned for a brief moment, and another shot fired. "I will deal with *you* in a fucking minute."

"Wait in the hall." Mason commanded me. I could feel the rage building in his voice. "I'll be right there."

"Mason–"

"Hallway." He said firmly, and was already turned back to Shah.

I stumbled across the room, and steadied myself using the leather sofa that was halfway between me and the door, and that was as far as I made it.

I suddenly zoned in on Shah wide eyed and bleeding on the floor. Mason took the butt of his gun and smashed Shah's left kneecap. The sound of it made me want to hurl, and I did. I felt my eyes fluttering shut, and I wanted to lay on the floor so badly. Everything was swirling, my heart was racing, my grip on the couch slipped and I crumpled to the floor. I strained to keep my eyes open, my cheek pressed into such soft carpet, and I blinked as I looked at the dust bunnies under the sofa.

"Fuck." I felt Mason's arms slip under me, and I was going up, up, up, and then the room was spinning. Finally, the spinning slowed, and Mason gently set me on the floor in the hallway. "Keep your eyes closed." I felt him sweep my hair out of my face, and pull my dress back down over my hips, and then his footsteps got farther and farther away on the plush carpet.

I looked to my right, and the two security guards were unconscious and bleeding out on the floor. It was so much blood; I reached out to grip something, anything, but there was nothing to ground myself to.

So I leaned against the wall and hurled. Over and over again. From the sight of the blood, from the nausea of the drugs in my system, from what I had just thought was about to happen to me. It was all too much.

I struggled to scoot to the side of my vomit and I leaned against the wall, slowly sinking down onto the cool marble floor that laid at the edge of the thick carpeted hallway runner. The marble felt so incredibly cool against my hot skin; it was a welcome sensation.

I sank to the floor and laid my cheek against the cool marble and stared at the carpet fibers in front of me, looking at how they twisted and curled in on one another. I ran my hand over it lazily, so dense, so soft.

There was more screaming from the room, and what was left of the door suddenly closed, and I squeezed my eyes shut and tried to block out the sound of the screams.

Finally, Mason appeared, and he gently propped me up. I could hardly focus my eyes, but as I did, I saw the blood all over his hands, the way it speckled the white of his shirt.

I watched him wipe his hands on his pants and then I felt the floor steadily moving away from me, as my body went up, up, up. Finally, I settled against a familiar chest, and breathed in his comforting smell, as the hallway spun with each step he took.

21

MASON

I LOCKED THE BATHROOM DOOR, and I turned around and lunged forward and barely caught Emma just as she was about to keel off the padded stool in the bathroom.

I gripped her under the shoulders, keeping her upright. "Emma?" I couldn't make out what she said. She mumbled incoherently again, and just blinked at me. I checked her pulse. It was racing, her eyes were glazed over. As I gazed at her, I tried to steady my rage at the realization that she'd been drugged.

My chest heaved as I held her. If I'd been– I couldn't think about what nearly happened. That I nearly didn't get to her in time, that I'd been gone long enough that she was nearly rendered vulnerable and unconscious by that sleazy piece of shit.

"Did you kill him?" She asked, as I moved her to the sofa. I grimaced, and she continued, "Did you– that was the guy. Shah–" She mumbled.

"I'm gonna take you home, Emma. So you can sleep. Can you try to keep your eyes open a little longer for me?" She slumped lower into the couch in response.

With her securely on the couch for the moment, I
quickly went to the sink and turned on the hot water, and
began scrubbing the blood off my hands furiously. The
white sink basin turned pink as I scrubbed the layers of
blood off my hands. I quickly dabbed my shirt and face,
trying to clean myself up the best I could.

We didn't have much time, and with Emma like this, I
needed to get her out of here quickly. I'd successfully copied
the hard drive, and when I came back down to the ballroom
and didn't see Emma, I'd panicked and I'd raced down
multiple hallways before I heard her screaming. I was
halfway down the hall when my blood went cold when I
heard Emma. I knew the sound of that scream. I'd heard it
before.

Now the source of the man who'd inflicted that scream
not once, but twice, had paid. I'd killed him for it. I knew I
should have taken him in for interrogation, but I'd lost it.

Seeing another man putting his hands all over Emma,
against her will. I'd lost it. The built up anger I'd fostered
since Iran. I'd made him suffer too, before I finally put him
out. If I'd had more time, I would have made him suffer
longer, but I didn't want to leave Emma alone, not when
she'd nearly been– I couldn't hardly think the words. No,
she needed me now more than ever. I hadn't even realized
she'd been drugged when I'd carried her out. I'd just
thought she was just in shock. In that, Shah had been lucky
I hadn't dragged it out longer. He deserved to suffer. I panted
as I gripped the sink basin, my wild eyes looking back at me
in the reflection.

Behind me, Emma stumbled up and raced into the
nearest stall and heaved into the toilet. I quickly grabbed the
single use hand towels and dampened several under cool
water. I squatted next to her in the stall, the two of us barely

fitting, and I held back her hair. When she was done, I wiped her mouth with the cool towel, and then her face removing the smeared blood I'd left with my own two hands. I shook my head looking at the all the places my hands had been on her body, and how as I'd checked her, I'd marked each place with the blood on my own hands. I went around the rest of her and spot cleaned the blood off her as best I could. Some of it was on her red dress, and thankfully it wasn't quite as horrifically obvious as it was on my white button-up shirt.

I moved to pick her up off the bathroom floor. "Did you get it all out?" I asked gently, before I moved her.

She nodded, the color drained from her face, and her hands trembled. "Did you kill him?"

"I did what I had to do." I said, and she nodded. I gently tried to stand her up. "Can you walk?" I knew she wouldn't be able to, but I let her try anyway and I was right there to catch her before she pitched forward.

I ran a hand over my face. How was I going to explain this? Get her out of here on her own two feet. And we did need to get out of here quickly before someone realized what had happened to Shah. It wouldn't be long now.

"Fuck it." I picked her up and threw her over my shoulder, the only way I could hold her and still keep one hand free in case I needed to pull my gun on the way out.

"Just hang in there, baby. I'm gonna get you home."

She grumbled in response, but she hung limply over me, not bothering to argue, which in and of itself told me how out-of-it she was.

I unlocked the bathroom door and quickly waltzed right through the ballroom. And all the same eyes that had been drooling over Emma just an hour ago, now looked utterly shocked. I just gritted my teeth and made a beeline down the long, carpeted stairs without a word or explanation.

I quickly flagged our driver over, and in the back seat, I pulled her into my lap, cradling her against me as she struggled to stay awake.

"It's alright baby, you can sleep now. I've got you." That seemed to be the comfort she needed, knowing we were out of that horrible place, because I felt her fully relax against me.

By the time I carried her back up to my bed, she was out like a light. I slipped her heels off and I shook my head as I tucked her in, cocktail dress and all. There was no point in jostling her, for now she just needed to rest, to sleep off the drugs. And covered in my bloody handprints. This was the only time she was going to get to wear her new dress because it was effectively ruined. I knew even if the blood came out, the emotional scars would never wash out of this dress. So for now, I'd let her sleep, fully clothed, peacefully, deeply, fully, while I stayed up, making sure she was safe.

I peeled off my own suit and showered and changed into sweats and a hoodie. I grabbed the data drive out of my suit pocket and I went downstairs to my laptop. I plugged it in and blew out a breath, leaning my lips against my clasped hands as I waited.

I'd downloaded the hard drive quickly, and now it was time to see what was on it. If I was right, Shah was The Viper, and I'd effectively just ended him, and cut the head off the snake.

And I seriously hoped I was right. I'd had a sneaking suspicion that the man from Iran was the man hosting the party tonight, but I hadn't known it until I'd broken down the doors to his office and seen his mask less face.

I dragged a hand over my face. Emma had called him by

his name. She'd recognized him... she never should have been there. I'd let the love bubble I'd been in for the last few weeks cloud my judgment. She wasn't built for this, trained for this. She had already been carrying the weight of the world on her shoulders after Iran, and now this. She was so strong, but I was so worried about her. How would she ever bounce back after this?

I began clicking through the hard drive, searching, looking for the answers to everything, hoping it'd be here. Shah's final begging words played in my head, that he wasn't The Viper, that it was someone internally. A mole. A piece of information in exchange for his life. But I took his life, anyway.

I hoped he was lying. I hoped it was a final effort to protect himself, because if it was true, Emma had been right the entire time, and I hadn't listened.

I felt the pit in my stomach grow, knowing that if we did have an internal mole, that Emma was in more danger than ever. Her and that suspiciously talented little brain of hers, just working away, solving one question after another, until she was too close to a truth she wasn't equipped to handle. Or at least that's what I tried to tell myself. The alternative being that on her way to unravel this issue; I was worried she'd get to the bottom of who'd attacked her in the house. If she was smart enough to dig through classified documents, and I didn't doubt that she could, then it'd be a glowing nose in a snowy storm. Obvious and right there.

I grabbed a cold beer out of the fridge and sat staring at the computer, scrolling through documents while I drank it. I sat there calmly while the rage rolled through me like a thunderstorm waiting to strike.

My head snapped up when I heard the bathroom flush upstairs and I checked the time and realized it was early in the morning already. I rubbed my eyes and promptly pushed myself up and quickly made my way upstairs to check on Emma.

I pushed the bedroom door open and found Emma pulling one of my shirts on, her red dress in a pile on the floor at her feet.

"How are you doing?" I said softly, sitting on the edge of the bed.

She sighed heavily and then sat down next to me, but she didn't say anything. I would never tell her this, but she looked like shit, dark bags under her eyes, her face was pale, the life in her eyes snuffed out. It broke my heart to see her like this, this worn down, this affected. I leaned forward and scooped her up, my own eyes suddenly feeling heavy, and I crawled into the bed with her. She snuggled against me silently, all of her limbs tucked into herself, protecting herself as I wrapped my arms around her, protecting her too.

"I thought –" She pulled back to look at me, "I didn't think you were coming."

I brought her face to mine and gave her a soft kiss. "I should have checked on you sooner. I'm sorry that happened. About what almost happened."

She didn't cry, she just numbly slumped against me.

I held her tightly to me, and I felt my own eyes fluttering shut.

Then I flicked my eyes open as she spoke, slight amusement in her voice. "I broke his fucking vase." She said.

I chuckled, "I broke his..." And then I realized I didn't need to list the various bones and body parts I'd broken. She'd had enough trauma for a lifetime.

"You can say you know, I'm not going to freak out."

I slipped my hand up under the arm of her T-shirt and massaged her neck. "I know. I know you won't."

I AWOKE SEVERAL HOURS LATER, and Emma lightly stirred against me. We'd fallen asleep and hadn't budged. Each of us was thoroughly exhausted.

Emma's eyes finally flickered open.

"How are you feeling?"

She groaned. "My arms are asleep."

I gave her a pointed look.

She sighed and her shoulders sagged. "I don't know... I'm as good as one can be, I guess."

I'd had this idea last night, and I didn't want to wait a moment longer. "I want to show you something." I winked at her.

"Now?" she pulled back in surprise. "I just woke up from the worst drug induced nap."

"We can wait until tomorrow." I offered.

"Ugh." She sighed. "Now you've got me curious. What?"

I motioned for her to follow me with my finger, and she rolled her eyes.

I stood waiting for her a few steps down from the top of the stairs, and she slipped onto my back, and I carried her piggy back downstairs with her arms tightly wrapped around my neck, and her head resting in the crook of my neck.

I kissed her arms in front of me and then plopped her onto the armchair.

I went and pulled the couch cushions off the couch and lined them up on the floor, creating a DIY crash mat.

Emma winked, one eye shut and made a face. "You want to *do it* on the floor?"

"Come here." I grinned at her. She stood up, and she closed the gap between us and I grabbed her wrists tightly. "Try to get away."

She pulled, and I didn't budge. "I can't." She rolled her eyes.

"Really try."

"Come on, Mace, we both know I'm not going to be able to."

"Just try."

She huffed and made a minimal effort. "See?"

"I'm going to teach you how. You should know some basic self defense, and I don't know why I didn't think of this sooner."

She raised her eyebrows. "Ok."

I let go of one wrist and while I held the other, I used my free hand to guide her elbow up, pivoting it to ninety degrees. "It's all about leverage, using someone's body against them. See." I lifted her elbow all the way up, and she twisted her wrist out.

"Ok, but you *let* me get out."

"Try again. Twist *fast* and *hard*." I gripped one wrist and she twisted her arm out. The look on her face was priceless, and it made my heart swell. "Good. Now try the other side." I could see the little grin that was sliding out from under her skeptical expression.

"See?" I grinned. "Not too difficult, huh?"

She pursed her lips to conceal her skeptical smile, but her eyes were twinkling.

"Now let's try, with me sitting on you." I stepped forward, closing the gap between us, and pressed a kiss to her lips just as I swiped her leg out from under her, causing her to fall back onto the pillows I'd laid out.

"Hey." She complained, but her breathing shifted as I kneeled on either side of her, and slowly lowered down until my hips met hers.

"I want you to roll over onto your belly, and using your elbows and your hips, push yourself up, and throw me off."

She was pleasantly surprised that she was able to do it. "But you're not going full force."

"Neither are you." I returned. "If someone attacks you, you do everything you can to get away. You fight dirty. If someone's attacking you, they've already broken the rules. There are no rules, Emma. You bite, you claw, you kick, you scream. You're little, so you might not be able to out muscle someone, but you do have a good chance of slipping out of someone's grip if you do it right." I got up and headed to the basement. "One more thing." I winked at her. "Don't move a muscle."

I came back upstairs and held my hands behind my back.

"What?" she groaned.

"Pick a hand– actually wait." I shifted the items in my hands all to my left hand and reached into my pocket with my right hand. I pulled out a tube of pepper spray. "Oh, but first, pepper spray. This is for you. You can put it on your keys, okay?" I set it on the side table where we kept the car keys.

She narrowed her eyes and nodded. "Okay." She dragged the word out.

I came to stand in front of her again. "Okay, *now*, pick a hand."

She was propped up on her elbows, and she lazily pointed to my right hand. I pulled it out from behind my back and showed her the zip ties in my hand, and then I pulled my other hand out and I showed her the duct tape. She sat up and her eyes widened a little bit, but she didn't say anything.

I knelt in front of her. "Hands." I commanded her with a chuckle. She bit her lip and gave me a glimmering look as she put her hands out, with her wrists touching. I looped the tie around her wrists and pulled it mostly tight. Her expression flashed with uncertainty for just a moment.

I squatted in front of her. "Are you ok?"

"Mhmmm." She just watched me for a moment, but didn't say anything.

"You sure?" I watched her closely to see if this was too much. If she was ready for this. I didn't want to push her past her limits too fast, or too soon.

"Yeah." She said softly.

"Good." I nodded, but kept monitoring her. "If you're ever zip tied and you want to get out, you need to tighten the tie first. She gave me an incredulous look.

"Tighten it?" She said in disbelief.

"Go ahead." She took the loose end between her teeth and pulled it tight.

"More. As tight as you can."

"Is this a joke? You are going to let me out of this, aren't you?"

"You can get out of it anytime you want." I reached across and pulled it tight against her skin just before it started digging in. I demonstrated as I spoke, "Elbows out, and bring your wrists down hard against your hips. She tried, and it didn't break. "Hard. Like your life depends on it, like if you don't get out, I'm going to tickle you to death."

Her eyes went wide, and she stumbled back, tripping over the pillows. "Don't you dare Mason Reynolds. Don't you dare." Her eyes were gleaming as she backed up around the couch.

"You can get out anytime you want." I teased her as I prowled forward. She threw her hands down hard and the zip tie snapped. She looked delighted, but when her eyes met mine, they went wide and I chased her around the couch, anyway. I chased her around the couch and back to the pillow crash mat I'd made. She screamed with delight as I tackled us to the floor, and I tickled her.

"Mason!" She shrieked between laughs. She pulled me to her lips and kissed me in an attempt to seduce me, so I'd stop tickling her.

"I see what you're trying to do, and it won't work." I pushed her shirt up and blew a raspberry against her stomach. She screamed in delight.

"It works with duct tape, too."

"What does?" She arched her back and moaned as my tickling turned to hot open mouth kisses all over her stomach.

"You can get out of the tape the same way, just slam your wrists down."

"Good to know." She panted. She sat up on her elbows and bit her lip. "I can think of a few other ways we can use those zip ties."

I growled into her stomach, "You naughty girl." And then I stood up and swiftly threw her over my shoulders and headed up towards the stairs. "I'm taking you to bed."

22

EMMA

"YOU FORGOT THE ZIP TIES." I grumbled as Mason carried me towards the stairs. "It would be kind of hot." I offered in a sing-song voice. I felt slightly nervous at the offer, but I knew I was safe with Mason.

"If you want me to tie you up and fuck you senseless, I have much softer things upstairs I can use." He chuckled and rubbed my ass and then spanked me as he started up the stairs.

My core tightened with longing at the suggestion. As he carried me over his shoulder, I bobbed up the steps and my head swung with each step. Halfway up the stairs, I started to get an odd feeling, and I gripped Mason's waist. I felt something bulky under his shirt, and I lifted it up, and it all came flooding back to me. The sensation of being carried on the stairs in my own home, the height where my hands fell at his waist.

I stared at the bandage in horror as I suddenly pieced it together.

Mason was the one who'd attacked me that night my computer had corrupted. Mason was the one who broke into my house, who'd *zip tied* me. And it was Mason who I'd stabbed trying to get away.

His foot hit the top of the stairs, and I couldn't breathe.

"Put me down." I whispered.

"Hmmm." Mason rubbed my ass again.

"Put me down." I screamed and railed against him.

He quickly pulled me down over his shoulder. "Emma, what's the matter?" Concern sprinkled his face, and horror washed over mine.

My heart thundered in my ears. I backed up as I eyed Mason, who stood in front of the stairs blocking my only exit out. I pressed myself against the wall in the hallway, willing to create more distance between the two of us.

"It was you." I finally managed to say it out loud. "It was *you.*"

His stance changed in such a subtle way, I knew. I was right.

"Emma." He said it cautiously as he put his hands up. "Emma, I would never intentionally hurt you."

I inched down the wall. "Except you did. You *did.*"

I felt like I was suffocating. I felt like my head was right back in that bucket of water again. All my senses were on high alert. I could feel the subtle texture of the drywall under my fingers as I inched down the hallway.

Mason stepped forward and tried to close the gap.

"Don't come any closer, Mason. Don't."

I must have sounded convincing because he put his hands out, palms up, but I knew better than to let him get close. I lunged for the bedroom door and slammed it shut, locking it. It was just one of those flimsy little bedroom locks that could be opened with a bobby pin. I frantically looked around, knowing Mason would be through that door in no time flat. My eyes darted around the room, trying to make sense of it, feeling like a trapped animal looking for a way out. I couldn't tell up from down.

I had trusted him. I had let him comfort me when I was afraid. Now I realized he'd been the perpetrator. He'd been the cause of the fear, the cause of the pain. What once felt safe suddenly felt threatening. Life threatening. And I didn't know what to do with it. My heart was breaking into a thousand pieces and simultaneously threatening to implode in on itself as my chest tightened with fear.

"I'm coming in." Mason called out, and the door split in two as he burst through it.

I screamed and lunged for Mason's nightstand, where I knew he kept his firearm. I ripped the drawer open and pulled the gun out and aimed it at him.

"Emma, put the gun down."

My whole body quivered, and suddenly Mason didn't seem like a warm cocoon, no my eyes saw him for what he truly was.

A towering, muscled, trained killer.

A threat.

No longer my safe haven.

Adrenaline coursed through my veins, and terror coursed through my heart. At the idea that I could shoot him, that maybe I *should* shoot him.

"Emma." He inched toward me with his hands up. "Emma, put–"

I screamed, "Stop. Saying. My name. Stop. Stop. Stop." I tightened my grip on the gun.

"Let me explain." His tone changed.

"Show me your side." I demanded.

"Let's just talk, ok?" I could hear the false calmness with which he spoke, I knew it was part of his training, to subdue me, to earn my trust back, just long enough so he could get the gun from me. It wasn't real.

"Show me your side." I snapped.

He reluctantly lifted his shirt.

"Where did you get that?"

"Iran."

"Liar!" I screamed.

"I think you know where I got it."

"All this time... you moved me into your house... into your bed!" I kept the gun aimed at him. The fight or flight was taking over, and mostly the fight was starting to kick in. "All this time."

"Just let me explain."

"You... you hit me. You drugged me, you made me think I was going to die." I started to thread all the horrible things together that had happened to me over the last few months. "You dragged me to Iran. You dragged me to that gala where I almost got killed again. You are a killer, Mason. Are you *trying* to kill me?"

"Just think it through. Wouldn't I have already killed you if I wanted you dead? Hmmm?" He tried to take a step forward, his hands were still up.

"Back the fuck up." I screamed.

He stayed in place, not moving forward or backward, and he spoke calmly, too calmly. I didn't blink; I watched him, making sure he didn't try anything. "Viktor was going to send a team in after you fucked up with the security breach in June."

"Bullshit."

"He was going to send a team in to scare you. Emma... they don't fuck around, they break bones, they were really going to hurt you. I told Viktor I'd come smack you around, scare you a bit. So you'd be safe."

"I wasn't safe." I blurted out as I tried to steady my breath. My arms were starting to burn as I held the gun with my arms straight out, and that fact pissed me off. My senses were getting muddied by my emotions as I stood in this room, his *bedroom*, with him. Where he'd made me feel things I never knew I could feel, where he'd made me love him.

Mason stepped forward, and I did too, finger on the trigger. "Back the fuck up. Against the wall." He didn't move. "Against the fucking wall." I screamed, and I fired the gun into the wall to the right of him.

He hissed, "Fuck, Emma. Just–"

"Who the fuck are you?" I could feel tears starting to well up in my eyes, and I blinked my eyes furiously, begging them to remain focused on my target. I knew one long blink, and that was it for me. He'd have me disarmed, and he'd have the gun.

"Emma."

"Stop. Saying. My. Name." I gritted out, and I wiped the tears from my face. They burned, and my vision started to become blurry as my eyes filled with water.

"I want answers. Now." I said. "Did you order my kidnapping just so you could get into my pants?" I laughed maniacally at the thought.

"Are you fucking serious?" Now Mason raised his voice. "You think I *let* someone snatch you up and torture you? *You* were the one who left that apartment. *You* made that decision despite how many times I told you to stay put. *You* were the one that had to meddle in things you weren't supposed to be looking at. *I* have been bailing you out since the day you started." He was fuming angry. "*I* have been the one saving your ass, time and time again, and you so carelessly throw every second chance away. *I* can't keep protecting you if you don't *let* me."

"Protecting me!" I cut him off. "I wouldn't have been in *any* of these situations... if it were not for *you*!"

"No, you'd be in prison!" Mason yelled back before running his hand over his face. "Just..."

"No. No." I kept the gun pointed at him and I moved towards the door. He made like he was going to move. "No." I said firmly, and the look in my eye must have convinced him because he stayed put.

I stood in the doorway, with my exit now within my reach. "I want the cliff notes, what do you do? What does Viktor do?"

He shook his head, "Viktor runs the agency, I'm..." He shook his head and scoffed. "I'm your team leader."

I laughed hysterically. "*You're* my team leader... *you're* the one I've been messaging for all these years... *you're* the one I messaged that night... un-fucking-believable, Mason." I backed out towards the door and raised my eyebrows. "Are you the mole? Are you the one selling information? Is that why we were in Iran so you could make a little deal? Are you The Viper? Is that why you went to the gala? To do business with Shah? Was I a little side deal?"

"Jesus Christ, Emma, I'm not–"

And I didn't wait for him to finish. I turned my back and sprinted down the stairs, gun in hand. I snatched the pepper spray and the keys off the table and bolted towards the garage. I could hear him thundering down the stairs, and terror pulsed through me. I raced into the garage in a panic, and threw myself into the car. I started the engine, and locked the doors. I punched the garage door opener, and when it wouldn't open fast enough, I peeled out, driving

through the lower half of the door, as Mason pounded the
back of the car while I drove away.

23

EMMA

Four A.M. the next day...

I CAUTIOUSLY MADE my way into the gym, barefoot and wearing just Mason's giant T-shirt. I tried to discreetly tuck Mason's gun under the shirt. I didn't dare leave it in the car in case I needed it.

I'd spent yesterday driving around, thinking, strategizing, trying to figure out where to go, and what to do. I had finally pulled into the gym parking lot after dark, when the gas tank had gotten too low, and I'd spent the night in the car, waiting for the gym to open.

Now I was on the hunt for a shower, shoes, and clothes. I looked around the gym, nothing seemed out of place. Having just opened for the day, the front desk person was hardly awake and didn't even look up as I walked past shoeless... with a gun tucked under my shirt. I blew out a breath and shook my head at the ease of it.

I didn't glance over my shoulder at the front desk

person, I just hurried into the locker room. I needed to shower desperately, and I had hoped I left an extra set of clothes and shoes in my locker. I needed a full outfit asap, and I especially needed to get this shirt that smelled like Mason off of me immediately. I couldn't stand to be trapped by his smell, it made me sick.

I quickly found my locker and looked around before cautiously setting the gun on the changing bench while I attempted to open my locker. I tried to turn the dial on my combination lock, but my hands trembled and I missed the second number in my combination.

I looked around, I needed to get this gun into my locker, soon, before anyone came in and saw it. I shook my hands out and tried again, and finally managed to get the lock open. I blew out a breath of relief and quickly shoved the gun into the back corner. Another breath of relief at seeing my shower flip flops and an extra sports bra and leggings were shoved into the corner.

Thank God.

I shut my locker, but left the lock off, hiding it under the changing bench, in case I needed to grab my stuff and run. I seriously hoped no one was digging through lockers to steal something this morning. It was quiet enough, so I doubted it would be a problem, but with my luck, it wasn't impossible. I decided I'd have to hurry in the shower just to be safe. I looked around and strained my ear, listening for a moment, before finally deciding I was safe. I grabbed a towel off the complimentary towel cart and headed for the shower.

I turned the water on scalding hot, which was only halfway as hot as it could get. I'd made the mistake of cranking it all the way up and nearly giving myself third-degree burns when I first started showering at the gym. A mistake I would not make again.

I peeled Mason's shirt off and angrily chucked it into the trash can that was nearby before I stepped into the shower stall, and closed the opaque white shower curtain.

I closed my eyes and let out a breath as the hot water soothed me, and drowned out the other physical sensations in my body. The trembling, both the numbness and the high alert awareness of every physical sensation.

As I stood there letting the droplets beat against my skin, rhythmic drops, one after another, the thrumming and buzzing slowly started to quiet. I braced myself against the back tile wall with my hands and let the hot water pour down my head and face.

After standing there for a while, I finally pumped some of the complimentary citrus shampoo into my hands and started to lather my hair. As I felt the blunt ends of my shoulder length hair against my fingertips, I felt the anger bloom in me once again. It had been God damned fucking Mason who'd cut my beautiful long hair off.

I growled low and sharp in my throat, and it echoed against the walls in the empty locker room. As I lathered my hair, I tried to piece everything together in a clear line. Mason not only worked for the same agency, but he was my boss. He'd been the one *keeping me in line*. AKA beating the shit out of me and then rescuing me, like he had nothing to do with it.

Fucking asshole.

I called him every name under the sun silently in my mind, because the alternative was that the love of my life betrayed me. I couldn't bear it, so all the terrible names I could think of filtered through my head one after another, drowning out the chance for heartbreak to rear its ugly head.

I played his words over and over in my mind. 'I did it to save you... They would have broken your bones. I can explain.'

How was there any explaining, anything? I didn't even know if I believed him. But I'd been through enough at this point to know that I had to keep my wits about me. I'd allow myself this shower, and then I'd game plan. I'd figure out where to go and what to do. But for now, I would just stand in this shower and have this moment.

As I rinsed my hair, I wondered if Mason truly was the inside man. I would have never seriously suspected him unless I'd caught him red-handed like I had hours ago... but the more I thought about it, everything added up so flawlessly. It would have been easy. Too easy for him to be the one selling the weapons information.

I shook my head. It was no wonder he got me a job instead of treason charges, he'd been expertly maneuvering that himself, for God knows how long.

Fucking traitor.

No wonder he didn't want out of the agency.

He *was* the agency. He was benefiting from his situation on so many levels. No wonder he brought me in with the snap of his fingers. He'd been gaming the system for God knows how long.

I didn't bother running for the toilet when the sickening truth of it all finally blasted through my numb nerves. I just leaned over the shower drain and vomited. The idea of being his pawn, of sleeping in the same bed with the man who'd dragged me out from under my own bed, who'd fired a weapon at me, who'd drugged me, it made me sick. Even if he had saved me in Iran, and then again at the gala, it didn't excuse a damn thing he'd done to me. It was a thick web, and I struggled to see through it, feeling like the realization of it all was getting tighter and tighter around me. The web he'd spun, the lies he'd told. I was trapped by my own denial. I hadn't wanted to see what was right in front of me. I braced myself against the shower wall as I weakly wretched over and over until finally nothing more came up.

I stood trembling under the hot water, letting it soothe me as much as it was able. The man I thought I loved was the biggest piece of shit I'd ever laid eyes on. And if I didn't get it together, he could easily put an end to me if he wanted to.

That was what I had to figure out... what his motives were.

What he would do to me, now that I knew.

I didn't know who to trust, who to go to. I was utterly alone and in danger. Life-threatening danger.

While I knew I didn't love him anymore, part of me wondered if for that brief moment that I did, as a token of what I thought we'd had. If I could keep my mouth shut, and just go my way, and let him go his. Maybe if I just kept my mouth shut about what I knew, he'd let me be. Maybe.

Even that would require a level of trust I knew I couldn't risk. Even if I wanted to, I knew I couldn't count on him to just let me go. Not that it was right, but maybe it was safe?

I shook my head, but the reality was, I was one of his loose ends now.

I shuddered, wondering what he was capable of... if he'd tie me up like all the other loose ends he had over the last few weeks.

The thought made my chest tighten.

The feeling of those big calloused hands and how many times they'd brought me to ecstasy, and now all I could think about, is how those were the hands of a killer. Those were the hands of a man who killed in cold blood, and they could snap me in half without a second thought if they wanted to.

Grief and fear swirled around, mixing, mingling, causing confusion and panic to stir up in my chest.

It was so incredibly painful.

Being betrayed by him was so incredibly painful.

Losing him... was even more painful.

As the water poured down my face, I was sure it was also washing away big heartbroken tears. But they disappeared into the stream of water without an ounce of recognition.

I had no one. And the one person I could trust in my life, my dad, I couldn't bear the thought of putting him in danger by asking for help. Even if he could help, I knew the truth of the situation would break him. Knowing what his best friend had done, what he was *doing*.

Suddenly, I heard an odd noise, and the hair on the back of my neck raised.

24

EMMA

I STILLED in the shower stall and listened for a moment, trying to calm myself.

You're fine. You're safe. You're just being paranoid.

I bent over and looked between the gap of the shower curtain and the floor, peering into the locker room.

I stifled a gasp, softly sucking in a breath as I snapped back up, steadying myself on the shower stall walls.

Two sets of black men's boots fanned out around me, walking in my direction.

My heart caught in my throat, and my head suddenly felt fuzzy as adrenaline crashed through my system like a hurricane taking over.

I silently waved my hands, cursing without uttering a single sound. I frantically looked around the shower. Mason had said, use what you have. Use what you have.

I silently mouthed the words as I waved my hands around.

What do I fucking have?

Shampoo?

My fucking naked body?

I scoffed at myself for taking his advice now, of all times, wondering if it was him on the other side of this curtain. Not sure if it was better or worse, if it was him. I ducked down and glanced again, finding possibly a third set of shoes, though I couldn't be sure now.

I could feel my heart starting to palpitate as the heat from the water ripped through me. I suddenly realized just how hot the shower was, and suddenly I got an idea.

I quickly covered myself in shampoo, and stepped out of the stream of water and turned the shower temperature all the way hot and then I quickly slipped under the stall into the adjacent shower. I quickly turned on the following four showers, easily slithering under the stalls into the next one until the steam began to steadily billow into the locker room.

The cold tile floor chilled my bare skin, a sharp contrast against the thick steamy air, as I moved from shower to shower, trying not to think about how dirty or clean the tile floor was.

In the last shower stall, I tried to steady my breath as I stood up and pressed myself against the wall. The hot water threatened to scald my skin mere inches away, the steam licked my skin in hot swirls, but I didn't dare reach up and point the shower head away from me.

I stared at the tile floor and it disappeared as I visualized the locker room, trying to navigate the fastest way back to my locker.

The fastest way to the gun.

If I could just get to my locker, maybe I'd be okay. But not knowing how many pairs of boots were out there, or where they were between me and my locker, it made my heart sink.

I tried to steady my breath and calm myself.

Don't panic. Don't give up.

And I finally made the choice that I wasn't going to go down without a fight. If it *was* Mason out there... *fuck him*, he was going to have to deal with everything he'd just taught me. If I was going down, it was going to be clawing, and fighting, and screaming. If I was going out, I was going to shred up the bastard that did it.

I leaned into the fight instinct and adrenaline exploded through my body, my breathing ragged and wild.

My mind wandered back to the prison cell in Iran, how Shah had said, 'Isn't it fun when they fight'. And I swallowed hard, suddenly wondering if this was all some big game, if I was just playing right into Mason's hand. If he'd orchestrated every single event leading up to this.

I shook my head, I couldn't think about that, not right now.

By now, the entire locker room was hot and filled with thick steam. I peeked through the shower curtain and saw a dark frame moving across the locker room, blocking my path to my locker.

Fuck!

I chewed my lip and looked at the sauna on the other side of the locker room, and quickly snaked my hand out and grabbed a towel in each hand off the cart next to the shower. I didn't bother wrapping one around myself. I had to move fast, and I did. Softly and quietly as I could, I sprinted low into the sauna and clenched my teeth as I gently closed the door behind me.

I waited for a moment to see if the door would open behind me. Through the glass door, I could see the steam slowly creating a thick veil in the locker room. With my window of time, I quickly grabbed the towels and eyed the hot stones in the corner of the sauna.

I laid one towel on the ground. Then, using the other towel, I carefully pulled the metal grate off the hot sauna stones, trying to move quickly as I felt the heat swiftly seeping through the towel.

I quietly deposited the stones one by one onto the towel on the floor. Working quickly and methodically, releasing each stone before it burned me through the towel.

As I grabbed the fourth stone, the towel shifted and the hot stone made contact with my bare skin. I jolted, losing my grip and the stone descended the rest of the way to the floor with a soft thud.

Fucking shit!

Fucking, motherfucking shit!

I bit my lip so hard it bled, I could taste metal in my mouth, but I didn't dare make a sound. I silently screamed as the side of my hand throbbed, the burn ripping through me.

I stood waiting, panting, forcing back tears, but still no one came.

Quickly I grabbed the corners of the towel and as quietly as I could I propped the sauna door open, and I held my breath as I dragged the stone filled towel to the edge of the lockers. I pressed my back against the cool metal of the lockers and dared a tiny peek around the corner. It was steamy, and I couldn't be completely sure, but I didn't see any dark figures on this side.

I grabbed one of the rocks with the towel and hucked it across the floor back into the sauna. The noise as it clattered against the tile and then rolled into the sauna was startling in the silence of the locker room, and yet the sound was still more muted than I expected as the steam devoured the sound hungrily.

My chest pulsed up and down as I tried to pull in silent

breaths, feeling like I didn't dare breathe. God forbid, the sound of my breath, be the thing to give me away.

Out of the corner of my eye, something moved, and I froze. From the other side of the locker, a dark figure appeared and headed towards the sauna. As he passed by, the steam swirled and I got a close enough glimpse of the back of him. Masked in tactical gear. Whoever this was, they were here for me. I had no doubt about that in my mind.

I held my breath as he quickly made his way into the sauna and I crept up as close as I dared and quickly closed the door behind him. I frantically struggled to thread the towel through the handle and knot the handle shut, effectively locking him inside. It wouldn't hold forever, but maybe it would buy me a few minutes.

I heard approaching footsteps, and I panicked, darting into the adjacent steam room. I turned the knob all the way on and steam burst into the room, creating an even thicker, suffocating veil of moisture. I raced to the wall next to the door, and crouched down, holding my breath while a second shadow stepped over the threshold.

I struggled to steady my breath, my body trembling with fear, courage, adrenaline. I didn't know what, my body just trembled uncontrollably. I waited as long as I dared and as he stepped past me and I lunged out of the door and slammed it shut, the noise deafening in the silent locker room.

I sprinted toward the middle row of lockers, towards *my* locker. I was out of extra towels and there was no lock on the outside of the steam room door. If anything, I probably shouldn't have slammed the door, but I didn't have time to think. I was surviving now.

Living second by second.

That's all I had.

I had to move fast.

Faster.

I had to get to my locker.

I *had* to get that gun.

Still completely naked, my feet slipped on the wet tile floor as I rounded the corner. I sprinted down the row and ripped open my locker door.

I was fumbling, panicked, as I dug for the gun.

My clothes tangled around my damp hand, sticking to my skin as I reached for the gun.

I got it!

Suddenly, I was being yanked backwards and then the sensation of falling through the air.

I slammed into the floor; the breath whooshed out of my lungs as my back flattened forcefully against the ground. In a flash, a giant body pinned me down with knees on either side, and I gasped, struggling to pull in a breath.

I screamed and squirmed and writhed under his death grip, gasping for each breath as I struggled to pull in breath, my lungs still flattened in my chest.

My skin was wet from the moisture in the air and slick from the shampoo I'd doused myself in. It was giving me some movement under him.

The slippery tile floor, my ally in this moment.

But still, I couldn't get my hand free. I couldn't get my arm up to shoot him.

I was so close, and yet so far away, time seemed to slow as I watched him reaching for my throat, and his other hand reached back to his utility belt for God knows what. I could feel the cool metal of the gun in my right hand, and it didn't do me a damned favor.

I remembered what Mason had said, and I instinctively bit the man's arm as his hand reached across me for my throat. He growled out in pain, and I suddenly knew it wasn't Mason under that mask.

A small part of me felt relief.

I struggled to flip over onto my belly and push up, push him off balance, like Mason had shown me. Now the tile floor, wet from the steam, was working with *and* against me simultaneously. I wasn't stuck; I wasn't pinned, but I couldn't get enough of a grip on anything to get out from under him. I was sliding around and going nowhere.

I grunted as I grabbed his own leg, gripping onto the fabric, using it for leverage as I wriggled out from under him and scrambled up.

I whirled around and trained the gun on him, and I didn't pull the trigger.

It all happened at once...

He lunged at me.

The sound of breaking glass behind me.

My scream.

I pulled the trigger.

Time slowed down.

My hand violently jerked back, the power, the force utterly shocking.

The motion of my finger pulling the trigger, so minimal, so slight, so easy, for such a deadly consequence.

I fired the gun over and over again until he finally stopped moving. We were so close together that I didn't miss a single shot. We were so close that I was splattered in the red sticky evidence of what I'd done.

Suddenly, arms came barreling around me from behind, pinning my own arms to my sides, I screamed and kicked as I was thrown a few feet onto the ground again.

I pushed myself up frantically, searching for the gun that was no longer in my hands. The dark figure stood between me and the gun, and I scrambled up, around to the other side of the locker. Panting, I saw my sauna stones, and I grabbed the corners of my towel full of rocks and swung it just as the dark figure rounded the corner and he cried out in pain, stumbling back.

I screamed with terror, a war cry as I hit him again and he stumbled backward to the ground. My body took over, and I climbed on top of him and pounded one of the stones into his head, over and over again. The sounds, the crack of bone, all muted as the world around me went silent.

Finally, my hearing came back a muffled sound over the ringing in my ears and I heard myself screaming. I pushed myself up, realizing he wasn't going anywhere. Ever. Again.

By now I was covered in more than just blood. My skin itched with the dampness and the stickiness of it all. I felt dizzy as I looked down at my naked body, at the red that dripped and streaked down me, how the vapor in the air bonded with the slick shampoo and blood and created a wet sticky coating, sealing me into it entirely.

I staggered backwards and pushed my wet hair out of my face, feeling the sting of shampoo in my eyes. I had to get out of here. I had to get out of here before the other man figured out how to get out of the steam room, or the sauna, or whichever one was still stuck.

I fought to see through the stinging tears in my eyes, my hands, my body trembled, and I cursed as I pulled my leggings on over my sticky legs. The stretchy fabric protested the entire way as I wrenched against it, trying to pull them up my legs. I cursed as I fought my sports bra. It rolled and snagged against my damp skin, refusing to uncoil so I could get it on properly.

Finally, I pulled it down over my breasts. I grabbed my duffle bag and shoved the gun into it and sprinted out into the gym towards the exit. I caught the eyes of a horrified woman as she jogged mouth agape on a treadmill.

"Don't go in there." I said to her as I sprinted by. The sound of my own voice shocked me, so animalistic and hoarse.

Covered in my hard earned war paint, I climbed into the jeep and started the engine.

I was going to end this.

My pulse thundered in my ears. If Mason wanted me dead, he had another thing coming.

I was going to fucking kill him first.

I was going to *kill* Mason Reynolds.

25

MASON

I SAT on my laptop at the kitchen island and dragged a hand over my face. I'd spent hours going through this damn hard drive and I was going nowhere fast. I needed someone who knew how to navigate what they were looking for.

I needed Emma.

Suddenly, something caught my eye in the window. I tensed for a moment and then relaxed, seeing it was Emma's small frame in the reflection. I watched, slightly amused, as she edged along the side of the house, not realizing she was in plain view, the angled kitchen window catching her reflection and completely giving her away.

Then my chest tightened. Her arms went up as she moved closer to the back door. She still had the gun. *My* gun.

What the fuck is she doing?

I stayed put, knowing it was probably best if *I* didn't come at her. I'd let *her* come to me.

She disappeared out of the window reflection and I couldn't help but smile to myself as I heard the back door softly jiggle and then finally stop. She hadn't come barging in through the front door, and she had my keys, so she was certainly up to something.

Apparently coming to shoot me.

I tried to decide what I thought she was really going to do. She *had* shot the wall in my bedroom, far too close to my head for comfort.

I sat listening for a moment. I craned my ear, waiting for the next sign of her. The garage door handle jiggled and then it went quiet.

After a moment, I heard a key turn in the lock, and the door opened softly.

I was impressed and slightly proud as Emma crept up on me. I almost couldn't hear her, she moved softly and carefully. Despite her best efforts, I still knew exactly where she was behind me. But I stayed put, not wanting to startle her. After everything, I'd at least give her the courtesy of not scaring the shit out of her again.

I wondered if it was a bad gamble.

She might shoot me before I could get another word out.

Then, before I had the chance to change my mind, the cold barrel of the gun pressed against my neck.

I tried not to smile at the naivety of it. "Emma." I said evenly.

"Mason." She ground out.

"Can you put the gun down?" I asked gently. "I think we have a lot to talk about."

She pressed the barrel more firmly against my neck in response. "I know it was you." I could hear the hysteria in her voice, it unsettled me, and I didn't dare let her go a moment longer with the gun pressed against my neck.

In one swift motion, I spun around and twisted the gun out of her hand. She stumbled back, crashing into the wall wide eyed. In another swift motion, I pulled the clip out and emptied the remaining bullet out of the chamber.

I set the gun and the ammo on the counter, but my eyes didn't leave hers as I did so. Then it registered. My eyes trailed over her fully, taking her in.

My throat went dry.

She was completely and utterly plastered in blood. Who's blood I didn't know. Her wet hair was plastered against her face, and she had a wild, crazed look in her eyes.

I took a step towards her, my protective instinct kicking in. "Emma, what happened?" I asked. I needed to check her to make sure she wasn't injured. "Whose blood is that?" Panic laced my voice as I moved towards her.

Before I could blink, she lunged for the kitchen knives and pulled the biggest one out of the knife block. "Don't come any fucking closer." She screamed at me.

I realized I had unintentionally cornered her. Not good. And like a wild animal, she was panting, her eyes frantic, racing. My heart twisted at the fear she held in her eyes, the fear of me. The fear of whatever hell she'd just been through to be covered in that much blood. Her own or someone else's, I didn't know.

I held my hands up and spoke slowly, gently. "Emma... is that your blood? Are you hurt?"

"Don't you fucking play stupid."

I eyed the knife in her hand. If I'd had any doubt earlier that she'd shoot me, it was misplaced, because looking at her now, I knew she'd use that knife if she felt like she had to.

"What happened?" I pressed gently again.

"Oh." She growled it out, as she held the knife towards me. "You want to know what happened?" She sounded maniacal as she inched down the length of the kitchen towards the breakfast nook. "I killed those men you sent after me, so I guess *you'll* have to finish the job." She panted and her eyes flicked away from mine for just a second. "If you can."

The boldness and the terror in her eyes made for an interesting combination as she watched me closely. "Let's just think this through. Let's be logical." I had my hands up, I had to play my cards carefully. She was unpredictable right now.

She bolted around the far side of the kitchen island and headed for the sliding door to the backyard.

I cut her off, and she lunged at me. I instantly felt searing pain as she sliced my arm with the kitchen knife.

Fuck.

Before she could take another step, I lunged forward and grabbed her wrist. With my other hand, I took the hilt of the knife and twisted it out of her hand. She quickly threw her elbow up, and she twisted out of my grip, exactly like I'd taught her.

I whirled around as my own warm blood dripped down my arm and lunged towards her, tripping her. She went tumbling to the floor and was nearly up again as I grabbed her. I pinned her as gently as I could, holding her shoulders to the ground as I sat on her, trying to get her attention as she screamed and writhed underneath me, struggling. Her arms were pinned under my legs. Despite her best efforts, she wasn't going anywhere.

"Emma." I said softly. "Emma, I'm not going to hurt you. Okay?" I pleaded with her, taking her face and forcing her to look at me. "I need you to tell me what happened so we can figure out what's going on. Okay?" Her eyes were so wild, so distrusting, and I continued. "I just want to keep you safe."

She panted underneath me struggling, and finally she stilled, realizing she wasn't going anywhere. "Fine."

Her immediate submission surprised me and I knew better. "Are you going to try to run when I get up, darling?" I raised my brow.

"No." She grunted out. "Just get the fuck off me."

I blew a breath out, "Alright, let's just–" I moved slightly, and no sooner had I shifted than I was crying out, my eyes suddenly burning.

Pepper spray.

It burned my eyes and singed my lungs with my next inhale.

I growled out a string of curse words as my hand went to my eyes. I felt Emma writhing around under me coughing as well. She managed to flip over on her stomach and push up. Push me off balance, just enough to scramble up, just like I'd taught her. The fucking timing of it all.

"Fuck!" I grabbed her around the waist and hauled her up, her feet no longer on the ground. "Give me the fucking pepper spray, Emma." I growled.

I fought her for the pepper spray, twisting her wrist until she cried out and finally released it. I threw her over my shoulder and hauled her upstairs. With every step I took, she railed against me, harder than she had the night I'd broken into her house. She was fighting now, like she meant it. She bit my shoulder blade, and I cursed. She bashed where she'd stabbed me weeks ago, again and again. I gripped her tightly, my jaw clenched with every hit she delivered onto my still healing wound, and then I reached the upstairs hallway closet. I swung open the door and pushed her into the hall closet, slamming the door behind her.

"Don't bother trying to get out." I snapped. "Take a

breather. You're safe. You hear me? You're fucking safe." I was breathing heavily as I pressed my head against the door. I tried to speak in a more soothing voice, but I could hear my tone. She'd gotten me all worked up and my voice was far from comforting.

I panted as I shoved the hallway table in front of the door to keep it shut while I dealt with my eyes. I stalked down the hall to the bathroom, where I rinsed my eyes and mouth out. I blew out a breath and leaned on the counter before hearing the hallway door rattling violently and I quickly went back into the hallway.

The door remained closed, blocked by the table, but the table rocked as she shoved against it. I leaned against the wall. I would give her a minute to calm down. Hell, I needed a minute to calm down.

Finally, after what felt like a lifetime, the door stopped rattling. I moved the table, and opened the door. Emma sat curled up in a ball on the floor, crying. She didn't even look up as I opened the door.

And then I didn't have to try. Softness and gentleness rushed through me as I gazed at her. "Emma?" I squatted down in front of her.

She didn't look up; she didn't say a word.

"Whose blood is that- are you hurt?"

"Are you fucking joking?" She sobbed, her voice muffled as she kept herself tucked all together.

I wanted so badly to reach out, to touch her, to pull her into my lap. She still hadn't answered my question. Was that her blood or someone else's?

"Please?" I pleaded softly. "Please don't shut me out."

Nothing.

"If you don't want to be with me, I understand, but I need to make sure you're not hurt. Can I check you?" I lowered down to my knee, putting us a hair closer. I wasn't sure if I should reach out and touch her just yet.

Her eyes snapped up, and she finally responded, her voice trembling. "Are you going to kill me?"

The air whooshed out of my lungs at the sincerity she held in her question. It hurt more than my side being stabbed or my arm being sliced. It cut into the deepest caverns of my heart. "You think I want you dead?" I asked softly. I couldn't help it. I reached out and took her chin in my hand. She tried to jerk away, but I held her face firmly, forcing her to meet my eyes fully.

"I don't know what you want." She hissed, her chest still heaved as if she were ready to run. "I don't know who you are."

"Yes, you do. You do." I encouraged her, taking her face with both hands, so gently.

"Did you fucking send those men after me?" She looked at me with purpose, carefully watching my face, her body ready to uncoil and spring if needed.

"Emma." What words could I even find to convince her to trust me? There weren't enough words in the English language to convince her. So I just simply answered, "Of course not."

"Then who the fuck did?" She snapped. "Who?"

"I don't know. Emma. I don't know." I kept my eyes on her as I inched a bit closer. "But I have that hard drive, and I could really use your help. Everything we need is on it."

She waited for a moment before responding, "Why did you attack me that night?"

I blew my cheeks out. Here it was, the big question that had brought it all crashing down. "I told you, I did it to protect you."

"Bull-fucking-shit." She tried to jerk away, but I held her face firmly.

Now I spoke more sternly. "You know as well as I do that Viktor does not give two shits about you." I could see that she recognized that as the truth in her eyes. "You fucked up. Big time. Viktor was sending a team to deal with you. And if I didn't give Viktor what he wanted, you would have been done." Something in her shifted. I was gaining a little bit of ground here. "They were going to fuck you up, and then the agency would have dropped you, and your deal, your contract keeping you out of prison, would have been gone."

She didn't say anything.

I continued, "Would you have preferred that I let you go to prison, huh? Would you have preferred if I let the team fuck you up?" I looked at her. "Why... are you covered in blood?"

"I trusted you, Mason." Her voice was softer, edging on crying.

I dared let my eyes rake over her and I slowly started checking her for injuries. "You can still trust me." I gently worked my way over her arms, and then her bare stomach. If she was injured, it was under her leggings. I couldn't see anything so far. Nothing around any vital organs was bleeding, at least. I nodded my head to her blood covered hands. "Are you going to tell me what happened?"

She looked at me for a long moment, her eyes discerning, and deciding. "You didn't send those men?"

"If I wanted you dead, don't you think I'd have done it by now?" I asked with a raised brow. "Were you followed?" I realized the length of time we'd been in the closet. If someone had attacked her, she'd likely led them here.

She pulled her lips between her teeth and watched me, trying to decide if she was going to trust me. "I don't think–"

Suddenly, a noise came from downstairs. I looked at her. "Don't move." I pressed a finger to my lips, motioning for her to be quiet, and I softly shut the closet door with her tucked inside.

I stood at the stop of the stairs, listening. Nothing. It could have been the wind shifting the door into the garage. I cautiously made my way downstairs, going straight for the kitchen island. I grabbed the gun off the counter and swiftly reloaded it.

Then I spun around and fired.

A big masked burly man laid on the floor, no longer moving.

I glanced up at the top of the stairs and shook my head. Despite my instructions, Emma stood there, silently, with no reaction or shock on her face. She was surprisingly calm for what had just happened.

"Is this?" I motioned to the man, and she nodded. I pulled the weapons off his body and looked at Emma. "We have to go. Now."

I sprinted up the stairs and quickly returned with a handful of clothes. I shoved Emma into one of my hoodies, and she let me stuff her into it and I threw a baseball cap on her head. This would have to do until we got to my safe house. Hopefully, we didn't have to make any stops, and hopefully we didn't get pulled over. I grabbed my go bag out of the downstairs closet and my laptop off the counter and took her hand guiding her out to the jeep that she'd parked right in the driveway. She only hesitated for a moment before getting into the car with me.

I started the engine and peeled onto the road.

"Where are we going?" She finally asked.

"My safe house." I responded.

26

MASON

IT WAS a little over an hour to the beach house and Emma sat silently, looking out the car window. Finally, I spoke first. "Are you going to tell me what happened?"

She didn't look at me, and kept staring out the window. "There's not much to tell." Her voice was hollow, empty. She was probably in shock. Judging by the state of her, whatever had happened had been rough. Really rough. I was proud of her. I didn't even need to know what had happened, to know that she was strong and capable of so much. She'd endured so much already, and she was surviving and fighting to survive more now than ever. I was proud of her for that.

"This is important. Every detail is important." I tried to invite her to share. And it was. I needed to know what had happened in the hours she'd left the house. If we had any chance of getting out of this alive, we had to stick together, at least for now. As much as it broke my heart, I knew I'd let her go when the time was right. Once she was safe, if that's what she wanted, I'd let her go.

"The longer you wait to tell me, the more risk we're in." I offered that morsel of truth gently, but she needed to understand the situation we were in. She was most certainly in shock.

"I don't–" She finally looked over at me, and there was so much hesitation, so much fear as her eyes spoke volumes all on their own. "I don't even know where to start." She whispered.

I slowly reached out and rested my hand on her knee, waiting to see if she'd let me. She looked nervous and finally, whether she decided to trust me or decided she was too tired to care, I wasn't sure, but I felt her relax under my hand. I gently rubbed her knee, a small comfort, and her eyes found mine. I could tell she so desperately wanted things to go back to the way they were.

"Start with where you were." I continued caressing her leg, and she ever so subtly leaned into it. The fraction of shift in body language sent relief through my entire being. She wasn't embracing me with open arms, but she wasn't pushing me away either.

"I was at the gym." She chewed her lip, her eyes flickering, reliving it all. I nodded, waiting for her to continue.

She softly detailed out what had happened, how she'd narrowly escaped. When she finished, my chest tightened knowing she'd been clever and brave, but mostly she'd been really, really lucky. I'd been lucky too, that I hadn't lost her.

I didn't know how I felt about the information I now knew, the fact that, in order to defend herself, she'd had to kill two men. Killing someone, even if your life depended on it, was such a heavy burden for anyone to bear. I wished I could carry the weight of it for her, but I couldn't. I couldn't spare her from this.

I lost myself in thought for a moment. The way she had talked about killing the second man, I could hear it in the strain of her voice, in the smallness of her body language. It had changed her, and the muscle in my jaw fanned knowing there was no undoing it. There was only moving forward now, doing the best anyone could to cope, to regain her confidence as she moved through the world. I knew it would be a long road to any sort of normalcy for her.

We sat in silence for some time after she finished, my hand still rested against her leg, holding her as closely as I could, the pads of my fingers caressing, soothing her, while I drove. I could tell she was so tired, but she wouldn't let herself drift off.

Finally, we pulled up in front of the house.

"Where are we?" Emma asked.

"We're at one of my vacation houses."

"Won't they know to look here?"

"No, this address isn't traceable." I hummed and got out of the car and walked to her side and opened her door. "Let's go inside."

Emma slid out of the car a bit stiffly.

Instinct kicked in and I reached for her. "Can you walk? Are you–?" I still wasn't entirely sure that she wasn't injured. But she shook her head and slipped past me, heading for the front door. She waited while I punched in the door code and then I pushed the front door open. I motioned for her to go in first, and I could tell that she was still slightly on edge. She didn't love the idea of me walking behind her. She wasn't running from me, but we were far from okay.

"Why didn't I know you had a house at the beach?" She asked somewhat suspiciously. Another surprise to add to her growing list.

"Because I rarely come here. It's specifically for situations like these, when I need to lay low for a bit."

She wrapped her arms around herself protectively.

"Mmm." She hummed, the sound was barely audible, a grunt almost in place of words.

There was an awkwardness between us, a stiffness that I didn't quite know how to fix.

I set my bag down on the floor and closed the distance between us. I picked Emma up and slid her onto the counter, standing between her legs, trying to be slow and intentional in my movements. "You know I would never intentionally hurt you, right?" My palms rested on her knees, and she didn't push me away. My eyes searched hers desperately for the hope that she knew that, that she believed she was safe with me.

She whispered in response, "I don't know what's real anymore, Mason." Her arms were still wrapped around herself, and she looked away. "I want to believe you, I do. I just don't know yet." She continued, "You've kept so many secrets from me."

I nodded. "Yes, and I'm sorry for that." I reached up and stroked her cheek with my knuckles. Her breath hitched for a moment and then continued at a steady pace. "I am." I emphasized.

The only problem was, I had one more *big* secret. I needed to tell her about the chip I'd put in her shoulder, to track her, but I doubted now was the appropriate time for that.

I just wanted to come clean, to share everything with her. I was so sick and tired of there being so many barriers and secrets between us. But I stopped myself from telling her anything more that might upset her. It would be selfish for me to offload the rest of my secrets now. Right now, as she sat in front of me, I was watching the life drain out of her. I was watching her essence fade into a dull flicker.

Somehow, I needed her to trust me, though, to know

that she was safe with me. Probably the safest she'd ever be. I needed her to *feel* that safety, to be able to relax into it, to understand I was a wide safety net spread out for her. Even if she didn't want me anymore, she had to know I'd go to the ends of the earth for her. I'd die for her. To keep her safe, and from enduring even an iota more pain.

She stared past me blankly. I pushed off her knees and went to my bag, pulling my laptop out. "Everything you need to see is right here." I waved my laptop in the air, an invitation. "We're going to bring whoever the sick bastard is down. I promise you that." I hesitated. "When you're ready, I could really use your help with this." I gripped the back of my neck, unsure if I should even be asking her to think about work right now. Maybe it was just the distraction she needed, though.

"Okay." She nodded before sliding off the counter and going to sit on the couch. "I'll look at it later."

The muscle in my jaw fanned. She was so... I didn't know exactly what. I worked for a while on my laptop, letting her settle into the new environment before I finally got up.

For hours she sat unmoving on the couch, so long she sat there silently while the daylight started to fade. She silently stared out the large windows at the ocean, her eyes seemingly peered out at nothing, registering nothing. Her eyes were empty, blank, and she was still covered in blood.

Internally I fought against myself, the need to go to her, the understanding that she probably wanted space. My body took over, and I came to stand in front of her. She didn't acknowledge me at all. "I–" I started, but my voice choked out, my emotions rippling through me. I cleared my throat, starting again. "I think we should get you into the shower." I couldn't bear to let her sit like this, covered in the muck of what had happened today, not for a second longer.

"Mmm." She barely hummed out, but she didn't budge.

I gripped the back of my neck, struggling with what to do. How to take care of her right now, not knowing if I should give her space or scoop her up.

"I'll heat the shower up for you." I offered.

She didn't say anything.

I blew out a breath and headed for the bedroom and the adjacent ensuite bathroom. I started the shower and stood there until the steam started swirling in the bathroom. I came back out, "Showers hot and ready." I tried a smile, but it fell flat as she stared empty eyed out the window.

I closed the distance between us and knelt in front of her. "Em?" Her eyes met mine, and I searched them desperately for some of that spice and sass she loved to give me, nothing. "I'm going to help you into the shower. Okay?" She nodded, hardly moving her head enough to be considered agreement.

She let me slide my arms under her, and she weakly slumped against me as I pulled her against my chest. She felt so small and vulnerable. Even between the layers of grime on her, I could still smell her sweet essence peeking through, and it sent a bolt straight through me. This was the woman I loved, and was going to spend every day for the rest of my life trying to prove it to her, if that's how long it took.

I carried her into the bathroom and carefully set her down in front of me. Part of me thought she might collapse if I let go. I waited, and she didn't move.

I opened my mouth, but no words came out. She didn't move for the shower, or do anything, she just stood there staring straight ahead.

I'd never felt this way in my life. I was watching the woman I cared most about disappear into a shell of herself, and she took a piece of me with her, into that darkness. I cleared my throat and steadied my voice. "I'm going to help you undress. Okay?"

She didn't say anything. I clenched my jaw as my eyes started to water up. I tried to speak in a comforting tone, but panic was bubbling up in my throat. "Can you just let me know if that's okay?" I asked.

Finally she looked up at me and nodded.

I nodded back in mild relief. "Okay." I gently slipped the baseball hat off her head, careful not to snag any of her hair that was now a bit matted, and I set the hat on the counter. "It's alright, I've got you now, baby." I hummed as I gently pulled at the zipper on my hoodie she was wearing. She limply let me slide it off her, pulling each of her arms out. "I'm gonna get you all cleaned up, and then you can sleep." I slid the pads of my fingers up her rib cage and slipped my fingers under the band of her sports bra. Before I could ease it up over her head, I froze as she sucked a sharp breath in.

Panic flooded through me. Was she injured? Was she afraid of me? Was she afraid to let me see her naked in this moment? I stood still, waiting, not daring to make a sudden movement.

She finally looked at me nodding, permission to continue.

I blew a breath out and struggled to slide the sports bra up. It was all twisted, and I didn't know how the fuck she'd gotten the damn thing on. I finally worked it up over her ribcage. "Arms up." I instructed.

She lifted her arms and as I went to pull it over her head; it got stuck on her face, jerking her head around a bit. "Oh shit! Sorry." I hissed out before I readjusted and slid it up over her arms. I had to bite my cheek and stifle a laugh at the absurdity of it. What a time to jostle her around like that.

When my eyes met hers, there was a flicker of something there. Not quite a smile, not quite amusement, but something. She'd found it just as humorous as I had, and this was the most she could muster to show me that.

I slipped my thumbs into the waistband of her pants and she gripped my shoulders as I slid her leggings and underwear to the floor so she could step out of them. I looked at her body, and again felt the startling urge of emotion bubbling up as I took in the dark bruises, and all the streaks and smears of rust red that marred her from top to bottom.

I guided her to the shower, and she stepped under the stream of water, just letting it pour over her. Finally, *I* stepped into the shower, clothes and all, and I so, *so* gently began to wash her.

I tenderly scrubbed her from head to toe until there were no more rust colored streaks left. The water, surprisingly bubbly as I rinsed her over and over again. Finally, she leaned against my chest, as we both stood under the spray of water and I washed her hair. She let out the softest sigh, relaxing against me as I held her up with one arm and massaged her scalp with my free hand, taking extra time to not just clean her hair, and detangle the mats but to touch her in a safe and comforting way.

Finally, when she was rinsed, and after what felt like an eternity, no more bubbles magically formed from her skin, and I turned the shower off and wrapped her in a giant towel and carried her to the bed. I stood dripping wet on the carpet as I pulled one of my large T-shirts that I knew she loved to wear over her head, and then tucked her into the covers.

I turned to get myself cleaned up, and as I turned, I felt her small hand slip into mine. Her hand communicated a wealth of information as she gripped my fingers so weakly. My eyes flicked to her, surprise no doubt etched on my face, and I found her expression panicked. Panicked at the idea of now being separated from me. An olive branch, a request to be comforted. Relief flooded through my being and I simply peeled off my wet clothes, and crawled into bed and pulled her against me.

This was a start.

27

EMMA

I WAS SCREAMING; I was fighting for my life; I was about to die.

I couldn't breathe.

If I couldn't get my head out of the bucket, I was going to drown. I tried to scream again this time no sound came out. My lungs burned, and I started choking.

Suddenly, I pushed myself up with ease. I was no longer drowning; I wasn't even wet. Except for my hands, something warm trickled over them. I looked down, and they were covered in so much blood.

I could see my own body. I was hovering above myself and I watched as I ruthlessly cracked his skull open, pounding a rock against his skull over and over again. Both of us screamed, the me that was watching, and the me that was doing. I was trapped watching. I couldn't stop. I was trapped in a loop, frozen in place, watching myself kill someone in cold blood.

A sickening feeling gripped my insides. Something was not right.

I watched myself scramble up knowing, something was not right.

In horror, I then saw the man's face.

It was Mason.

Someone was shouting in the distance. I couldn't hear them. All I could hear in my own ears was you killed him, you killed him; you killed him.

I had killed Mason. I had killed the love of my life.

Hands gripped my shoulders. I couldn't get away. Someone was coming for me. I screamed.

I looked down at his blood all over my hands. I couldn't get it off me. I wiped it on my pants over and over again, but more just appeared. It was sticky, coating my skin, making me itchy and sick.

"EMMA!" I heard my name, again and again.

I stared down at my hands and then back at a lifeless Mason, and I crumpled to the ground in devastation.

I had killed the love of my life. What had I done?

Someone was shaking me.

"WAKE UP!" It was dark, and I jostled as someone gripped my shoulders.

Finally, I came back into my body, my eyes flicked open and I screamed as panic bolted through me, registering a dark shadow looming over me.

"Emma, it's Mason!"

I panted, and it slowly came back to me, where I was, who I was with.

"You're just dreaming." He said, his voice shifted, softer, controlled, commanding, gentle. "I've got you now. You were just dreaming, baby." I felt this hand stroke over my head gingerly.

My eyes adjusted to the darkness, and I began to make out

the sharp outline of Mason's jaw that was hovering over me. "Mason?" I breathed. The words were nearly inaudible. I reached up and searched his face with my hand. His stubble, another reassuring detail of what was real. "You were dead." My words came out strange sounding, strangled almost. "You were dead." The words came out in a sharp sob, and I collapsed against his bare chest. His arms crushed me to him. The pressure of his arms around me was the only sensation I could feel in my body. His touch a welcome balm as my limbs trembled, buzzing with numbness, while my stomach rolled with nausea.

I sobbed against him, the sounds in and of themselves, terrifying as they clawed their way out of me. "I'm right here." He whispered against my ear. The heat of his breath sent warmth to my core. "And you're right here. In this room, with me. Nothing bad is happening." He stroked my face as I gulped deep breaths. "That's it, just breathe."

And slowly I did, slowly I started to come back into my body. I felt his hard chest against my skin, and with each deep calming breath he took, I slowly synced my own breathing up with his, taking long, full breaths.

The dream had felt so real. Real memories mixed with lies creating horrifying nightmares of alternate realities. I felt lost at sea, unsure of what was real as I lay here in the darkness. The only thing bringing me back to reality was Mason's body pressed against my own. Real. Here with me.

"I killed you." I whispered, feeling a hot tear streak down my cheek.

"I'm right here." He hummed, and I devoured the feeling of his deep baritone voice as it vibrated through my body. His arms were still tightly wound around me, but he pulled his face back enough that I could see him. He kissed where the tear had streaked down my face, his brows crinkling.

My mind still raced. It wandered back to the house, how

I'd been moments away from pulling that trigger when I'd shoved the gun against the back of his neck. I wasn't entirely sure why I hadn't pulled the trigger in that moment. But in this moment, I was so, so grateful that I hadn't.

I didn't know if I could trust him. I didn't know who to trust right now. But at this moment, right here in his arms, I needed him. I needed him more than I needed air. The fear of what it would be like to lose him consumed me.

I tilted my chin up, my lips parting, and I reached for him. He was too far away, and I snaked my hands around his neck and frantically pulled his mouth to mine. My mouth crashed into his, hungry, desperate for the return of affection. His pillowy soft lips caressed mine and gently he pulled back.

My heart cracked in two.

In the darkness that my eyes had now adjusted to, I could see such conflict in his expression. I could sense *such* hesitation.

But...I *needed* him.

I was desperate for the comfort I had once found in his strong arms.

If I didn't have Mason, I didn't have anything. I didn't have ground to stand on or air to breathe. I let out a sharp sob. "Please." I whispered against his throat, and when his breathing became husky, I pressed him further, letting my hands wander lower, lower, lower.

The pads of my fingers grazed over hard muscle, down the carved valley of his obliques, until my hand found the reassurance it was looking for. He groaned as my fingers grazed his firm velvet length, but before I could grasp it, his hand shot out, gripping my wrist, stopping me.

"Please, Mason." I whimpered. "I–" I would disintegrate if he rejected me. I'd given all the strength I had in the last

few weeks, and I was empty. I had nothing left. I needed him
to fill me up. I needed to feel something other than hollow
and empty. It was selfish, I knew that, and maybe he didn't
trust *me,* after what had happened. I didn't blame him if he
did. "I *need* you." I begged. "Please."

He shifted up to one elbow, his breathing husky. His eyes
were on my mouth, and I shuddered as he ran the pad of his
thumb over my lips slowly. So slowly. My eyes fluttered shut
and the hot burn of desire exploded into every nerve,
making me feel a pulsating hunger where everything had
been lifeless and numb just moments before.

I felt his face lowering to mine, and I waited in desperate
anticipation. With my eyes still shut, I waited for his mouth
to descend, for him to accept or deny me. Hope and fear
blossomed through me in those short seconds that felt like
eternity.

Finally, I opened my eyes to find his expression wide
eyed, boyish, vulnerable. He hovered above me, his forehead came to rest against mine. I heard soft words, uttered
in deep unguarded vulnerability. "I *love* you, Emma." He
breathed it against my skin, the heat burning, and then the
cool absence of his breath suddenly stinging. "I love you
with everything I am." He panted, "I can't– I can't just have a
taste, I have to have all of you." His breath was ragged, laced
with an uncollected nervousness that I'd never witnessed
before. "If you're going to leave me, if it's what you want, I'll
let you go. I'll never stop protecting you, but I'll let you go, if
that's what you want." He continued nearly breathlessly
with more urgency, "But I *can't* touch you– I can't taste you,
not knowing if this is the last time you'll ever be in my
arms–" His voice choked out. "I can't make love to you
tonight and let you go tomorrow." He continued, his voice
quivering. "I'm not strong enough." My eyes flicked between

his in the darkness. I waited with bated breath for him to continue. "I understand if you don't trust me, you have every reason not to. But if you're going to make me let you go–" He couldn't breathe. He was so overcome with emotion, the words getting caught in his throat. "I can't make love to you tonight and let you go tomorrow. *I love you....* And I just can't..."

Tears streamed down my face in relief, in joy. I took his face in my hands. "Then make love to me now, and tomorrow, and the next day, and all the days after that." I whispered, as I nudged his nose with mine. "Don't let me go, fight for me, and I'll fight for you–" I'd no less than gotten the words out before his lips were crashing against my own.

His mouth devoured mine with equal desperation as he rolled over and pulled me up onto his chest. His callused hands roamed over my body with reverence and familiarity. I felt my slickness work its way down my thighs and his hands gripped my thighs, pulling me apart and down, his length now snugly against my slick folds. I whimpered at the contact, rolling my hips to meet his as his length massaged my sensitive nub. He kissed me like he needed my lips to survive, our tongues dancing and swirling, sweeping over each other. His hands free to roam, touch, tease, and play, as I grew more and more slick against him.

Wordlessly, he rolled us over and flipped me onto my back, pushing my T-shirt up to expose my stomach and my tight aching breasts. My back arched with each new hot bolt of desire that shot through me as he kissed my stomach.

"I love you Emma Mitchell."

Another hot kiss on my stomach, and I moaned while he breathed adoration into my very skin.

"I love you."

He chanted it.

His tongue flicked over a nipple, and I jolted under him, moaning at the contact. "I love you." His mouth panted at my ear.

I raked my nails down his back, gripping his ass, bucking up, trying to earn more friction, I clenched around nothing as he worked his way back down my jaw, my neck, the tender place above my collarbone, over and between the slope of my breasts. And then down, down, down his mouth kissed, until he finally buried his face in my center.

I cried out at the sudden fire that uncoiled within me. "Oh God–" I pulled at his hair. "Oh God–" I writhed underneath him.

"*My* name." He growled into my core. It liquified me further. "Say *my* name when you come, baby."

I squeezed my eyes shut, losing everything but the feel of his wide tongue working relentlessly against my pulsating nerves. "Mason." I whimpered.

"That's right." He growled between strokes. "Again." A command I obeyed.

"Mason." Speaking became difficult. My back arched, and his hands shot out to pin me to the mattress, to stop my escape, as the intensity built.

"I'm going to–" I squeezed my eyes shut even tighter, "Oh God."

"Say *my* name, and I'll let you come." He panted.

"*Mason*." I was nearly falling off a mountaintop.

"Good girl." He lapped me up like he was starving. "That's it, you're almost there, baby." Two thick fingers plunged into me, curving against my sweet spot as his mouth continued on my bud.

I screamed out, cursing, writhing, chanting Mason's name as I erupted from within, exploding into a million little sparkling pieces.

"I need you inside me." I begged. "Make *love* to me, Mason. Fill me up."

With two fingers still pulsing inside me, milking the residual waves of pleasure that surged through me, he reached for the nightstand and brought a condom to his mouth, and then I heard the rip of foil opening.

His mouth found mine, and he kissed me more slowly, more passionately, like he was committing the shape and feel of my mouth to memory.

His fingers slid out of me for a moment, and then grazed over my still sensitive bud, and I whimpered into his mouth as he gently spread my legs open and lowered himself between them.

His hands threaded through mine above my head, and held them there, pinned to the mattress as he eased into my slick warmth. "Oh..." I breathed, remembering the fullness. My head fell back, and he wasted no time making a meal out of my neck as he slowly sank into me.

"You're so wet for me, baby." His hands floated over the sensitive skin on the inside of my arms as he trailed his fingers towards my face. Then his thumbs grazed over my eyelids, and my temples as he slid out of me and then so torturously, and slowly back in.

I gripped his hips, desperate to feel his full length. "Deeper." I begged, and he greedily obliged, sinking all the way into me this time, causing me to arch my back as he swept over my sweet spot.

"You like that?" He growled into my ear.

"You're *so* hard." I panted as his hips molded against mine. There was no escaping the rigid, unforgiving length of him.

"I'm always hard for you, baby." He rocked against me, and I gasped as my sweet spot came alive with need. He rocked in and out of me as, once again, the world faded away. Only the slick sweat of our bodies and the ragged sound of our breathing existed now.

"You're mine." He growled into my ear as I approached another climax. "Riding my cock like such a good girl." He praised me as I writhed under him, beginning to see white.

And then I shattered once more, clenching around his incredible fullness, the walls of my center fluttering around his length as he jerked into me. I screamed as the pleasure rippled through me, again and again.

With the words of love in the air, and the fear of nightmares under both our closed eyes, we ravished each other's bodies until the early hours of the morning; until we were both thoroughly and completely incapable of staying awake for another second.

I drifted off, wrapped in corded muscle, riding out the waves of my dizzy pleasure.

MASON PATTED HIS KNEE, and I gave him a glimmering look before sitting down on his lap. He went back to typing on his laptop with both arms on either side of me. I was wearing another one of his giant T-shirts and a pair of panties, and my stomach tightened as I pushed back and rolled my hips against him, feeling his fullness pressing into me from behind.

His breath was husky in my ear, but still he continued typing. I leaned back, letting my head rest in the crook of his shoulder and neck and began touching myself, running my hands over my stomach, and then up over my breasts.

I watched as Mason made a mistake typing and went back and corrected it. Three times he corrected what he was writing. I nipped at his throat, and his fingers went still, his own eyes closing.

"What's the matter? Can't focus?" I taunted while he stilled against me. I loved that when I touched him. His body responded just as much as my body responded to him. I was finally getting all of him, as he relaxed more fully into his desires for me. "Fuck me on this table, Mason." I breathed.

We'd made love all night, and this morning there was nothing but thick sexual tension in the air. I wanted more of him, but he was determined to prove his innocence to me, that he wasn't some international terrorist conspirator. He'd said the key to what we needed was on the hard drive, and I knew we needed to work quickly, anyway. This was so much bigger than just the two of us. But something in me had shifted in those early morning hours in his arms, here in this quiet beach house, just me and him.

Coming off the biggest adrenaline spike of my life, and what was undoubtedly the trauma of my life... I had thought for a solid twenty-four hours that he was going to kill me. So I went to kill him first, only, I realized I couldn't do it, I couldn't pull the trigger. In that brief moment of hesitation, I'd given him a window, and he'd taken it. When he'd disarmed me in the kitchen, I'd both felt relieved that I wouldn't have to kill him, and terrified that he was going to kill me instead. And then, to my shock, he hadn't...

Maybe I'd gotten everything twisted up, maybe I wasn't thinking clearly. Instead of killing me, he'd cared for me, bathed me, held me, while I screamed in my nightmares, and then... he'd said those three little words.

Those three little words that I'd been feeling for years. Hearing his love confession, feeling my affections being returned in full. It was a dream come true; it was intoxicating.

He was all I could focus on.

I realized, even without the evidence, that was likely sitting at the edge of his fingertips at the moment... I believed him, and believing him meant that I could forget some of the reasons I'd run in the first place.

It was complicated, and layered, but in Mason's arms last night, I knew deep in the fibers of my being that he was *my person*, and that maybe he'd made some shitty choices, but that I was safe with him, ultimately.

And that was all I needed to know that I wasn't playing into some veiled, sinister plan. I didn't have the evidence right now, but what I did have was the feeling in my gut. I believed him when he'd said Viktor was going to send a team for me. I'd understood why he'd made that choice now. I understood that it was the shittiest way he'd been able to protect me, but in its way, that's what it was, him protecting me.

And if his motivation had been to protect me, then not only was I safe with him, but I was loved by him. And after everything that happened, I needed to be loved. Because the alternative was that I let the darkness inside me consume me, and snuff out my light.

For a moment there, I'd wanted to succumb to it, to slip into the darkness, but Mason was a tether, guiding me back into the daylight.

So I made a choice to forgive him, to receive the love I so desperately needed.

To stay in the light.

At least that's what I told myself.

I rolled my hips against him again, feeling his hands finally surrender and drift to my inner thighs. I hummed as his fingers slowly grazed closer and closer to my inner thighs, as I pushed myself back, grinding against his length.

We had a lot to sort out, but I was exhausted and right now our physicality was creating a bridge between us, a pathway back to the light.

And I wanted to cross that bridge over and over again.

With a huff, he shoved the laptop off the table and swiftly pulled my shirt up over my head, throwing it to the floor. I groaned as his fingers pinched and rolled my nipples. He swiftly stood up and bent me over the table, and ripped my panties off, causing me to gasp.

I'd wound him up, and now he was unleashed.

He gently bit my left butt cheek and then the right, and it sent a jolt through my body, and heat to my core. He knelt behind me and he gripped my ankles, rubbing the sensitive skin there before he guided my legs apart. I clenched around nothing as I felt his hot breath at my entrance. "Don't. Move." He growled.

I whimpered as his touch suddenly disappeared. I heard him go into the bedroom, presumably for a condom, and then I heard him come back into the living room. I waited for what felt like forever, and when I finally looked over my shoulder, he was standing with dark eyes gazing at my hot dripping center.

"So beautiful, baby. You're so fucking beautiful."

I pushed myself up to my elbows, and in a flash, he was pressed against the back of me. "What did I say?"

I grumbled.

"Be a good girl, and stay still." I could hear the amusement in his voice at making me wait. Then finally the rip of the condom, and his mouth at my ear, as his fingers trailed down my back, leaving a wake of fire behind them. "How does *my girl* want it?" He kissed the back of my neck and moved to my other ear. "Tell me what you want, Emma."

His girl.

Fuck.

And then, the sound of my name in his mouth nearly made me come right then and there. I panted, "Fuck me hard, Mason." The hard cool table crushed against my hot aching breasts and it aroused me even more, as his teasing touch grazed everywhere but where I needed it most.

"Are you sure you don't want it slow?" His fingers trailed tantalizingly slowly across my skin.

"Fast, I want it fast." I complained, trying to push my hips back and find him.

"If you insist." He rumbled. "How can I deny what my baby wants?"

Thank God.

I felt his head thick at my entrance and I cried out as he sank into me hard and fast. I gripped the sides of the table as he gripped my hips and drove into me over and over. Against the table there was no give, and I shifted so my clit rubbed against the edge of the table with each thrust. We both quickly reached the edge, finally tumbling over together in a vortex of hot white fire.

He pulled out of me, kissing my back as he did so, and I felt disappointment when he was no longer against me. Fully spent, running on minimal sleep, I stayed pressed against the table catching my breath, and before I could muster the energy to push myself up, he quickly returned and I shuddered as he cleaned me up with a warm wash-cloth and slid clean panties up over my hips.

I pulled his shirt back on and he pulled me right back into his lap with a chuckle that warmed me to the core. I leaned back against him, still breathless, as he reached for his laptop on the floor.

He kissed my temple and then began typing again. I watched him pour through the hard drive, watched as he searched, partly paying attention to his work, but mostly paying attention to the way his body felt against my own. He caught my attention as he struggled to access an encrypted file, and my eyes flicked up to his.

He nodded at the computer. "Want to take a whack at it?" I sat up and took a deep breath. Not sure if I was ready to come out of the love bubble. But I quickly went to work, and my eyes widened as the information started to form a clearer picture.

28

MASON

EMMA'S FINGERS flew across the keyboard. She sat in my lap and it took everything within me not to start another game of lovemaking all over again. I left my hands resting against her bare legs, and my fingers twitched at the stillness I kept, despite my longing for more of her.

I held her as she steadily typed away, and I could feel myself hardening at the closeness of her yet again. I could tell when she felt me against the backside of her because her breathing changed. Oh, how I loved that subtle little change in her.

I slipped my hand up under her T-shirt and grazed her bare skin. She shifted, but continued working.

I ran my fingers along the rim of her waistband, desire pulsing through me. The need to dip into that tight warmth again and bring the taste of her, the smell of her glistening desire, to my lips.

There wasn't enough of the drug that was Emma Mitchell.

My Emma.

My girl.

Mine.

We'd been teetering on destruction, and in the matter of seconds, she'd yanked me off the edge of the cliff I'd been teetering on. The fear of losing her dissipated as we confessed our affections for each other in those early morning hours.

She was mine.

And I wanted to have her over and over again. The newness of this place we were in, needing to live in it, to gratify the realness of it, over and over.

We had a long way to go, so many things to work through, but she wasn't running. She was mine. Today, tomorrow, and all the days following, she was mine.

I would make sure of that soon.

My fingers inched closer and closer to the soft place under her breasts. Each of us teetering between responsibility, and giving in to desire *again*.

"I think I'm getting close." Emma said, her voice raspy, and I tried to decipher if she was referring to her work, or the effect my hands were having as they caressed her. "I can't make sense of it yet. I'm going to need more time." The crease between her brows deepened as she focused on her work. "Maybe if I can figure this out, I can get out of my contract." She sounded hopeful.

I stroked her hair. I doubted that. "We can certainly try."

"I have to try." She said simply.

Emma continued steadily clacking away at the keyboard, and suddenly she turned over her shoulder and looked at me. "You've been my boss this whole time?"

My hand stilled against her belly, and I nodded.

"That is *so* fucked up, you know?"

"I know." I said apologetically. "I wanted to tell you."

She went back to typing, and I held her in my lap, watching as she quickly and skillfully worked through the hard drive, cross-referencing the military contracts I'd told her she had free range to dig through now. It was all or nothing. Clearly, both our lives were on the line now.

Multiple assassins had been sent after us. This was life or death. For the moment, I knew we were safe. Emma was safe, as long as I was with her, she'd be safe.

I glanced up at the clock. It was nearly lunchtime, and we'd been love making all night, and lovemaking all morning. We were in desperate need of some sustenance, and I knew Emma's tendency not to eat when she was stressed.

I nudged her. "Let's take a break. You need to get something to eat. We're going to figure this out. *You're* going to figure this out. I know you are." And I had full confidence in her abilities. She was smart and clever beyond anyone I'd ever worked with, let alone what she knew how to do, especially for her age.

She leaned back against me. "No, I can't take a break."

I nuzzled her neck. "You need to eat something before you melt away, especially if you want more of this." I flexed my throbbing dick against her backside.

She grumbled. "Fine." I chuckled at what motivators she responded to.

I stood up and placed her back in the chair. "I'll go pick something up. Any requests?" I asked as I gathered my wallet and keys.

"I don't really know what's around here, so I guess you pick." She went right back to working.

"Ok, I'll be back in twenty, maybe thirty... don't go anywhere." I said, rather seriously. I watched her carefully as she barely registered my words, humming in response.

My deepest fear had been losing her, and now that I'd said the words 'I love you' out loud, I knew it was more than a fear for me. It would be a death sentence if I lost her. For the time being, she needed to stay inside, or with me, where she'd be safe.

29

EMMA

I WATCHED Mason walk out the front door, and I heard the door lock click into place. Now alone with my thoughts, a teeny tiny part of me wondered if I believed Mason. The part of me that I'd shoved into the back of my brain last night and this morning reared its ugly head. Part of me wondered if he was playing me, if I was stupid to trust him, and if I was just falling exactly into the trap that he'd laid for me.

I shook my head. No, I had to trust my instincts, otherwise what else did I have?

I continued steadily working, and my pulse quickened as I finally worked through the encryption on one of the files. What I saw stunned me.

If I hadn't been clever, I might have fallen immediately for what I saw, but I knew better.

But still, my heart pounded.

A perfect collection of breadcrumbs that led straight to one person.

Mason.

My breath caught in my throat for a moment... but I steadied my breathing and kept going.

So much for trusting my instincts.

No, I had to be sure.

Looking at it... It was too obvious. It was too up front. It was *so* clean and so direct that someone had to be framing him.

They *had* to be.

At least that's what I used to soothe myself as I tried to continue working quickly, searching for more evidence, either for or against Mason. Because if I was wrong, if Mason was the culprit, he was going to be back at any minute, and I didn't know what I'd do.

I had to be sure. My eyes flicked up at the clock, watching the time as I steadily worked, cross-referencing account numbers, locations, contracts.

Someone had to have taken Mason's foot steps and carefully tracked directly in them, using his tracks to conceal their own, while making it look like it was all Mason.

Right?

My pulse rang in my ears.

Or maybe I was in denial at what was in front of me, clear as day. My brain buzzed as I wondered if I was wrong. But I kept going. I had to be on the side of the man I loved. I had to be, because if someone was framing him, I was going to put them in the ground.

And if he wasn't being framed, if this was all accurate, he hadn't killed me yet... So, I'd play things cool until I knew for sure.

Slowly, I connected a series of shell companies and bank accounts that led a strong clear trail right to Mason.

Getting more and more frustrated, I continued to dig.

Nothing but giant arrows pointing to Mason, Mason, Mason.

My stomach sank, and I hated when I looked over my shoulder to see if he'd snuck up on me. I hated that I distrusted him.

But was my distrust misplaced?

Maybe I'd put too much faith in him, maybe I'd been naïve, and he'd said those three little words last night that I'd been waiting to hear for so long. Maybe he was just a master manipulator, and I was the stupid little puppet, letting my strings be pulled all over the place.

Suddenly, the fear of everything I'd been through hit me like a wall. I dialed his phone and quickly called him, not sure if I was relieved when he picked up.

"Where are you?" I asked, trying to steady my voice, searching to see if something felt off.

"I'm almost back. I went to this cafe, and grabbed you some pasta and some eclairs for dessert, though I know what *I'm* going to have for dessert." He chuckled.

A shiver ran up my spine at the sentiment, and I licked my lips that *I'd* be just the thing for his sweet tooth. Conflict raged within me.

"I'll see you in a few minutes... I love you." He said, and I could feel his smile through the phone. My breath hitched in my throat at the casualness of ending a phone call with those words.

Did he even mean them? I wondered.

"Okay, see you soon... I love *you*." I bit my lip as uncertainty swirled in my mind, but I couldn't let him know anything was up.

I hung up and drummed my fingers on the table. If it *was* Mason, he wouldn't have given me the evidence to prove him guilty. He wouldn't have just left me with his laptop and the tools to give him a life sentence. No, that wouldn't have made any sense.

Something felt off, and I needed to figure out what it was.

My mind buzzed with the events from the day before, now that I was by myself. There was an edge in my system, the prick of fear that had reared its ugly head again. What if it *was* Mason? I wrung my hands as I paced around the living room, wondering what to do. Wondering if I should run now while I had the chance.

I suddenly realized my window of escape was nearly gone. Mason would be back at any second. He was probably pulling into the driveway at this very moment. I slumped back down in front of his laptop and, with my brain fuzzy, I struggled to find the focus to keep working. To see what else I could dig up. What would I do when he showed up with eclairs and lunch with that big warm smile? Would that smile change when he realized what I'd seen? Was I teetering on the edge of danger again? The anxiety started to build.

Where the fuck is he? He should have been back by now.

I chewed my lip and called him again, and he didn't pick up.

Fuck.

What the hell is going on?

What do I do?

I stood up, looking around.

I need to get out of here.

Now.

My fear turned into the urge to run, and I ran to the bedroom and dug out an odd tangle of clothes that were partly my own and partly his, pulling them on. I grabbed his gun and shoved it into the back of my pants and then I cautiously peeked out of the front door window towards the street.

Nothing.

I opened the door and hurried out.

As I rounded the edge of the garage, confused fear raked over me.

Mason's Jeep sat running, with the keys in the engine, the driver's door wide open, but no Mason. I cautiously walked into the driveway and looked all around, before finally looking into the car. The food was still in the takeout bag sitting in the passenger seat, and Mason was nowhere to be found.

Fuck.

Oh fuck...

30

EMMA

I QUICKLY GRABBED the food as I took the keys out of the ignition and sprinted inside, locking the door behind me.

What do I do now!?

I frantically racked my brain.

Do I leave?

Do I stay?

Was this some sort of trick?

What if Mason was hurt? What if one of those assassins already killed him?

I steadied myself on the kitchen counter, focusing on my breathing. Oh God, I wasn't cut out for this. What the fuck was I doing here?

I cursed myself for ever rerouting that plane back in high school. I cursed Mason for dragging me into this job.

Maybe prison was better off. You got outdoor time, after all, and you could take classes or have hobbies. Maybe prison wasn't so bad. Maybe I'd just terminate my contract myself, let them lock me away.

I shuddered at the realization that the agency could probably get to me, even if I was locked up. No, I needed to figure out a real solution, not relive my greatest regret as a stupid teenager right now.

I felt so nauseous, but suddenly I realized maybe it was because I was hungry. I smelled the food in the takeout bag, and I shook my head, feeling incredibly guilty. Mason was either fucking me over right now, or he was getting fucked over, and I... was hungry.

Well, if I was going to save him, or end up having to kill him, I supposed I'd better not do it on an empty stomach.

I rolled my eyes, stuffing half an eclair into my mouth. I groaned as it melted in my mouth.

Oh, it was *so* good.

I knew I needed to eat some protein, though, something a bit more solid than sweets. I licked my fingers and quickly pulled out a container of lemon pasta and grilled chicken. My heart twisted at the fact that Mason went out to get me lunch and while he had mysteriously disappeared, I was doubting his loyalty. Not to mention eating. But I had to. I could feel the shakiness of my low blood sugar setting in. I quickly scarfed down a few bites of the chicken pasta while I stood at the counter.

Chewing, I blew out a breath as the food started to hit my system, and my shakiness slowly started to subside. I needed to figure out what to do. Plopping back down in front of the laptop as I chewed, I went back to work following the breadcrumbs. While I searched for what I hoped I would find, my anxiety continued to build, causing my nausea to come back

Suddenly, I snapped the puzzle pieces together, the picture clear in my mind.

My hand flew to my mouth, and goosebumps pebbled over my skin.

Oh... shit.

Shit, shit, shit.

It *wasn't* Mason.

My heart pounded in relief and horror.

It wasn't Mason, but this realization of who it was might be worse. It meant Mason, and I were in even more danger than I realized.

My stomach turned while I contemplated it. Why hadn't I put it together sooner? It all made so much sense now that it was laid out in front of me. The ease with which the breaches kept happening over and over. I'd known it had to be someone on the inside, but this... this was catastrophic.

They'd been able to push me off their trail at every turn.

Time and time again.

No wonder it had been so easy for them to redirect me every time I went digging.

My blood began to boil.

This person within the agency had been authorizing the backdoor access the whole time. Nearly every security breach had been allowed at their discretion. Not only had they been allowing classified information to be stolen from right under our noses, but they'd been *actively* selling the information. They were enthusiastically lining their pockets as they equipped terrorists with military grade weapons, to enact mass suffering on innocent people.

I was hot on the trail; I quickly traced the bank accounts and found that they went to a shell company.

They had made a trail straight to Mason in case of exposure, and I'd bought it for long enough that it nearly cost me.

This, the reason Mason had come to my house that night, the reason I was stuck in this for life.

I hated the fucking agency, and everyone in it. I hated it.

My fingers flew over the keyboard.

I didn't hesitate for a moment, and I emptied the accounts, sending them to random ones. I could amend that messy solution later. Right now I was going to drain those mother fucking accounts for all they were worth.

Mason, oh he was lucky that I was as good at my job as I was. He was about to become the fall man if they didn't kill him first.

My pulse thundered in my ears as I quickly worked to erase my own tracks as I toggled between our stolen hard drive and the system I was responsible for protecting.

If I wasn't careful, someone would know my sticky little fingers had gone where they weren't supposed to go, and suddenly I panicked, wishing Mason hadn't left me.

I sat at the computer furiously hacking into the agency system. If they had framed Mason, maybe this was it, maybe they were taking him out. Or maybe it had been the terrorist organization that had taken him. I couldn't be sure.

I went straight into the main system. If the agency had taken Mason, I'd be able to find him on the security cameras, and I prayed it was the agency. Because if it wasn't, I didn't know how I was going to find him.

And I had to find him.

I *loved* him.

I hacked through the agency network, searching for any sign of Mason. Finally, I hacked into the security system and pulled up a live stream, as I frantically flicked through the video feed one after another.

And there he was.

I flicked back to the live feed of Mason strapped to a table, similar to the one I'd been strapped to months ago. He laid there with a bright light shining on him, not moving.

The hair on the back of my neck raised, wondering if someone had been tracking my work on Mason's computer all morning. It would make sense, it *was* a company computer, and if the traitor at the agency wanted to frame someone, they'd certainly keep tabs on that person to make sure they stayed in the dark, until the traitor was ready to drop the curtain and blame their fall guy, Mason.

My fingers froze over the keyboard, hesitant if I should even continue working on the company computer. Wondering if they knew I was here, too.

I studied the live feed for just a moment longer, waiting, watching for his chest to rise and fall. The feed wasn't clear enough, I couldn't tell if he was unconscious or... I couldn't think the words. I wouldn't, not until I knew for sure.

The thought made me sick.

Fear prickled over my skin.

What if they knew I was still here?

What if someone came back for me?

I had enough information to go off of. I needed to figure out how to get Mason out... if he was still alive. The thought made me sick.

And then I ran to the bathroom and was sick.

I tried to steady my breathing.

I stood up and steadied myself in the bathroom mirror. I dug around the drawers but didn't find my toothbrush. I looked at Mason's and decided otherwise. I squatted down and frantically dug under the sink, looking for mouthwash or a new toothbrush, hoping maybe Mason had an extra.

I found a drawer full of new toothbrushes, and as I went to stand up, I curiously opened the organizing drawer next to it. Tampons and pads, of course, he would have everything a woman would need here too. He was thoughtful like that.

I stood up and started to brush my teeth, and I slowly

stopped, resting my toothbrush against the sink, as I looked at my reflection... When was the last time I used a tampon?

My eyes searched in the mirror. When was the last time I'd had a period?

My hand flew to my mouth, and I gasped in realization.

Oh, my God.

No.

My horrified reflection stared back at me.

Not right now. Please God, not right now.

I'd been through hell and back the last few months, I was stressed. I hadn't been paying attention to my period at all. It'd been the last thing on my mind.

Mason and I had been using protection, except for the incident in Iran. I wasn't on birth control; I wasn't sexually active, so I'd never seen the need. When Mason and I had started sleeping together regularly, he'd just automatically started using protection I hadn't considered...

I whirled around to the towel closet and dug around. He had everything else in this damn safe house; I doubted he'd have what I was looking for... but maybe. I finally found a first aid kit, it was in a large black zippered bag. I blew out a breath, shaking my head as I dug through it. It was the most jam-packed first aid kit I'd ever seen, if you could even call it a first aid kit. It was more like an emergency crash cart. I set aside a defibrillator and a stethoscope and began frantically unzipping the many pouches. Some contained syringes and vial after vial of God knows what. I opened another zippered pouch and sure enough, pregnancy tests.

Of course, he would have these.

I stared at it and then, realizing I had zero time to waste, I ripped the packet open and quickly took the test.

I set it on the counter feeling anxious and I frantically

finished brushing my teeth and then paced the bathroom for the remaining minute while the test processed.

My eyes were wild when I peered over the counter, as if the test would jump up and bite me.

Holy Shit.

Two lines.

Positive.

I was pregnant.

I was carrying Mason's child.

A strangled sob erupted out of me, and I held my belly as I sank to the floor, taking it in.

I'm pregnant.

Mason's the father.

My child is going to lose their father.

I'm going to be a single mother...

I erupted into uncontrollable sobs.

I was going to have a walking, talking reminder of the love of my life, and the room closed in on me when I realized how painful that would be.

Why was everything so fucking complicated? Why couldn't everything just be simple, easy? Why did we have to be wrapped up in this nightmare?

I didn't know how Mason would feel if he knew. Then fear ripped through me, knowing he may never get the chance.

I vomited into the toilet again, and this time I just rinsed my mouth and wiped my mouth with the back of my hand. I *had* to get moving. I had to save Mason. If I could do it, I would.

I raced around the house, ripping open drawers, searching for anything and everything that could help me. I clipped on a utility belt and loaded it up with knives, and strapped a gun to my thigh, and another to my calf under my pants. I quickly glanced over a mask and decided to leave it. If I did go in there, guns blazing, they were going to know who it was, anyway.

I shoved Mason's laptop into my bag, along with the defibrillator just in case, and drove to the location that I assumed was the agency, the location where they were keeping Mason.

I was going to save him, or we were all going to die as a sad little family trying.

I couldn't bear the thought of trying to live without him, let alone raise a child without him.

It was freedom or bust now.

I realized the agency knew that Mason had the hard drive, the hard drive that would expose the traitor, and I had to get to Mason and let him know who it was before they tied off the loose end that Mason was.

I swallowed hard... if they hadn't done it already.

31

MASON

"Fuck." I groaned, realizing everything hurt. My eyes fluttered open groggily and when I went to move, my arms jerked to a stop. I struggled to lift my head and get my eyes to bring the room into focus.

Shit.

Strapped to a table, my pulse quickened when I realized where I was. I was at the agency, and this time I was on the other side of the one-way glass.

Not good.

Slowly, my eyes flicked to the room around me, and I steeled myself. I'd been in many rooms like this before. A variety of instruments were laid out on the table. A bright light shone in my eyes.

I stared up at the ceiling, recalling the last thing I remembered. The moment I'd pulled into the driveway, the bastards had blocked me in, and outnumbered, they'd sedated and bagged me immediately. I sucked a sharp breath in. They'd taken me back at the house, where Emma had been lounging inside in her underwear, completely

unaware. Had they grabbed her too? How long had it been?
Was she still at the house? Did she know I was missing?

I had to get the fuck out of here and find Emma before
they did.

I yanked against the restraints in frustration, but I felt
the residual effects of the sedative I'd been drugged with
inviting me to slip back under. I fought the sleepiness with
everything I had. It could have been hours, or days, I wasn't
entirely sure at this point. The room I was being detained in
didn't have a clock, or much to go off of.

It was a simple room, easy to clean and sterilize between
interrogations if needed. Just white tile walls, with a row of
stainless steel cabinets along one side, and the one-way
glass along the other. In the corner of the room, a security
camera blinked at me with an irritating little red light. A
reminder that my every move was being watched.

I took a second glance at the little red light on the security camera.

Was that?

It blinked at odd intervals.

Almost as if...

Morse Code.

I concentrated on the small blinking red light.

P...

E...

R...

Per?

I waited for the next set of letters.

V...

I...

K...

I heard footsteps coming down the hall. I missed the
next few letters.

Per Vik?

I racked my brain, playing a life or death game of scrabble in my mind.

I kept watching... my eyes felt blurry, bile coated the back of my throat, as the morse code raced the clock against the steps approaching closer and closer.

I missed the next letter as I strained my eyes blinking.
Come on. Focus.

I...

P...

The footsteps neared. I ignored it despite the thundering in my ears and focused on the blinking light.

E...

R...

Iper?

Oh my God.

Viper.

Someone's trying to tell me, warn me.

V...

I...

K...

Vik–

My eyes snapped up as Viktor waltzed into the room.

The dots clicked into place; the code realized.

Viktor, Viper.

Fuck.

Of course, Viktor was the man they referred to as The Viper.

That's exactly what he was, a snake.

I gritted my teeth angrily, trying to keep my new discovery under wraps. He didn't know I knew, and if for some reason he hadn't dragged me in here to end me, then he certainly would kill me as soon as he realized what I knew.

"Ah, Reynolds." He sang and pulled up a rolling stool. "Comfortable? Can I get you anything?" He loved to toy with people when he brought them in for interrogation. I knew it was a mask over the real sinister capabilities he had.

"You can start by telling me why you've got me strapped to this table, you motherfucker." I spat at him.

He grinned, completely amused, as he usually did. It was easy being on that side of the table. "You've become a real thorn in my side lately, you know that?"

He stood up and yanked on the straps that held my ankles, making sure they were tight. As he damn well should, because as soon as I got out of these restraints, I was going to shred that traitorous motherfucker into tiny pieces.

I scoffed, shaking my head, suddenly piecing together why he was always so hard on Emma. Because she was the only one who'd gotten even remotely close to tracking him down, she was the one always putting her nose in things she wasn't supposed to. She was the one who threatened to expose him.

I blinked back up at the camera, and it continued to play the morse code. She'd probably hacked in and set it up on a recurring loop. I glanced away from the camera, not wanting to draw Viktor's attention to it. God forbid he realized there was a message silently blaring across the room, outing his dirty little secret.

I realized the incriminating evidence must have been on that hard drive, and that's likely why Viktor had dragged me in here, to see how much I knew already. It was all coming together lightning quick. Emma had likely pieced it together back at the house, and she knew where I was. She was sending me this message in an effort to try to help me. As glad as I was for the intel, I seriously hoped she was far, far away from me right now.

If Viktor had been working closely with Shah, he'd have realized the moment the incriminating hard drive had gone missing. That's why Emma had been attacked at the gym, and then another team had been sent to collect me at the house. I shook my head. If I'd realized it was the agency sending these assassins one after another, I'd have left the company electronics, but instead I'd let them track me straight to the safe house.

My chest tightened thinking of Emma. I seriously hoped she'd escaped.

I glanced at Viktor, who I realized had been drawling on about God knows what. He now stood over the tray of metal instruments, fingering them with delight in his eyes.

He whirled around. "Don't you think?"

I made eye contact with him, burning him to the ground with my eyes.

"Hmmm?" He asked again, and I had no idea what he was referring to.

"I could start now, I suppose." He grinned with a wicked grin. "Though I know you won't talk on your own, so I suppose we should just get straight to the fun part."

Fucking hell.

I steeled myself. Knowing what was to come wasn't going to be fun.

Viktor leaned over the table, looking at me with glimmering delight. He was so fucking thin and gangly, like a spider. I could snap him in half with my bare hands. It'd be easy. And that's why he'd had me sedated and then restrained. He was wise to do that. He knew what I'd do to him if my hands were free. "You're still so very sleepy, I see. I think I'll wait to start until you're completely awake, and then you can fully enjoy what I have in store for you." He snickered.

I played into it, pretending that I was still out of it, still heavily under the effects of the sedation. And I was, but not nearly as much as he thought. My willpower was stronger than the lingering sedative in my system. This was going to buy me a little time, at least.

"See you soon Reynolds." He left the room, and I let my head sink back onto the table.

My mind was running a thousand miles a minute. If I could just get these damn restraints off, it'd be game over.

But getting these off was going to be a bitch.

My eyes wandered around the room, wishing that the tray of sharp instruments was so much closer to me.

I thought of Emma, and what they'd do to her if they had grabbed her too. The thought reminded me I had no time to waste.

The last time Viktor had strapped her to one of these tables, it was just to scare her, to warn her of what he was capable of, but thankfully, they hadn't actually tortured her. If Viktor got his hands on her now, knowing what she knew...

I had zero time to waste.

I yanked against the restraints.

Over my dead body was I going to let that fucking bastard lay a finger on her.

I heaved in a few breaths and then pulled hard on my left hand.

I kept pulling even as the pain began to radiate up into my arm.

I pushed through the pain, and I broke out in a cold sweat, biting my cheek until it bled.

My hand reached a threshold of pain, and I knew this was it.

I grunted and yanked hard as I felt something snap.

I nearly passed out from the pain, and I steadied myself, gasping for breath as I wretched my now broken hand through the restraint.

Pulsating throbbing pain radiated through me, making me nauseous.

I ignored it entirely.

I had to move quickly. If anyone was watching the cameras, they'd have seen me, and if I didn't at least get my other hand out before they came back in, I was done. I'd have broken my hand for nothing.

I panted as I reached across my body and gingerly started pulling the straps loose on my right hand. I nearly couldn't get it undone with the radiating pain shooting through me, my broken hand hardly able to grip the restraint firmly enough to pull it open.

Finally, sweating and cursing silently, my right hand was free. I swallowed hard and quickly loosened the restraints on my waist and ankles.

I stumbled off the table and tried to cradle my broken hand against me as best as I could.

Suddenly, I heard a dull boom somewhere far away, and then a security alarm was blaring. I jiggled the door handle. It was, of course, locked from the outside. I pressed myself against the wall and waited for someone to open the door and give me access to my escape.

Whoever walked through that door was about to take a very long nap.

32

EMMA

I SAT outside the agency in the Jeep and tried to steady my breathing through my tight chest. I eyed the door on the back side of the building that I had decided was my best chance at entry. So far, I hadn't seen anyone guarding, entering, lingering.

It had been so eerily quiet back here I wondered if I was walking straight into a trap. The only thing guarding the door was a security camera, with a red light, steadily blinking the morse code message I had set up on a loop. I hadn't been able to isolate the light specifically in Mason's cell, and I figured the more people that figured out who Viktor was, the better anyway. So my morse code message steadily blinked across all the security cameras in the facility.

I blew out a breath. I'd been watching the door for some time, and it was now or never. I looked over the utility belts and the weapons I'd strapped all over my body, as if it would help me. I'd hardly fired a gun except for the chaotic moment in the locker room. I shivered at the thought and pushed it out of my head. Though escaping that attack in the locker room had convinced me that I wasn't totally inept, maybe this was a death sentence going in there; but maybe, just maybe, with a little luck, it might work.

The only thing standing between me and getting into the building was an electronic keypad into the back door.

I pulled the laptop into my lap and quickly pulled up the security camera feed inside. I sucked in a sharp breath, watching Viktor standing over Mason. I had to do something quickly. It was time to pull up my big girl pants and just do it.

I wondered if Mason had gotten my message, if he knew what Viktor was, who he was.

I toggled over to the next tab and studied the schematic of the building, willing myself to remember where Mason's cell was, and then I started worming my way into the security system to bypass the exterior door lock.

It took me all of three minutes, but it felt like eternity as I wondered how long I had before Viktor started carving Mason up. Finally, I was in, and I disabled the exterior door locks. I slammed my laptop shut. I was really going to do this.

My chest heaved as I checked all the weapons I had strapped to various places on my body one final time. I didn't have the muscle memory like Mason did, but hopefully I'd reach for the right thing at the right time if it came to that. I didn't know what the hell I was going to do when I got in there, but I was going to shoot down anyone and anything that tried to stop me.

I set the defibrillator out on the passenger seat in case I'd need it later.

Then I slid out of the Jeep and quickly sprinted into the bushes, waiting outside the back door.

My hands trembled as I flexed them, listening for any

sounds inside. I finally mustered my courage and shot up, ready to do the damn thing. I froze when I heard a soft click. It was like time started moving in slow motion as I looked down and saw the grenade pin dangling, snagged on a branch.

I ripped the grenade off the tactical belt and threw it hard, before I turned to sprint. I was thrown face first into the bushes from the impact, and heat seared my body from behind.

I groaned as I pushed myself up blinking. My ears were ringing, wait, no, that was the security alarm. Shit! So much for sneaking in unnoticed.

I staggered up and took the gun from the holster on my hip. I fired a practice shot into the ground to get the feel of it and trotted to the door. I'd already announced my entrance, so I wasn't concerned about being quiet anymore. What was one gun shot after the sound of that explosion? Waving the smoke to the side, I listened for a moment and didn't hear anything.

I slipped inside using the giant hole I'd just made and staggered down the hallway in the direction I thought I was supposed to go. I turned to look down each hallway and everything looked the same, just long hallway after long hallway. There were no distinguishing marks.

I sprinted down one hallway, and the numbers on the doors went down.

Shit. I was going the wrong way. I tried to shake the fog out of my head and I whirled around and sprinted the other direction. I could hear heavy footsteps somewhere in one of the hallways and I knew I was running out of time.

Just get to Mason, I chanted it to myself, knowing if I could get to him, he'd be able to get us out of here.

I ducked as gunshots rang out in the air and bolted around the corner to the next hallway. Just keep moving.

Room 155, I sprinted to the end of the hallway. Room 166.

Fuck. Where was it? Where the hell was his cell? I was too high.

It must have been across the other side of the hallway.

I inched to the corner of the wall and listened. Nothing.

I raced across the hall and tripped to the ground as more shots rang out. I pushed myself up, and stumbled hard into the wall, before I braced myself, and kept moving.

I sprinted past several more rooms feeling like I could collapse. There it was!

Room 142.

Yes! I tried the handle. It was locked, of course it was locked.

I fired the gun again and again at the door handle, and it finally fell to a clatter on the floor and I shoved the door open.

I hardly got a scream out as an arm immediately snaked around my throat.

No sooner than the arm had closed around my neck, it suddenly released. "Emma!" Mason sputtered in surprise. "What the fuck are you doing here?"

As he released me from the choke hold, I stumbled forward and braced myself on the nearby table coughing and trying to catch my breath. I looked over my shoulder and just gave him a smirk, and then I went down.

My leg suddenly gave out underneath me.

"Shit." Mason lunged for me as I crumpled. His eyes were wide with horror. I followed his gaze down to my leg, and my eyes widened in equal surprise.

I'd been shot.

I gingerly touched the wound, shocked. I brought my

hand to my face and gazed at the blood on my fingertips with confusion.

When had I been shot?

In a flash, Mason's hand snaked up under my pant leg and whipped the gun out, firing it two times into the hallway, as I screamed, covering my head.

"You're shot." He breathed, talking more to himself than to me. His eyes were wide, I could see them working, quickly making a plan. Suddenly, he shifted. I could tell he was forcing the panic out; his demeanor became calm, in control. "We're going to have a long conversation about why the hell you thought it was a good idea to come storming in here." He growled, but I sensed his tone was more fearful than angry. His eyes were manic as he looked at me, wild with equal parts fury, confusion, awe, and pride.

"Yeah okay. Hi to you too, ya big dummy." I winced. "Can't believe you let them catch you." I hardly got the words out before crying out, as I tried to stand, I earned myself the most intense pain I'd ever felt in my life.

Mason grimaced. "Don't put any weight on it." He gently eased me back to the floor. "I'm going to get us out of here." He stroked my face gently, gazing into my eyes for less than a millisecond. Mason quickly took one of the many utility belts I had strapped to me, and stripped all the knives and weapons off it and quickly looped it around my leg, positioning it just below my knee. He pulled the makeshift tourniquet so freaking tight I cried out in pain.

That registering of pain started to fan out all over my body, and I could feel my whole body now trembling involuntarily. I struggled to hold in little sobs as the adrenaline subsided enough that I could feel my pain in its fullness.

"I'm sorry, baby." Mason's brow crinkled in guilt as he tied off the tourniquet. Pain inflicted to keep me from bleeding out. "Just keep breathing, in and out." He said in an eerily calm voice.

He quickly pulled the other utility belt off me, as well as the gun holsters, and strapped them to himself. Then he hauled me up and threw me over his shoulder, and I nearly blacked out from the flurry of it.

He raced into the hallway, it was a flurry of smoke, and gunshots as I swung wildly over Mason's shoulder. I wasn't sure if it was gunshots coming towards us, or Mason shooting at someone. I panicked as he groaned in pain, worried that he himself had been shot. But I couldn't focus on the fear because my own pain was radiating through me more and more intensely with every breath. The pain pushed out all other sensations and thoughts. It railed against my senses with ruthless relentlessness.

Then we were outside, the fresh air pulling into my nose. We'd made it, Mason had gotten us out. The world swirled again as Mason deposited me into the front seat of the jeep, shoving the defibrillator onto the floor with a manic laugh, and then he frantically buckled me in.

His hands worked over my entire body. "Keys, where'd you put the keys, baby?" I could hear the terror in his voice.

My throat was so dry, I could hardly swallow. I winced as I nodded to the ignition.

Mason laughed maniacally, "Of course you left them in the ignition." He kissed me on the forehead in gratitude and relief, and then sprinted around the car, hauling himself into the drivers seat before peeling out onto the road.

"Just hang in there." Mason encouraged me. "You did so good." I slumped against the door and watched his eyes flash with concern as he flicked his gaze between the road and me. "I'm tempted to throw you over my knee and remind you why you should never do that again." I could hear the strain in his voice. I knew he was trying to make a joke, to distract me, but I couldn't muster enough energy to even chuckle at the statement.

I felt my eyes fluttering shut. Mason's hand was on my shoulder. "Emma." He drew the words out in frustration. "Stay awake, baby. Can you keep your eyes open for me?" He continued moving me gently by the shoulder. "Can you talk to me?"

My brain was fuzzy. I needed to tell him something. It was important. What was it?

"I have to tell you something." I mumbled out.

"Good, tell me all about it," Mason encouraged.

"Baby..." I struggled to pull in breath as the pain radiated through me. I just wanted to sleep so badly.

"That's it, keep talking."

"We're going to have–" I gasped for breath, "A baby." I breathed.

I stared at the backs of my eyelids, as Mason processed what I just said.

"We're– you're pregnant?"

"Uh huh." I hummed as the blackness dampened everything out.

33

MASON

"At least tell me how she's doing. Give me an update. Something!" I struck the counter at the nurses' station with my good hand. I wasn't even supposed to be back here, but I was desperate for an update on Emma. I'd pushed my way back here moments ago. The security guard finally had given up trying to stop me. He'd gone pale and wide eye'd after I'd threatened to throw him through a wall if he didn't let me through.

The nurse huffed out an irritated breath. "Mr. Reynolds, she's still in surgery." Her tone softened ever so slightly. "I will give you an update as soon as I have one."

I paced the hall in front of the desk before finally shooting another look back at the nurse. "She's fucking pregnant." I didn't know if I was talking to her or myself anymore. I was on the verge of tears, and I rubbed the back of my neck before I collapsed against the wall and sank down to the floor. My head fell into my hands as the weight of the situation came crashing down onto me. The adrenaline from our escape had dissipated, and I felt every ache in my body, and every tremor of worry in my mind. "She's the mother of my child. I can't lose her." I mumbled into my hands, feeling the words come out of my mouth for the very first time. I cursed when I'd absentmindedly bumped my own broken hand.

The nurse stood with the clipboard as if she was debating smacking me with it. "I know. We're doing everything we can." She said it in such a way that I knew she had said those words a dozen times today already. "I would really like to look at that hand." She stood lingering in front of me with a stern look on her face.

I blew out a breath and looked at her numbly. "Fine." I pushed myself off the floor and lumbered down the hall after her into a room.

As I followed her, I went numb, considering the worst-case scenario. The possibility that Emma had come to save me, and that now there was nothing I could do to save her. It was in someone else's hands entirely. Emma had been so brave, and also so, so stupid. I was livid at her for coming to save me. And I was terrified of the consequences.

Just when I'd finally gotten something good in my life, it threatened to be ripped away. I shook my head. She was so fucking smart and clever, she'd even pieced together the information on that hard drive and figured out who Viktor was, in mere hours. She was too clever for her own good to have figured out exactly where I was and how to come get me.

And now I was out here, and she was in there.

I was so grateful to have escaped from Viktor's clutches, but I was horrified at what it had cost. I didn't like that I had to bring her to the hospital. We were both too vulnerable here, but there was no way around it. Emma needed medical care immediately, and I'd been on edge the moment they'd wheeled her away from me. A sickening pit had settled in my stomach when the hospital doors had swung shut, with me on one side and her disappearing somewhere on the other. I couldn't keep her safe if I wasn't with her, and I grew more and more agitated the longer I waited. I was just waiting for the agency to slip in and finish us both. Every minute that passed left me more terrified than the last.

I warily let the nurse inspect my hand, not bothering to cry out in pain anytime it shifted. I was holding the fear and pain of a thousand lifetimes in my chest, what was a few broken bones. As she looked over my broken hand, I leaned into the pain, the only thing that I could feel stronger than my terror of losing Emma.

"Agent Reynolds?"

My pulse quickened.

A woman in a slick pantsuit approached, and I instinctively reached for my gun, which I had subconsciously forgotten was no longer holstered to my leg. Security had promptly stripped me of my weapons when I raced into the emergency room earlier with Emma. They'd nearly tackled me, except for the wounded woman I carried in my arms.

I tensed, eyeing the woman in front of me, clearly another agent. I'd kept my eyes wide open for anyone Viktor would have sent immediately after. After several hours, I'd convinced myself that if he had intended to send the team after us, they would have come to the hospital already. If he had, we were sitting ducks, the job would have been finished before we could blink an eye. The fact that we were still alive was evidence that we were safe for the moment. That sentiment was clearly a mistake.

As I eyed the woman in front of me, it did not miss me that two burly men stood armed out in the hallway several paces away, lingering, watching, assessing.

"Agent Reynolds?" She asked again.

"Yes?" I asked cooly.

"I'm Agent Zuri with the CIA." She flashed a badge at me, and I watched her warily. "I'm aware you're part of a special black ops division, and we're going to need to bring you in for questioning."

"Yeah, listen." I glanced at the men in the hallway. "There's not a chance in hell you're bringing me in." I stood up, and she immediately pulled a gun on me that I hadn't realized she'd been wearing. The two men in the hallway now also had their guns aimed at me. One was now inside the room and the other blocking the doorway.

The nurse backed wide eyed into the corner.

Agent Zuri, with her gun still drawn on me, smiled, amused at me. "I suppose with what you've been through, I'd understand that." Her amused smile was pissing me the fuck off as she continued. "I hate to do this to you, Reynolds, but I see we're going to have to do this the hard way."

As the words came out of her mouth, I growled and shoved a heart monitor at the male agent and lunged forward towards her, but I didn't make it two steps before I felt a sharp sting sink into my chest.

"I'm going to fucking kill you." I growled, as I blacked out.

I BLINKED as light started to filter through my eyelids.

Fuck.

My head was pounding as I struggled to get my bearings. I instinctively reached up and rubbed my chest where I'd been hit. The simple action made me realize I wasn't strapped down.

Odd but good.

I lifted my shirt to inspect where I'd been hit. A tranquilizer dart bruise was starting to form where I'd felt the sting.

I flicked my eyes around. They'd tranq'd me, not shot me. It surprised me.

They hadn't killed me yet.

What the fuck is this?

It was a relief finding myself not being chained or strapped down, but I was equally panicked about being locked up again. Equally panicked that I wasn't with Emma. If they hadn't taken her too, she'd be a sitting duck when she came out of surgery with no one to keep her safe.

"Agent Reynolds." The voice came crackling through the speaker into the room. "I'm going to come in, and I'd really like to have a conversation with you. But I *will* have you tranq'd again if I have to."

I blew out a breath and cocked my head at the camera in the corner of the room. The red light on this security camera blinked evenly, no sign of Emma's morse code loop. That was one piece of information. I was likely in a different building now.

I backed up and leaned on the wall farthest from the door, putting my hands up in mock surrender. I glanced at my left hand and noticed it had been put into a cast while I was under. I took a moment to take that fact in, knowing that was another odd but good sign.

"Agent Zuri." I said sarcastically as she stepped into the room. The door clicked shut behind her, and she leaned against the wall next to the door, gun now obviously holstered to her hip, for easy access.

We watched each other for a moment, each taking each other in, gathering data. I realized she was surprisingly young for someone in her position. If she was from the agency, I'd never seen her before.

She wore her dark coiled hair parted down the middle and pulled back, slicked away from her face, the ends of her full pony tail gently swayed and bounced as she moved. Her caramel skin and somewhat innocent face was quite beautiful, though I could tell by the cool, calculated look in her sharp eyes that underestimating her would be a mistake.

She stood unfazed, confidently taking an equal assessment of me.

I smiled wickedly at her, letting her know that I could cross the room and snap her delicate little neck before she even thought about getting the door open.

She gave me a look back that said she would fill me full of lead if I tried.

I smirked, knowing even if she emptied her clip into my chest, I'd still have time to break her in half before I went down.

Her eyes narrowed, and I knew she understood the threat. It was clear, my expression, though silent, might as well have been screaming the words into the air for her to hear audibly.

She finally spoke. "This may come as a huge shock to you, Mason, but I'm actually on your side." She said evenly.

"Oh, really?" I asked. I didn't dare ask about Emma, hoping they hadn't nabbed her from the hospital, hoping that she still had a chance of escaping. I was sure they knew she was there, but on the off chance they didn't, I wasn't giving anything away.

"Miss Mitchell is out of surgery." She tossed out, but she watched me like a hawk gauging my reaction.

Fucking Hell. They know about Emma.

"We have a lot to talk about, you and I." She motioned to the table. "Why don't we have a seat?"

"I'd like to see Emma." I shot back, a request, but also I was testing the water just as much as she was.

"I can arrange that." Agent Zuri nodded.

We were playing a game of cat and mouse, but I was getting the sense that she thought I was the cat.

Good. Let her sweat.

She scanned my hand. "It must have been pretty urgent for you to escape if you broke your own hand. Quite clever, the morse code bit."

Fucking hell, maybe I was at the agency.

She continued, "Miss Mitchell would do well in the field. She's been quite resilient, all things considered."

I watched her, trying to figure out where this was going. She was putting out feelers; she was fishing, something felt off.

Curious, I finally took the seat across the table, and Agent Zuri nodded, clearly pleased, and took the seat across from me. I began to notice this room while it did have the one-way glass. It did not seem to be equipped with the nasty interrogation supplies in the last room I'd been detained in. I was taking it all in, suspicious, wary, and completely skeptical. Maybe we were doing the good cop, bad cop bit now.

Agent Zuri laced her fingers together and rested them on the table, leaning forward. "Reynolds, what do you know about Viktor Ivanov?"

I mirrored her body language, leaning forward, hands on the table, "I think the better question is, what do *you* know about Viktor Ivanov? You seem to have all the answers here, huh, cupcake?"

She smirked slightly and tapped on the table.

Morse code.

She was tapping. "Fuck you."

The corner of my mouth twitched.

"So you did get Emma's message then." Agent Zuri smiled deviously.

She was spunky, and she reminded me a bit of Emma. "Perhaps." I responded coyly, still not willing to give up any solid intel.

"Then you know that Viktor has been selling classified information, putting military weapons into the hands of our enemies."

"*Our* enemies?" I countered.

"Alright, here it is, Reynolds." The cockiness disappeared, and she got serious. "I've been tracking your work for some time. What you may not know is that the black op division you were working for is not part of the U.S. government." She paused, watching me before she continued. "After your time serving as a SEAL, you were unknowingly recruited into a terrorist syndicate. Your black ops division, led by Viktor Ivanov, is *not* a covert branch of the CIA, despite what you've been told." She continued carefully as my mind began to reel. "You're not working for the good guys, Reynolds. Viktor has been poaching high performance agents and analysts posing as a black ops division of the CIA for the last twenty years." She paused as I struggled to absorb what she was even saying, to decipher if it was true. I knew Viktor was a scumbag, but the idea of having the wool pulled over my own eyes was nearly unfathomable. She continued, "Do you think the U.S. government would order assassins to track down and eliminate every agent that made a mistake? We wouldn't have a department left if we did that."

I said nothing as the information raced through my

mind a million miles a minute, trying to determine if she was speaking the truth or spinning lies.

"I've been watching you both for the last year, and we had intended to reach out to Emma Mitchell among a few others, to use her as a double agent. We knew she was hot on Viktor's trail. But after that slip up in June, when you moved her in with you, we hardly were able to get in contact with her. You kept such a close eye on her, we couldn't get in touch without risking her safety." I smiled, knowing that was true. I had hardly let her out of my sight. Agent Zuri continued. "At the time, I wasn't sure if you were aware of Viktors' dealings, if you were being used as a pawn, or if you were actively supporting the syndicate. Once you obtained the hard drive from Shah, and Viktors agency sent a team after you, we knew you'd likely been kept in the dark."

"If you are telling me the truth, then you have no reason to detain me, and I'd like to see Emma." I responded, this was a whole truckload of shit she'd just unloaded on me, but my main concern right now was still Emma's safety. If this was true, she was still a sitting duck. I watched Agent Zuri, unsure of how she'd respond.

"Very well. We have lots of time to discuss all this." Agent Zuri nodded. "Come with me." She stood up, and the door buzzed open.

I hesitantly followed Agent Zuri out into the hallway, surprised at what I saw. I was in a large office that was hustling and bustling with agents. She turned and gave me a subtle smirk. "Welcome to the *real* CIA, Reynolds. Try to keep up."

I clicked my tongue, still unsure of what I believed. I just needed to see Emma. That was the most important thing right now.

We navigated across a sky bridge into an adjacent building, and I followed her into an elevator. The elevator music was a vast juxtaposition of pleasant music amidst my skepticism towards Agent Zuri.

I watched her out of the corner of my eye, knowing I could take her down right now if I wanted.

She stared forward as if she was unaware, but she responded. "I dare you."

I scoffed, rolling my eyes at her cockiness. We rode the elevator up a few more floors in tense silence, and finally we stepped out into a light-filled building with large windows, some sort of medical floor, not quite a hospital, not quite an office.

She turned down a hallway, not bothering to see if I was following, and stepped into a room.

I followed her through the doorway and nearly collapsed when I saw her.

Emma.

I raced to the side of the bed where she slept peacefully. The light from the large windows poured into the room, illuminating the creamy white walls with a few decorative pictures of nature; hardly a prison cell. I scanned Emma frantically, a few wires led to a monitor that softly clicked and beeped near the bed.

I pulled the chair up to the side of the bed and stroked her hair, taking her hand in mine. The color was back in her cheeks, and she looked okay. I felt my eyes misting as I looked up at Agent Zuri.

"She did beautifully, and the baby looks like it's going to be just fine."

"Is she sedated?" I asked, nearly unable to get the words out.

"She'll be waking up soon." Agent Zuri smiled. "I'll be back later, but we have a lot more to discuss. You're a great

Agent, Reynolds." She nodded at Emma. "You two make quite the team." She paused. "I'd love to have you working for the good guys when you're ready."

I looked back and forth between Emma and Agent Zuri, who was eyeing her. "There is not a chance in hell you're recruiting her." I scoffed.

She just smiled. "We'll see about that." She lingered a moment longer, "Reynolds... she'll be safe here. Viktor and his team couldn't get in here, even if they dared to try." She gave me a smile and with that, she disappeared into the hallway.

34

EMMA

I SAT in the recovery room and slurped down a strawberry Jello cup, my eyes ping-ponging back and forth as Mason argued with Agent Zuri at the foot of the bed.

"There's no way in hell I'm letting you evaluate her for field work." Mason spat, "What are you going to do? Send her and my unborn child back into Viktor's clutches as bait."

"It wouldn't be like that." Agent Zuri was getting just as pissed at Mason as he was at her.

"It would be exactly like that," Mason thundered.

"All we need her to do is tell Viktor she wants to meet, and we'll take care of the rest. She'll be completely safe the whole time," Agent Zuri emphasized.

"You're telling me there is a one hundred percent guarantee she won't get hurt?"

Agent Zuri huffed, knowing that Mason had her. "I'm saying we will keep her safe. I can promise you that."

"It doesn't fucking matter. I don't know you from Adam. Your promise means nothing to me," Mason yelled.

I waved my hand. "Uh, hey, hello." I licked my lips. "We're talking about me here. Don't I get a say?"

In unison, they both spoke.

"No." Mason roared.

"Of course." Agent Zuri responded, immediately scowling at Mason.

I continued, "I just want assurance that my terrorism charges are dropped, permanently, erased from my file, that they won't even exist anymore. If you can do that, I'm in."

"Emma." Mason looked devastated.

Agent Zuri nodded. "I'll see what I can arrange." And with that, she pulled out her phone and slipped into the hallway.

Mason came to the side of the bed and knelt down, taking my hand. "I can't let you put yourself in harm's way."

I set my Jello cup down and raked my hand through his hair tenderly. "We have to end this, Mason. Let's help them put him away, and then you and I can just walk away if we want. I just want to be with you and not have to be looking over our shoulder every second of every day. You know?"

Mason nodded, reaching into his pocket and pulled out a twisty tie that was twisted into a small circle. "Speaking of being with you..." He took a breath. "I love you Emma Mitchell. I will love you until the day I die. I can't bear the thought of waiting even another second to make you mine. *Officially*." He smirked. "Will you marry me?" His concerned brow quirked into a nervous expression as he held the twisty tie ring. "I wish I had a proper ring with me right now, but I wouldn't dare let you out of my sight until this is over, so this will have to do for the time being. I love you with the depths of my being, with all that I am, and I will take care of you and our child, no matter what your answer is. But you'd make me the happiest man in the world if you said yes." His eyes misted over, "So I hope you say yes."

I was bursting at the seams and I threw my hands around his neck, knocking my Jello cup into my lap in the process. "Yes, of course, yes." I laughed ecstatically, joyfully, and squeezed his neck so hard he sputtered.

"Easy there, Rambo. You've been busting people out of jail and taking down assassins. I don't think you know your own strength."

All I could do was laugh so full of joy, and I grabbed his shirt, pulling him to me and kissed him. This was home. Mason was my home. After a long, passionate kiss, I finally pulled back breathless. "My dad's going to kill you." I said, sucking my lips between my teeth wide eyed.

Mason blew out a breath. "I know."

I BLEW out a breath and tried not to fuss with the earpiece in my ear as I walked towards the warehouse. "Can you hear me?" I whispered into the air.

"Yes, we can hear you. Everything is moving along as planned. You're doing great." Agent Zuri's calming voice reassured me through the earpiece.

I fussed with the earpiece, trying to get it just right.

Mason's soothing voice came through the earpiece next. "Stop fussing with it, love, you'll give yourself away."

"Right." I whispered back, and left it alone, but it still felt so obvious and so heavy in my ear. I pushed my hair forward to make sure it was fully covered.

I tensed when I saw Viktor come from the other side of the building.

"Where have you been?" He called out. He stopped in front of me, a little too close for comfort.

"I've been around." I said with false confidence.

"Do you have the drive?" He asked.

"Are you going to get me out of my contract for good?" I responded, knowing perfectly well that the CIA was already doing that for me, but I had to have a good reason for meeting him here like this. I had to pretend I still needed something from him.

"I'll see what I can do." He said smugly.

"Cut the shit Viktor, I can take this up the ladder and put you in the ground instead if you'd like."

Viktor smiled wickedly at me, sizing me up like prey.

"Easy." Were Mason's only words softly spoken through the earpiece.

Viktor spoke, "I see you've gotten a little better at negotiation since I last saw you." He gave me a dark look. "How are you holding up since your little escapade in the locker room?"

I clenched my teeth, willing myself not to flinch at the memory. But despite my best efforts, the panic began to wrap its barbed tendrils around me, sinking them into my mind. Everything started to tunnel as the PTSD of that day catapulted itself into my mind.

Mason's voice came through the earpiece again. "What do you see?"

I blew out a breath, looking at the speck of lint on Viktors' jacket.

Mason continued through the earpiece, "What do you smell?"

I took a deep breath in, forcing oxygen into my lungs. I smelled the crisp air, the recent rainfall.

"Taste?" Mason prompted me again, walking me through the grounding exercise he had taught me.

Taste... what did I taste, the metallic tang from how hard I was biting my cheek. I released my cheek and took another long breath in, finally coming back into my body with each continued breath. I wasn't in the locker room; I wasn't in Iran; I wasn't being attacked. I was safe. Sort of anyway.

"If you want the hard drive, I need your word." I said firmly, leaning hard into the bit Zuri and I had decided on.

"Very well." Viktor reached his hand out. "The drive, Emma."

I reached out and handed him the bag in my hand. As he reached for it, he pulled a gun on me.

"Such a silly girl." He said spitefully.

My pulse quickened, and I swallowed hard as I watched as half a dozen red dots suddenly appeared on his chest. "I could say the same to you." I nodded, and he followed my gaze to his chest.

He smirked, and I flinched as he steadied his stance; the look in his eye, his body language, despite the guns aimed at him, I knew I was about to get shot.

Fuck.

All at once, I heard a voice say, "Close your eyes." And I did. I squeezed my eyes shut, waiting to take the hit.

Two gunshots sliced through the air in unison.

One second passed, then two, then three, and I finally dared open my eyes.

Was I shot?

Was I hit?

The last time I'd been shot, I hadn't felt it initially.

The air whooshed back into my lungs as I gasped, and when I opened my eyes fully, Viktor was on the ground in front of me, dead.

I stood staring at him in shock, the feeling of numbness spreading through me. It was done. Viktor was dead in front of my very eyes as proof. He wouldn't be able to come after us anymore.

It was finished for good.

Relief flooded me.

"You did good." Mason breathed into my hair as his warm embrace suddenly appeared around my body. He turned me away from Viktors' body. "You did so good, baby."

Agent Zuri came stalking up. "Didn't trust my aim?" She smirked.

"No." Mason ground out. "I didn't."

"I'll take your bet on whose bullet hit him first." She said smugly.

"It was mine," Mason gritted possessively.

"We'll see about that." Agent Zuri wiggled her eyebrows at me.

Even though the plan had been to take him alive, I realized Agent Zuri had kept her word. Mason had only agreed to this if he was an additional sniper on the team. He'd broken protocol and shot Viktor to save me, and so had Agent Zuri. They'd both realized he was going to shoot me the moment I had as well.

"What now I asked?" Feeling dizzy with the relief that slowly washed over me.

"For now, you two are off the hook, but I'll be in touch." Agent Zuri nodded and went to speak with the rest of the team that now trickled down into the lot.

"Let's go home." Mason breathed into my hair before scooping me up in a bridal carry.

I smiled, leaning into his chest, feeling like everything might finally be ok. And then I remembered we still had to tell my dad about us.

35

EMMA

"I SHOULD HAVE KNOWN BETTER." My dad shook his head.

I took his hands across the table. "It's ok, you didn't know." I reassured him. Now that I was no longer in a super secret black ops division, I could actually fill him in, and it felt like such a relief to explain why I'd been so distant the last few years. Because I'd had this huge secret that I couldn't share with him. I, of course, had left out many of the more unsavory details of what I'd been through. I wanted to tell him, but I knew he'd be devastated if he knew the full extent of what I'd been through, and I had Mason, so I wasn't totally alone anymore.

My dad and I sat in the middle of the Italian restaurant, waiting for our guest to come sit at the empty place setting on the table. He eyed the ring on my finger. "So, is this the big news?" He asked warily.

I bit my lip and shook my head. "Yes." I couldn't help the beaming smile that escaped my lips. "It is."

"You're so young, Em–" He started.

"I'm not *that* young." I countered, trying to choose my next words wisely. Of all the things he could have said... that was not an ideal comment, given what I was about to tell him.

I took his hands again. "Dad." He gave me a look. "Dad." I said more firmly. "This is the man I love, okay? I really, really love him. He's– well, he's everything to me. So I would really, really appreciate it if you were nice."

He looked at me suspiciously. "What's the matter? Is he a musician or something?" He rolled his eyes.

"No." I said, annoyed.

"Well, does he at least have a job?"

"Yes, he has a job, and he's very good at it, and it pays him very well. More than enough to take care of me." I assured him.

"Good, because I will not settle for anything less for my only daughter." My dad said firmly.

"He is..." I tried to be strategic with my next words, "Older." I said simply.

My dad narrowed his eyes. "How much older, Em?"

I bit my lip and spat it out. "Seventeen years."

"Jesus Christ." My dad shook his head, getting upset. And oh boy, if he was upset now, he was going to be livid when he realized it was Mason.

"He's a really good guy." I said.

"Yeah, I bet he is."

"Dad." I said with as much attitude as I could muster, and his eyes finally softened.

"Alright fine, I'll be nice."

"Thank you." I texted Mason, who'd been waiting in the car.

"He could at least show up on time." My dad rolled his eyes.

Through gritted teeth I responded, "He's here. He was just waiting for us to talk first."

"Sure." My dad said, skeptical.

Mason strode into the restaurant, looking tall and hand-some in slacks and a crispy white button down that didn't hide the curve of his lean muscles. I tried to steady the nervous flutter that erupted in my stomach at the sight of him. That was my man, my baby daddy, my fiancé, the love of my life.

My dad perked up at seeing Mason. "Mason!" He excit-edly waved him over to the table. "What are you doing here?" My dad asked, elated to see his old buddy.

"What am I–" Mason shot me a look.

Oh shit. He doesn't get it.

My dad, thinking he was being devious, gave me a look. "Em here is engaged." Before Mason could speak, my dad continued. "Why don't you join us? I was just about to meet the dumb schmuck."

"Well–" Mason started.

"Apparently he's nearly my age." My dad rolled his eyes and elbowed Mason.

Mason looked green. "You don't say."

"Have a seat, have a seat." My dad pulled the chair out for him. "You don't mind, Em, do you?" My dad was giddy with delight, thinking he had a wingman to intimidate my arriving betrothed, but he didn't understand that he was already looking right at him.

We all sat down, and my dad looked at me, "So where is he? Huh?" He responded a bit too smug.

I grabbed Mason's hand under the table and pulled it up, resting our hands in plain sight.

My dad looked between us, confused.

"Dad–" I started.

He connected the dots as he stared between us, and I felt a bolt of anxiety shoot through me as he lunged over the table, knocking the breadsticks off the table. "You bastard!" He shouted.

"Dad!" I screamed as he knocked Mason backwards in his chair. They both fell to the ground, with my dad on top, and Mason let it all happen. I knew my dad couldn't have touched him unless Mason purposefully let him. My dad landed a solid punch to Mason's face before he stumbled back furiously. My dad grabbed his jacket and stormed out of the restaurant.

I crouched down over Mason, whose nose was bleeding. "*Oh*, Mason. I'm so sorry. Are you alright?" I asked, frantically dabbing him with a napkin, pulling him up.

He grumbled, waving me away. "It's alright, I deserved that." He grunted as he sat up. He nodded to the door. "You should go talk to him. I'll wait here."

I looked around at the shocked eyes watching us. "Are you sure about that?"

He chuckled, "I think after that punch, I can handle a few looky-loos."

I nodded and quickly raced after my dad. I found him sitting on the curb outside the restaurant with his head in his hands. As I approached, he looked up at me and shook his head, but said nothing as he stared blankly out into the parking lot.

"Listen, I'm just gonna lay it on you now. I'm pregnant, Mason's the father."

My dad's eyes snapped up even more furious.

I continued with my hand up as if to stop him from going right back inside and continuing what he started. "I love him dad, he's the father of my child, he's my fiancé and he's your best friend, which means not only do you like him, but you love him too." I continued, "I get that this is hard to digest. I really do. But this is my decision, and if you can't

accept that, then you can't be part of our relationship." I
chewed my lip. "And I really want you to be in my child's
life." I said, feeling my eyes get misty. "You're going to be a
grandpa, you know."

His eyes got misty too, and he stood up and for a
moment I thought he was going to go back inside, but he
wrapped his arms around me and hugged me.

He pulled me back and looked at me seriously. "Did he
try anything when you were a kid?"

"No, of course not." I shook my head, and he accepted
that answer and he pulled me back in for a hug.

"I love him, dad." I said into his chest.

"Okay." He whispered into my hair. "Okay."

He motioned for me to go back inside. "Alright, let's not
let this stop us from eating. I'm starving."

"Good." I patted his arm. "Me too."

I couldn't help but giggle at the sight of Mason when we
came back in. His dark brown hair ruffled, the ripped
napkin shoved up his nose, stopping the nose bleed.

My dad stopped in front of Mason before taking a seat.
"If you hurt her, I'll kill you." My dad said simply.

Mason responded, "I wouldn't expect anything less."

My dad shook his head, and then he stuck his hand out.
"Welcome to the family, I guess." And rolled his eyes.

36

EMMA

"THANK YOU." I smiled warmly as the woman finished the intricate swirling henna design on my hands. I admired the beautiful pattern that swept up to my forearms. In a mere few hours, I'd be bonded to Mason for the rest of my life. We'd be husband and wife.

And I smiled to myself, knowing my sixteen-year-old self would never have believed that my life turned out this way. That I'd find true love in Mason's arms, that we'd be a few months away from having a baby together.

I was lucky. Even with everything I'd endured, I felt truly lucky.

I pushed myself up off the colorful embroidered floor cushion and wandered through the ornate archway leading to my hotel balcony. I gazed out at the beautiful, bustling city below, as delicious smells and joyous music wafted up to me, inviting me to come play.

Mason and I had decided to elope, to tie the knot before the baby came. After the baby came, I had some big decisions to make, whether I wanted to start working for the CIA as a field analyst, or if I wanted to walk away from it all.

Part of me wanted to leave it all behind, but as I considered what else I'd do, I hadn't the faintest idea. While I'd been forced into the lifestyle initially to save my own skin, deep down a part of me realized that maybe I liked the work. Especially if I was working for the real government and not a terrorist syndicate posing as a special task force. The irony of it all, talk about a toxic work environment.

Agent Sophia Zuri and I had become fast friends over the last few months. I'd worked closely with her as we'd been debriefed, and I'd helped her and her team out as much as I could. I didn't know if I was going to accept the job offer long term, but I was certainly thrilled to help break the news to the other team members at the agency who'd also been through hell and back, just like me.

While the agency at its core was just a branch of The Crescent terrorist syndicate, there were many other people and agents like Mason and I who had unknowingly been going to work thinking they were helping people, protecting the country, and they deserved a second chance as much as I had been fortunate enough to get.

Now that the bulk of that was wrapped up, Mason and I could live in our little love bubble. We knew we needed to get away from it all, to reset, to heal from everything we'd been through.

I was so grateful that I had Mason. He'd held me night after night as I woke up from the nightmares, and slowly they'd started to dissipate. We both were in therapy, with a CIA approved therapist. We could share the darkest secrets we had without any fear of repercussion. We were in a good place, and there was no one I'd rather have gone into the depths of hell and back with, other than Mason.

With my new coping strategies in place, I knew I was

going to be okay, that Mason would be ok. And that gave me hope, reminded me that I was resilient and strong.

Suddenly there was a knock at the door, and I crossed into the room and opened my hotel door.

Mason.

I gasped playfully. "You're not supposed to see the bride before the ceremony." My eyebrows raised as I looked at him.

He wore a loose white linen button down and matching linen pants. The crispy linen contrasted against his tanned skin and his dark hair. I bit my lip, knowing I'd have to wait several more hours for him to quench the heat that had already started to pool at the apex of my thighs. With my pregnancy hormones, I was turned on all the time, ready to be taken to the edge with him, at a moment's notice, and today was no different.

He saw the lusty look in my eye, "I wanted to check on you, baby. See if you needed *anything*."

Breathily, I backed up, letting him come into the room. I lifted my hands to show him the wet henna. "I do, but I can't."

Mason gave me a wicked look, and his knuckles grazed up the henna free skin of my shoulder, and my eyes fluttered shut at the contact.

"I guess I'll just have to save what I had planned for later then." He chuckled. A promise of things to come.

"I guess so." I breathed, finally opening my eyes to find his dark glimmering eyes drinking me in with adoration.

He reached out and ran his hand over my swollen belly tenderly. "Feeling okay? Do you need anything else before tonight?"

I shook my head. "No, I feel good." I was out of my first

trimester and the morning sickness had mostly passed, which I was beyond grateful for.

"See you soon." He pressed a chaste kiss to my lips and disappeared into the hallway, giving me a wink before he closed the door behind him.

I smiled and flopped back on the bed, keeping my hands carefully propped up as the henna continued to dry.

Moments later, there was another knock at the door and I groaned and got up to answer it. One of the hotel staff had room service, and I thanked them and then rolled my eyes at the note.

> *Eat up. You'll need your strength for tonight, Rambo.*
>
> *XO,*
>
> *Mace*

I TOOK a sip of the refreshing mint tea on the platter. He knew I'd been trying to drink less diet coke since my pregnancy, and I'd been trying every herbal tea under the sun, trying to find something to scratch the itch. The tea was far from diet coke, but it was certainly delicious and refreshing.

I dug into the light meal he'd had sent up, Moroccan salad and a fragrant vegetable couscous, filling but light enough that it wouldn't upset my tender stomach.

Finally, it was time. I poked at the henna and, finding it dry, I gently brushed the henna crust off the top of my skin, revealing the light tan staining underneath. I slipped my white lace dress on and admired myself in the mirror. The delicate lace draped down to the floor and the intricate designs perfectly covered the important parts while beautifully accentuating my swollen belly. My skin, gently tanned from the time in the sun, glowed. I swiped a pink hue onto my lips and dabbed the extra onto my cheeks for a little bit of added color. I draped the veil over my head, and over my soft curls that had finally grown out a bit thanks to the pregnancy hormones.

I admired myself in the mirror for a moment before another knock at the door. The hotel manager smiled warmly at me and escorted me down to the wedding chapel.

The blue tile archway led me into the chapel, and candles glowed in the dimming light filtering in from the outside. Big sweeping bolts of fabric swept across the ceiling, giving the open-air chapel a warm and intimate feel.

At the end of the room, another archway opened up on the backside of the hotel into a stunning view of the desert, and the sun began to set, shooting brilliant orange hues through the sky.

And in the center of the archway stood Mason, misty eyed, handsome as ever, smiling at me.

"READY?" Mason gave me a wink as he took my hand.

"Ready." I whispered, hardly able to speak, as the joy of my emotions overcame me.

Standing here, hand in hand with Mason, I was getting everything I'd ever hoped and dreamed for and more. As I stared into those warm brown eyes, I knew I was the luckiest girl in the world.

The End

I hope you loved Emma and Mason's love story!

Find out what Emma does when she discovers Mason chipped her!

Bonus Chapter: Read Here

If the link won't open on your browser, visit LaurenColeBooks.com/Bonus

DON'T MISS WHAT EMMA, Mason, and Agent Sophia Zuri are up to next! Plus! Get a sneak peek into Agent Sophia Zuri's love story! Where she gets tangled up with a gorgeous, rich, Italian Criminal.

When you're done with the bonus chapter, be sure to check out Lucas and Brooke's book!

He needs a fiancee, she signed the contract. The only problem? She broke the most important rule, and she crossed it out with two pink lines! Standalone/ HEA

Read Now: Big Bossy Fake Fiance

REVIEWS

If you enjoyed this book, would you do me a huge favor? Would you leave a review? They help more than you'd think!

If you're shy (or in a hurry), you can always just leave a star review, anything helps!

Thank you lovely reader and I'll see you in the next one!

Amazon | Goodreads

SHOP DIRECT

Thank you for reading a Lauren Cole Romance!

Visit LaurenColeBooks.com to grab your next book or bookish merch!

Discount Code: RomanceReadsy10

When you shop direct from the author, you're supporting a small business! YAY! Please enjoy this discount code as a thank you!

Audiobooks are currently exclusive to the authors shop.

Be sure to check out the eBook bundles or browse cute and hilarious, bookish merch!

ALSO BY LAUREN COLE

Shop on Amazon

∾

Bossy Billionaire's Series

My Silver Fox Billionaire | Big Bossy Fake Fiancé

Big Bossy Billionaire | Big Bossy Ex's Brother

Action/Adventure Series

My Silver Fox Protector

Audio Books

Currently all audiobooks are exclusive to LaurenColeBooks.com

∾

Upcoming releases scheduled for 2025

A Society Of Shadows Series

Carter & Sarah

Liam & Julia

Hayley & Nolan

ABOUT THE AUTHOR

Lauren Cole is a Best Selling author of contemporary romance. She writes exciting, billionaire romances, that always end in happily ever afters.

Nestled between her page turning plots where danger is always lurking around the corner, you'll find witty banter, heartwarming friendships, and so much steam you'll be kicking your feet giggling.

Weeknights beware, your new favorite book boyfriend will sweep you off your feet, no matter how late it gets. With obsession inducing, possessive and morally gray hero's with hearts of gold, you'll be reading into the wee hours of the morning, panting for more!

When it finally gets cold enough in Texas, Lauren loves to read curled up under a fuzzy blanket with a cup of Throat Coat tea that will inevitably go cold. Though, sunning on the back patio, until her kindle overheats, is another kind of little luxury.

On the nights she's not reading you can catch her rewatching some of her all time favorite shows. Amongst which are The Office, Friends, and Grays Anatomy. The perfect mix of drama, friendship, and love!

An honorable mention must of course, be given to the deliciously, delightful British Baking Show. Which serves as mildly distracting background noise, while Lauren writes with two fur babies in her lap, and the frizziest messy bun you've ever seen.

If you love high stakes, feel good stories, with lots of heat, what are you waiting for? See you in the pages, Gorgeous!

Discover more at LaurenColeBooks.com
- eBooks, Audiobooks
- Save on Book Bundles
- Bookish Merch
- Affiliate Program
- Blog

Don't forget to signup for the Newsletter where you'll get anything worth knowing. Sneak peeks, bonus content, discounts, and more!